USEFUL FOOLS

C. A. SCHMIDT

□ □ □

DUTTON BOOKS

DUTTON CHILDREN'S BOOKS
A division of Penguin Young Readers Group

Published by the Penguin Group

Penguin Group (USA) Inc., 375 Hudson Street, New York, New York 10014, U.S.A. • Penguin Group
(Canada), 90 Eglinton Avenue East, Suite 700, Toronto, Ontario, Canada M4P 2Y3 (a division of Pearson
Penguin Canada Inc.) • Penguin Books Ltd., 80 Strand, London WC2R 0RL, England Penguin Ireland,
25 St. Stephen's Green, Dublin 2, Ireland (a division of Penguin Books Ltd.) • Penguin Group (Australia),
250 Camberwell Road, Camberwell, Victoria 3124, Australia (a division of Pearson Australia Group Pty Ltd.) •
Penguin Books India Pvt. Ltd., 11 Community Centre, Panchsheel Park, New Delhi - 110 017, India Penguin
Group (NZ), 67 Apollo Drive, Rosedale, North Shore 0745, Auckland, New Zealand (a division of Pearson
New Zealand Ltd.) • Penguin Books (South Africa) (Pty.) Ltd., 24 Sturdee Avenue, Rosebank, Johannesburg
2196, South Africa • Penguin Books Ltd., Registered Offices: 80 Strand, London WC2R 0RL, England

The song lyrics in this book are from the song *Las Torres* by Nosequien y los Nosecuantos. The song was
released in Peru in 1991.

LIBRARY OF CONGRESS CATALOGING-IN-PUBLICATION DATA
Schmidt, C. A.
Useful fools / by C.A. Schmidt.—1st ed.   p. cm.
Summary: A fifteen-year-old Peruvian boy, whose mother runs a clinic for poor village children,
becomes caught up in the war after Senderistas bomb the clinic, killing his mother and throwing his
family into turmoil.
ISBN 978-0-525-47814-0
1. Sendero Luminoso (Guerrilla group)—Juvenile fiction. 2. Peru—History—1980—Juvenile fiction.
[1. Shining Path (Guerrilla group)—Fiction. 2. Peru—History—1980—Fiction.
3. Family life—Peru—Fiction. 4. Violence—Fiction. 5. War—Fiction.] I. Title.
PZ7.S34996Use 2007   [Fic]—dc22   2006036508

Published in the United States by Dutton Books,
a member of Penguin Group (USA) Inc.
345 Hudson Street, New York, New York 10014
www.penguin.com/youngreaders

Designed by Abby Kuperstock

Printed in USA • First Edition
1 3 5 7 9 10 8 6 4 2

To my mother and father

▪ ACKNOWLEDGMENTS ▪

Writing a novel involves more people than I ever realized. In my case, Bob Becker, my first reader, knew how to be both honest and kind. Marieke Wyman and Brian Schmidt offered valuable teenage insights. Alice Hirata and Ann Pierson fought the winds on Assateague Island and helped fill the holes in my story. Lisa Simeone's sensitive criticism opened stylistic windows I didn't know existed. Adriana von Hagen, Sharon Stevenson, and Suzanne Timmons lived the war with me, read the book for me, and helped me survive both. Leslie Pietrzyk at the Writer's Center in Bethesda and Lee Bloxom at the Visual Arts Center in Richmond, as well as their students, gave helpful critiques. As for Steve Meltzer, my editor at Dutton, I can only quote Stephen King: "The editor is always right." (He was.) Finally, Alice, Peter, Jake, and Mark Hirata gave Gabriel a place to be happy while his mom was writing.

A novel like this is born from life. For me, it was a life in Peru, shared with Peruvians. *Gracias* to my stepdaughter, Jimena Lynch, for her love and friendship. *Gracias* to my godfamily, Octavia, Julián, Waldemar, Ann Mary, Sandra, and Alonso Rupaylla. *Tengo suerte de ser su madrina y su comadre.* I owe homage to María Elena Moyano and Barbara D'Achille, both horrifically martyred by Sendero Luminoso, and gratitude to Carlos Tapia and Carlos Iván Degregori, who helped me understand Sendero. And to the hundreds of Peruvians who amid war and terror found the courage to talk to me, thank you. *Mil gracias.*

Lastly, my heartfelt gratitude to Nicolás, for more reasons than I can say, and to Gabriel, for being the most wonderful son any writer—or mother—could have.

USEFUL FOOLS

▫ ONE ▫

Alonso took aim. There, right within his sights.

Terrorist scum, he thought. His muscles tightened. *You're mine.* The thought was warm honey, trickling down his throat.

Slowly, he drew his finger into a curl. Ever so gently, he squeezed the trigger.

BOOM!

The barrel slammed into his shoulder. The enemy crumpled. And then, with a scream of brakes, the bus jerked to a halt and Alonso lurched back into his own body. Not a superhero body. Just a lanky fifteen-year-old body crammed into a bus seat of torn vinyl and disintegrating foam. Alonso's foot had fallen asleep. The daydream was over, and so was the long ride from the shantytown. The ticket boy was yelling for them to get off, and Alonso's father was standing up. Passengers bumped and squeezed down the aisle and Alonso yawned.

"*Get off, get off!*" the ticket boy bellowed.

"*Ya, ya,*" Alonso muttered. He picked up his bag, a plastic sack stuffed with paintbrushes and drop cloths, and followed his father off the bus.

They were in Miraflores now. Two hours by bus from Alonso's home in Salvador, a dusty shantytown at the edge of Lima. They jumped down the steps onto an avenue lined with ficus trees and apartment buildings, with cafés and banks and travel agencies whose poster-dotted windows promised to take you everywhere, here in Peru or around the world.

The bus pulled away. Through the stink of diesel Alonso caught a whiff of the sea.

Traffic streamed down the avenue, cars and taxis and rattle-trap *microbuses* with their fenders falling off. A gap opened and Alonso and his father raced across, dodging like bullfighters around a speeding taxi. The cabbie screamed curses, and Alonso glared back, but his father kept his eyes down. A tall man, he always walked that way. Like he was reading a novel in the cracks veining the sidewalk.

At the corner, Alonso glanced up at a street sign, trying not to fidget while his father sounded out the letters. His old man didn't like to let on, but he'd never really learned to read.

"This is it," his father said, turning down a side street.

Big houses with barred windows hunkered behind cement and stucco walls. Atop each wall hummed a double strand of electric wire, with signs to warn intruders away. Yellow signs, with black lightning bolts. In case anybody wondered if those wires were really hot.

Alonso's old man stopped in front of a panel of doorbells set in a wall. A metal gate barred the way to glazed flagstones and a tower of glass and steel.

Alonso waited.

He used to like coming to Miraflores, helping his old man on the occasional paint job. But not anymore. He was sick of it. Sick of the smell of paint, of the stubble of latex on his skin. They'd spent the past four Saturdays in Miraflores, whitewashing cement walls covered in Sendero Luminoso graffiti. *Long live the People's War. Long Live Chairman Gonzalo.* Sendero—the Shining Path—loved dramatic strokes of red. It usually took three coats to cover the graffiti, but people in Miraflores were willing to pay.

Today it was an apartment lobby. Fashionable ocher or yellow. But what Alonso really wanted was to be back in Salvador at the clinic his mother ran, helping Dr. Pablo with the kids. Alonso wanted to be a doctor himself. Not a painter.

Staring upward, he counted. Twelve, maybe fourteen stories. From that penthouse up there, you'd see the Pacific Ocean. Waves, and a ragged line of cliffs. And atop one of those cliffs, Rosa's apartment building.

Rosa. Just the thought of her made Alonso's gut clench.

Rosa was Dr. Pablo's daughter. She came to the clinic with her father every Saturday. They'd been coming for years. But lately, just thinking about Rosa made Alonso's scalp tingle, like it was set with tiny electrodes. He kept imagining her hair. Brown hair, the color of mahogany. But shot through with fire, as though her curls had trapped the hot rays of the sun.

Alonso bounced his heels against the sidewalk. His father shot him a glance and pressed a button.

"Yeah?" The voice over the intercom was fuzzy.

"We're here to paint the lobby," Alonso's father grunted.

A surge of frustration shot through Alonso. Right at this moment, Rosa and her father were driving into Salvador.

As the gate buzzed open, he swallowed a curse. He followed his father over the flagstones and let the gate clang shut behind him.

The sooner they finished painting, the sooner he could get back to Salvador.

□ □ □

Rosa yawned as her father steered off the highway. They'd left home an hour ago, turning away from the sandstone cliffs of Miraflores, where their apartment's view gazed out over the Pacific. Driving east. Away from the sea and toward the hills. Toward Alonso, though that was a secret thought that made Rosa squirm, made her face heat up so she stared out the window, hoping her father wouldn't notice.

The car swung up the hill, wheels bumping over the dirt road. Rosa watched through the dusty glass as the first huts of Salvador appeared, faded shacks of woven cane that huddled like tired burros beside the road. Ahead of them, black and white and smeared with mud, with a dented rear bumper that hung by a string, a patrol car blocked the road.

A cop stepped out of the *patrullero* and stalked toward them. He had a machine gun slung from his shoulder and his hand encircled the pistol grip.

Rosa's heart fluttered like a fly against a windowpane. She glanced at her father, but Papá was rolling down his window, smiling. *"Buenos días, señor."*

The cop didn't smile back. *"Documentos,"* he barked.

With a sigh, Papá bent over, twisting below the steering wheel to grope for his wallet. The cop started to fidget, index finger hovering over the gun's trigger.

It's just a roadblock, Rosa told herself. At worst, the cop would ask for a bribe. *A few soles, señor. To fix the brakes on the patrol car.* He'd say it with an oily smile. He'd thank Papá afterward.

Wrists to belt, the cop hitched up his trousers and the gun twitched in Rosa's direction. Rosa sank in her seat, lower and lower, out of the line of fire. She was practically on the floor when her father finally popped up with his wallet in his hand. His glasses were skating down his nose and he looked so ridiculous—so Papá, somehow—that Rosa suddenly felt better. She straightened as her father handed over the documents.

Driver's license, voter I.D., physician's I.D., vehicle registration. Papá stuck his head out the window, trying to meet the cop's eyes. Papá always seemed to think that if he looked hard enough, he'd find the person inside.

The cop made a little jab with the machine gun. "Where are you going?"

"To the Cesip, *señor.*"

"The what?"

"The Cesip." The cop glared and Papá tried again. *"Say-SEEP,"* he pronounced. "The Center to Promote Children's Health. It's a clinic. I'm the pediatrician there." Papá started to explain about the Cesip, about the Mothers' Club and the volunteer doctors and the shantytown kids needing shots and checkups and—

"*Ya, ya.*" The cop shoved the documents back through the window, as though he no longer cared whether Papá were a terrorist or a doctor. Papá fumbled, trying to slip his documents into his wallet and go on explaining. But the cop stepped back and sent them on with a bored wave of his gun.

Papá dropped his wallet to the floor and popped the clutch.

"Why'd they set up a roadblock?" Rosa watched the cop walk back to his car. "Why here?"

Papá gunned the engine and sped up the hill.

Salvador. A panorama of dust and rocks and sand. Piles of bricks and endless rows of huts made of those woven cane mats, *esteras.* No telephone wires, though. No running water. And now a roadblock. "Papá?"

Her father glanced at the rearview mirror. "I don't know, Rosa. There's been a lot of graffiti lately."

Through the dust billowing around the car, Rosa made out a scribble of red on a wall. *Long live the People's War!* "There's graffiti everywhere." She tried to sound soothing. "Even Miraflores."

Papá frowned. "Salvador's different."

"You sound like Tía Virginia," Rosa teased.

A muscle twitched in her father's jaw. "This has nothing to do with your Tía Virginia." He slammed the stick into third gear. "Or anyone else in your mother's family."

Rosa slumped in her seat.

How had Tía Virginia put it last Sunday? *Salvador*—that final rolling *r* a landslide of aristocratic distaste—*is just FULL of* cholos.

Cholos. Citified Indians. Black-haired, dark-skinned, and poor. Like Alonso.

Rosa pressed her forehead against the window, watching an old man plod up the road. He carried a huge bundle of straw on his back, and his bare ankles were white with dust. *Cholos*, she thought.

If Alonso ever felt the way she wanted him to feel, what then? How would Mamá's family react? Rosa could just imagine.

Tía Virginia, this is Alonso. No, Tía, he's not the gardener. He's my boyfriend.

And Tía Virginia, a wrinkled old matriarch in saucer-sized sunglasses. Turning to Papá to hiss, "I *told* you so."

Because she had. Last Sunday at the beach house, in front of a dozen of Mamá's Alcázar relatives. All of them golden-haired and elegant in their Ray-Bans and imported sandals. And Papá in his flip-flops, a beetle amid a flock of butterflies. A *mestizo*. Not quite *cholo*, not quite white. Mamá had done the unthinkable, marrying him.

Tía Virginia had done her best. Waved an indulgent hand, that fat diamond sparkling in the sunlight. "When Rosa was a child, Pablo, a few *cholitos* as playmates . . ." *No harm done*, the hand said. All the Alcázars had played with *cholitos* at one time or another. The maid's kids. The gardener's nephew. "But Rosa is a *señorita* now! And Salvador is just *full* of *cholos*!"

Rosa sighed, remembering, as her father steered toward the low-slung blue building that was the Cesip.

Throughout the long drive up the hill, he hadn't said a word. But he'd been stroking his moustache every time his hand came off the gearshift, and Rosa knew what he was thinking. Roadblocks. Graffiti. Maybe Tía Virginia was right, for all the wrong reasons. Maybe he was crazy to bring Rosa to Salvador.

As they parked and the engine coughed and died, a black-haired wisp of a woman stepped from the Cesip's doorway. "Rosa!"

She was Alonso's mother, Magda. With Alonso's cinnamon-colored skin and black eyes, and with a gold-capped front tooth that glinted whenever she smiled. Magda enfolded Rosa in a hug and Rosa kissed her cheek and looked around for Alonso.

"They got some work, painting," Magda murmured. Rosa flinched, and Magda's voice dropped to a comforting whisper. "They'll be back by lunchtime."

"¡Caramba!" Papá slammed the car door. "What is *that?*"

Spidery red letters, crawling across the Cesip's facade. *PC del P.* Shorthand for Sendero Luminoso's name for itself, the Communist Party of Peru.

Papá flushed purple. "I thought we were off-limits! Magda, don't you—"

"That?" Magda waved a disparaging little hand. "It's just graffiti." She slipped an arm around Rosa's waist. "Your father's a mother hen, you know that?" Magda bobbed her head like an anxious chicken. "*Bok-bok,*" she clucked. "*Bok-bok-BOK!*"

Rosa burst out laughing and her father, still grumbling, followed them up the steps.

The day's work had begun.

◻ ◻ ◻

The apartment building had a wide lobby, with a ceramic tile floor and two elevators. Mejía, the building superintendent, spread paint-mottled drop cloths over the tile while Alonso dug brushes from his sack and his father jimmied open a can of paint.

It was Mejía who had hired Alonso's father for the job. They came from the same mountain village, and they had the same flat cheekbones, the same obsidian-chip eyes, spoke the same Quechua-accented Spanish. But Mejía's eyes glinted over a crooked-toothed smile, and he filled the lobby with chatter about his last visit home. He'd gone back for the village's annual festival, the *patronato*. The party had left everyone massively hung over. "Nobody knows how to drink anymore," Mejía complained. "We've all gone soft." He turned to Alonso. "Your grandfather used to go on three-day benders. On the fourth day he'd be up before dawn, watering the fields." He shook his head admiringly. "Strong as an ox. But your old man was a mean drunk, *no*, Carhuanca?" Alonso's father, pouring paint into a tray, didn't reply. Mejía winked at Alonso, then disappeared behind a door.

Alonso painted a glistening yellow stripe down the wall.

"Get moving, Alonso," his father said.

Alonso tried to speed up. Within seconds, it seemed, his father had painted an area the size of a pickup truck. Alonso looked at his own patch of yellow. A *Volkswagen*, he thought, dipping his brush. He stroked faster, and the Volkswagen grew.

A melodic beep sounded, and he turned to see the elevator doors slide open. A heavyset man stepped out, a hulking shadow with grease-slicked hair and a cheap brown suit. He fixed Alonso with a glare. "Who the hell are you?"

Cheeks reddening, Alonso glared back.

"*Buenos días, señor.*" Alonso's father gestured at the wall. "We're painting the lobby."

The man lumbered toward them, opening a trail of tile as his feet dragged through the drop cloths. "Lemme see your I.D.s."

"What are you, a cop? We—OW!" Alonso jumped as his father pinched his arm.

"Just show him your I.D.," his father muttered, pulling his own I.D. from a back pocket.

"But he can't . . ." Alonso gave a little bounce of impatience. "We have *rights*, Papá." They had just read the Constitution in school. His teacher had spent an hour talking about human rights. "Señorita Morales said—"

The Hulk frowned.

"Show him your I.D., Alonso!"

Hot-faced, Alonso reached into his pocket. Empty. Bouncing his heels against the tile, he groped in his other pocket. Nothing but lint. He looked sullenly at his father. "If he's a cop, he has to show us his badge," he muttered.

His father's eyes widened. "You forgot it?"

Stepping back, the Hulk swept open his jacket. Below his left arm, a semiautomatic pistol nestled in a holster.

"Papá, I—"

"Shut up!" Alonso's father shoved him, hard, against the wall, and stepped between him and the Hulk. "*Por favor, señor.*" He held out his hands, pleading. "Please. He's my son. Mejía hired us. The super. Just ask him."

The Hulk reached inside his jacket and pulled out a walkie-talkie.

"Mejía knows us, *señor*." Alonso winced as his father's wheedle sharpened to a whine. "Please, just . . ." His father stepped away and pounded on the super's door. "Mejía! Mejía! Come out here, please!"

The Hulk had eyes like a fattened pig, nearly hidden in folds of flesh. Sweating, Alonso met his gaze. The wall at his back felt sticky with paint.

Mejía stepped into the lobby with a piece of bread in his hand. He chewed slowly, glancing at the three of them. Then he swallowed and smiled at the Hulk. "Is something wrong, Señor Gálvez?"

"Who are they?"

"*Señor*, they are the painters." Still smiling, Mejía pointed at the half-painted wall.

"How long have you known them?"

Mejía spread his arms wide. "Carhuanca? He's from Mica, my *pueblo*. I've known him all my life." His expression shifted to one of mock concern. "Is something wrong, Señor Gálvez?"

"And the boy?"

"His son, Señor Gálvez. Alonso." Mejía turned to Alonso, and Alonso nodded.

The Hulk grunted and slipped the walkie-talkie back into his pocket. "Next time you bring a couple of *cholos* in here, you let me know first." He strode to the front door and turned to face them. "You hear me? If you wanna keep your job."

The front door slammed, and the Hulk's mountainous figure faded behind the smoked glass. Alonso's father blew out a whistling breath.

"Asshole," Alonso muttered.

"Bodyguard," Mejía corrected. "His boss, Señor Villanueva, sends him out to buy the newspaper every morning." He chuckled. "Gálvez hates that. Makes him feel so small, and he likes to feel so big."

Alonso thought of the Hulk, sent out like an errand boy with his pistol. Relief bubbled out in a laugh, but his father smacked him across the side of his head. "Idiot! You know what they'll do to you if they arrest you? Where the hell is your I.D.?"

Alonso rubbed his stinging scalp. "But Papá, he's not a cop! He had no right—"

"So what if he isn't a cop? You got any idea who his boss is? Villanueva?"

Mejía nodded solemnly. "Remember that banker Sendero killed?"

"That was Villanueva's brother," his father snapped. "So now Villanueva owns the bank." He picked up his paintbrush and slapped it against the wall. "My son the lawyer. Talkin' about his rights."

Alonso flushed, but Mejía cocked his head. "Forget rights," he told Alonso. "They got guns or money, you don't mess with them." He chuckled once more. Then he thumped Alonso on the shoulder and went back to his breakfast.

□ □ □

Seated at a desk in the cement hallway beside the Cesip's main exam room, Rosa put down her pen and stretched her fingers.

She'd been writing all morning. Heights, weights, names. Baby after baby. Pilar, Marco, Valentina. Every last one of them got a checkup and a line in the research log. She picked up her pen as another mother trailed past, clutching a fuzzy-haired baby and a yellow Cesip health card.

"Diego Quispe," Magda called. Rosa printed the name in the log. "Six kilos even." Magda hefted the baby off the scale. "You're feeding him well, *señora*."

Rosa watched as the baby's fat brown hand swiped at Papá's stethoscope. Then she glanced at her watch. It was already past noon, and no sign of Alonso. Would he ever come looking for her? Would he head straight for the *comedor*, the ramshackle lunchroom right across the street? In the exam room, Magda and Papá were taking their time checking the baby. Bantering with Diego's mother. Explaining about family planning and the cholera epidemic and how to keep Diego healthy.

They're a perfect team, Rosa thought. *It's hard to imagine one without the other.*

Magda jotted something down on Diego's health card. "Has the latrine brigade been by your house?"

Diego's mother nodded. "They gave us a sack of lime."

"Toss some into the pit every time you go. It kills the cholera germs." Magda wagged a warning finger. "Don't forget."

"No, *señora*." To Rosa's relief, Diego's mother snapped open a blanket. The exam was over, and the blanket flashed red as it settled across the examining table. Señora Quispe put Diego on it, grasped the corners, and with a little grunt swung baby and blanket onto her back. Handshakes and *gracias* all around, and then finally Señora Quispe was heading down the corridor, Diego jiggling on her back, flip-flops slapping the naked cement.

Rosa stood. "I'm hungry," she announced. Papá murmured something about doing charts, so Magda promised to bring him lunch, and she and Rosa left the Cesip together.

The *comedor* across the street had the rustic look of a stable, patched together of woven cane *esteras* and adobe. Feeling her pulse quicken, Rosa stuck her head inside. She smelled hot oil and garlic and cilantro, saw men, women, and children crowding hip-to-hip on the wooden benches. But no Alonso. Maybe he was farther back in the shadows, by the frayed *estera* wall. But wouldn't he have come to get her first, anyway?

Would he? Well, maybe not. Maybe he didn't care. Maybe she was an idiot, thinking that he and she—

"*Rosa!*"

Behind her, down the hill. Two figures stretched like lengthening shadows as they drew near. One was a tall man with a swift stride, the other a teenaged boy. As Rosa watched, the boy broke into a run.

Alonso, she thought. *Alonso, Alonso, Alonso!* She fought down a maniac urge to race into his arms.

He wore castoff jeans, double-rolled at the cuffs and streaked with yellow. Saffron grains of paint flecked his hair.

"*Hola.*" Alonso kissed Rosa's cheek, rueful. He hadn't been able to control himself. He'd seen her and his legs had taken off running.

Alonso's father nodded a greeting as Rosa stretched out her

hand. She would have liked to kiss Señor Tomás, the way everyone kisses everyone, but it was impossible. Not with those black eyes, gazing sternly down at her. That proud and unfriendly silence. They shook hands, and Tomás turned away.

Magda frowned. "Where are the kids? Didn't you stop by Ana's?"

Ducking to enter the *comedor*, Tomás jerked his head. "Go get the kids, Alonso."

"But Papá, I have to go downtown! I can't . . ." Alonso broke off in despair. Getting the kids would take at least half an hour. The way they dawdled . . . He turned to his mother. "Mamá, *por favor*! I have to go buy a book! For school!"

His father stepped back outside. "I told you to get the kids, Alonso."

Magda smiled. "I'll get them, *cholito*. You two worked all morning."

"Worked?" Alonso's father snorted. "Your brilliant son nearly got us arrested." He shook his head. "Forget it, Alonso. You've gotta disinfect those water barrels."

Rosa listened in horror. They'd send Alonso for the little ones, and then he'd go home. Saturday would end and she wouldn't have seen him at all.

Magda's voice was mild. "Can't he do the barrels tomorrow?"

Yes, Rosa thought. *Tomorrow*.

"No," Tomás snapped. "Tomorrow you'll be dragging him off to Mass."

Magda's smile evaporated. "Mass won't take all day."

"Don't baby him, Magda."

"I'm not babying him." Her voice softened. "Go on," she encouraged. "You must be starving."

Tomás scowled as Magda tilted her head and gazed up at him. Then, with an exasperated snort, he turned and stepped into the *comedor*.

Alonso grinned, but Magda turned on him with a frown. "Arrested?"

"I forgot my I.D.," he mumbled.

"You know better than that. Get it before you go downtown." She pulled a wrinkled bill from her pocket. "Have some lunch first."

"Ay, Mamá, can't we just get some *empanadas* off the cart?"

"We?"

"You want to come, Rosa?"

Rosa's heart rose, and the grin on Alonso's face spread to hers.

"You two . . ." Magda glanced sternly from one to the other, one finger up and ready to wag. Then she broke off with a laugh. "Okay." She held out her arms to Rosa. "Just tell your father where you're going. And don't forget. Remind your mother about the Cesip anniversary, okay? It's just two weeks now. You are all coming, *no*?"

Rosa stepped into the hug. "Of course," she promised. She thought of Tía Virginia and hugged back, hard. "We wouldn't miss it for anything."

▫ TWO ▫

"*¡Somos libres!*" Alonso's voice rang joyously across the Cesip's dusty front lot.

Rosa giggled. It was the national anthem. *We're free!* They had bus fares and permission to go and they were finally free. The two of them.

Alonso was bouncing by her side. He seemed delighted with himself. With her. With the way the sun was turning motes of dust into diamonds. Beyond them, the dirt road curved up, up toward the whitewashed parish church, and down, down, between shacks and flat-topped houses and pile after pile of bricks. Far below, sunlight struck silvery glints off the cars flitting along the highway. A bicycle horn bleated. The bakery man pedaled toward them, straining up the hill with his cartload of *empanadas*. The day had turned perfect.

Rosa bit into her *empanada*, powdered sugar and pastry and spiced meat. "What book do you need?"

Alonso didn't answer. He was licking the sugar off his *empanada*, his eyes on a gray Volkswagen toiling toward them. It sputtered to a halt and as the window rolled down, a thickset man in a priest's collar smiled up at them.

Alonso stepped to the open window. "*Hola*, Padre Manuel."

"*Hola* yourself. *Buenas tardes*, Rosa."

"*Buenas tardes*, Padre." Rosa bent through the window to kiss the priest's cheek. It was a soft cheek, oddly mismatched to the body below it. Padre Manuel's forearm, resting on the open window, was as sinewy as a wrestler's.

Padre Manuel glanced at his watch. "Coming to soccer practice, Alonso?"

Alonso shook his head. "I have to buy a book."

Padre Manuel frowned and Alonso knew what was coming. *You want to play on the team, you come to Mass and you come to practice.* He spoke before the priest could start in on one of his you-know-the-rules sermons. "You been saying Mass, Padre?"

The priest rubbed his neck tiredly. "No. I went to see the Archbishop. Your mother wants more food for the *comedor*."

"Too many mouths to feed, Padre?" Rosa teased.

The priest shook his head. "Not enough sharing, I think."

Rosa and Alonso grinned. *"Feed those dying of hunger,"* they intoned. *"Because if you haven't fed them you've killed them."*

Padre Manuel slapped a hand to his forehead. "I repeat myself that much?"

"As the early Christians used to say . . ." Alonso mimicked the priest's gravelly Spanish accent. Six years in Peru and he still sounded like he'd flown in from Madrid the night before.

"*Ya, ya*, get on with you." Laughing, the priest shifted into gear. "Have fun."

Alonso turned to Rosa as the Volkswagen gurgled up the hill. "Hey, Rosa." He kicked her a stone, passing it like a soccer ball. "When was the last time you saw Rodolfo?"

Toeing the stone, Rosa thought. Rodolfo was Alonso's best friend, a teasing broomstick of a boy who never stopped cracking jokes, even when he was too bruised to sit down. *An electrical cord! My old man went after me with an electrical cord! You shoulda seen me light up the shack!* When his father finally ran off, Rodolfo's family moved away from Salvador to live with Rodolfo's uncle. "Not since they went to Canto Grande," she replied.

Alonso stole the stone and began dribbling downhill. Rosa followed, watching his back. His shoulders had broadened in the last few months, and his sleeves didn't quite reach his wrists. "You want to go to Canto Grande?" she asked. "What about your book?"

Alonso turned with a sly wink. "Later," he said. "Let's have some fun."

Rosa shrugged, then laughed, then took off down the hill. "Race you!"

At the highway, they flagged down a battered purple *microbús.* "There's room at the back," the ticket boy yelled, and they shoved their way to the rear, wedging themselves among the other passengers. As the *micro* lurched forward, a woman's bosom squashed against Rosa's back.

"Good thing you didn't wear a watch." Alonso touched Rosa's wrist.

"I learned my lesson," she replied. On their last *micro* ride, a little boy had torn off her watch and jumped from the bus.

"I shouldn't have let that happen," Alonso said. His fingertip lingered on her wrist, tracing her birthmark. A little brown oval the size of a kiss.

"Don't be *machista*," Rosa retorted. "I should have known better." She could feel goose bumps speckling her birthmark. Her Alcázar birthmark. *La Huella*, Tía Virginia called it. The Mark.

Alonso thought for an instant of slipping his hand under Rosa's curls, hanging like loosely coiled springs down her back. Instead, he slid his fingers between hers. He felt a weird thump in his chest as their hands locked. *Contact!*

As his fingers twined with hers, Rosa stared out the window, struggling for the right look. Nonchalant, but not too nonchalant. Alonso's skin—on his fingers, the back of his hand—was so smooth. A baby's perfect skin, stretched over a man's sinew and bone. She wanted to caress it, to follow that skin up to those broadening shoulders, but she kept her hand still. Motionless.

The *micro* bounced down the highway, slamming into potholes that felt like craters. It stopped and started, rolling past factories and shantytowns. The crowd of passengers ebbed and flowed. Rosa and Alonso barely noticed. Rosa had the feeling that if she looked at Alonso she might burst into flames. Alonso was fighting a wild urge to pull her closer and touch her everywhere at once.

Hold on, he told himself. Knuckles, fingers, palm. *Just hold on.*

After a time they talked, standing side by side, their eyes on the garbage-strewn median. They talked about the new school year, which had just started. About Rosa's week at her grandparents' beach house and Alonso's morning in Miraflores. About everything they could think of. Every few minutes they fell into a hot-faced silence. By the time they reached Canto Grande, their hands were slippery with sweat.

"We're getting off at the corner," Alonso shouted.

"Getting off at the corner," the ticket boy echoed. "Getting off!" The *micro* ground to a halt and Rosa bumped once more into the soft bosom at her back. The ticket boy began to rush them, shouting. "Get off, get off!"

Rosa's hand slid from Alonso's as he jumped down the steps, but they had done it. They had held hands the entire trip. She followed him up a dirt road like the one into Salvador, all half-built houses and the flat taste of dust, and wondered how it would feel when he kissed her.

"Rodolfo's sister got into the teachers' college," Alonso said. He pulled Rosa off the road as a tricycle cart hurtled past. "Mariela."

"That's great," Rosa said. "I'd love to be a teacher."

Alonso snorted. "You're too pretty to be a teacher!"

Glancing at him, Rosa saw a flush spread up his neck like red wine over a tablecloth. She laughed in delight, and a half-naked baby, watching them from the doorway of a shack, laughed with her. Out of the shack's dusky interior came a woman's voice, cooing in response.

Alonso recovered quickly. "You like little kids, don't you?"

Rosa nodded. "I wish I had . . ." She broke off with a shrug. "You're lucky."

"I guess." Alonso laughed. "But I have to share everything." Even his bed. He didn't mention that. It embarrassed him, sleeping with his brother. Sometimes Gustavo wet the bed. "Hey." He bumped his shoulder against Rosa's. "You might get lucky. Baby sister?"

Rosa faked a laugh. "Nah." She looked down. The dust had

turned her sneakers gray and she had the niggling sense that the conversation was taking a wrong turn. Brothers and sisters. Soon it would be Mamá's condition, and she didn't want to spend her afternoon with Alonso talking about that!

Even the word was hard. Endometriosis.

Blood and pain, Mamá once told her. *Like childbirth, without the joy.* Sometimes it drove Mamá right over the edge. Sent her crying to the bedroom until Papá came home and gave her a shot to stop the hurting.

"Have you heard that new song?" she asked. "You know, about blowing up the electrical towers?" She sang, "*Un terrorista, dos terroristas . . .*"

"You never know," Alonso persisted. Babies were unpredictable things. Or mothers were. He wasn't sure if Gustavo had been planned or not.

"No," Rosa said. "I *do* know."

"No, really," he insisted. "Your mother might change her mind and—"

"Alonso, she *can't!*"

"What? She can't?" Alonso was quiet for a few steps. "Oh."

Rosa gave a little sigh of relief.

"I always wondered," he said. "I mean, your father's crazy about kids."

"It's not my mother's fault," Rosa snapped.

Startled, Alonso grabbed her hand. "Rosa, I didn't mean it that way."

She tried to pull free, but he wouldn't let go. "She just *can't,* okay?"

"Okay." Alonso brushed a curl from her temple. "I'm sorry." He started walking again, pulling her with him up the hill.

His palm was dry, his fingers wedged into the little V's between hers. They fit there, perfectly. Rosa took a deep breath, and they walked in silence up the hill.

They climbed for over a kilometer, past *estera* huts and wooden shanties. The roofs were plastic, the doors plywood or corrugated metal. Finally Alonso spoke, his voice light. "You know what I used to want to be when I grew up?"

"What?"

"You really want to know?" Theatrically, he looked around, as if someone might be eavesdropping. Then he lowered his voice. "A superhero."

"A superhero?" Rosa pictured Alonso in skintight red spandex and burst out laughing. "Going around saving people?"

He nodded, making fun of himself, trying to keep her smiling. "Zapping the bad guys. Changing the world." He squeezed her hand. "That was when I was a kid. Now I want to be a doctor."

"Right. And go around saving people." She smiled. "Change the world."

Her eyes met his. Green eyes, flecked with gold. Her lips parted and Alonso's heart gave another great thump. But then his mouth opened, and words tumbled out, and he looked away, hot and confused. "Rodolfo's house is around here somewhere," he mumbled. Across the street, a dozen teenaged boys stood in a tight circle. "Let's ask them." He heard Rosa sigh as they crossed the street.

Within the ring of teenagers, two boys were fighting. They grappled and broke apart, fists swinging. Then, with a great heave, the larger boy threw the smaller one down. The boy's head thudded against the ground and his attacker jumped him and started to punch. Blood surged from the little boy's nose.

"Stop!" Rosa cried.

Alonso rocked slightly on his heels. "Hey, that's enough, no?" Releasing her hand, he pushed through the jeering mob and pried the boys apart, grabbing the larger boy by the shirt collar.

Freed, the smaller boy scrambled to his feet and turned in a slow and wary pirouette. From beneath a dusty black forelock, he scanned the circle of boys. They moved inward, tightening the noose.

"Hey!" A tall boy, his head shaved in a black crewcut, stepped forward. "Why are you butting in?"

Alonso turned. "The little guy lost," he said. "Let him go."

"He's a *terrorista de mierda*," muttered the fighter in his grip. Alonso shook him, and the boy snarled. "He is! A terrorist piece of shit!"

Rosa was so surprised that she laughed. "A *terrorista*? He's only nine or ten!"

"He's from Ayacucho," one of the boys said.

"That doesn't make him a terrorist," Rosa replied.

"Oh, you're an expert?" The crewcut boy sneered. "Don't you know Sendero Luminoso comes from Ayacucho?" He looked her up and down, his gaze lingering on her imported sneakers, her jeans with their brand name sticking out like an expensive price tag. Then he spat. "*Pituca.*"

Pituca. Rich, white, and spoiled. The other boys stared at her. A few hissed.

"Take it easy," Alonso warned.

Crewcut wheeled on him. "And what are you? Her butler? Or maybe you're getting yourself some white meat?" The boys laughed.

"Come on, Alonso," Rosa snapped. "Let's go."

"Come on, Alonso." In a wicked falsetto, the boy mimicked her, then leaned closer, eyebrows raised. "You like dark meat, *mamita*? Let *me* give you some."

Alonso released his captive and shoved Crewcut. "Back off," he growled.

Lowering his head like a ram, the little boy from Ayacucho suddenly butted free of the circle and ran. The other boys swarmed Alonso, shouting and jostling. Red-faced, Alonso shoved back at them, one after another.

Rosa felt Crewcut watching her as waves of boys slammed against Alonso. What should she say? What if she made things worse? The shoving turned into a scuffle, and her fists clenched. What should she do? Punch someone?

Alonso stumbled. He felt himself going down and grabbed a boy's shirt. He pulled himself upright and was shoved into another boy's arms. There were too many of them. Crewcut grinned and reached for Rosa.

Just then another boy, slim, with dark curls and caramel-brown skin, slipped around her. With a quick, deft twist, left foot out and right hand shoving, he sent Crewcut flying. He seized Alonso's arm and dragged him backward till they stood shoulder to shoulder.

Alonso felt an exultant surge. There were two of them now.

"These are my friends," Rodolfo snapped. "You got a problem?"

"Some friends." Crewcut stood up, smacking the dust from his clothes. "A *pituca* and a *terrorista*."

"Watch your mouth," Rodolfo said sharply. "Don't you know the Party has a thousand eyes and a thousand ears?"

The boys gaped, the smaller ones flowing away like waves down the sand. Crewcut eyed Rodolfo. "You want to watch your own mouth, *amigo*." Lips pursed, he sent a loud kiss in Rosa's direction, then swaggered away.

Rosa's knees were trembling, but Alonso laughed and threw his arms around Rodolfo. "*¡Hermano!* My brother!" He thumped Rodolfo on the back. "Perfect timing!"

Rodolfo shook off Alonso's hand and gave Rosa a peck on the cheek. "You know better than to get into fights. What are you doing here, anyway?"

"Sightseeing." Alonso grinned. "What do you think? We came to see you!"

Rodolfo shrugged. "Come on. I was gonna get a drink." He led them to a cement hut, where a wooden board nailed to the windowsill served as a counter. "Inka Kola," he muttered. The woman inside passed out three bottles of soda.

They sat on a bench by a brick wall, beneath a scrawled red slogan. *Long Live the Armed Struggle.* Alonso tipped his bottle above his mouth and took a swig. "How've you been, *hermano?*"

"Okay." Rodolfo shrugged again. "You?"

"Pretty good. School, you know. Soccer up at the parish. We miss you on the team. And at Mass."

"You still an altar boy?" Rodolfo laughed, short and hard. "And still a superhero, no?"

Alonso lowered his bottle and stared.

"*Caramba*, Alonso." Rodolfo didn't try to mask his scorn. "Getting into a fight like that. Those guys would have massacred you, and God knows what they'd have done to Rosa."

"So what did you want us to do?" Alonso retorted. "Call the police?"

"Only if you've got a gun." Rodolfo wasn't smiling. "Take out a few cops. Now that'd be worth the trouble."

"Stop, Rodolfo," Rosa said. "You sound like a terrorist."

"Yeah? And how many terrorists have you met?" Rodolfo glared at her. "'Cuz I've met plenty, and they were all wearing uniforms."

"Oh, come on." Rosa frowned. "I don't like cops, but Sendero's worse."

"What do you know? Did the cops ever break down your door at two in the morning?" At her shocked expression Rodolfo laughed bitterly. "No, I guess that doesn't happen in places like Miraflores."

"You're kidding!" Alonso burst out. "When did that happen?"

"In February," Rodolfo snapped. "You think I'd joke about it? Eight of them, in ski masks. They broke down the door and started beating the crap out of everybody. Even my mother."

He was snarling like a hurt dog, dangerous. But Rosa suddenly saw him as he'd looked ten years ago, the day she'd met him. A tousle-haired shantytown kid, with skinny arms and dark curls and a black eye his father had given him. "Rodolfo," she breathed. She touched the bony ridge of his forearm.

Rodolfo blinked, staring down at her hand. "The cops hauled them all off in the back of a pickup truck. My mother, my uncle. Mariela." He looked up at Alonso. "You shoulda heard the kids. They went nuts!"

Alonso drew his brows together. "What about your neighbors?"

"My neighbors?" Rodolfo sounded bitter. "There's nobody like your mother around here, Alonso."

"But your mother . . . Is she . . . ?" Rosa didn't want to see the picture in her mind. Rodolfo's mother hauled away, screaming, by men in ski masks.

This didn't happen to your friends. You read about it in the newspaper. Doors beaten down in the middle of the night. Pistols and nightsticks. A new name on the long list of the disappeared.

She tried again. "Your *mamá*. Is she . . . ?"

"She came home with a black eye. And Mariela . . ." Rodolfo slammed his soda bottle on the bench. "Mariela came home pregnant." He jerked his arm free of Rosa's hand. "So don't tell me about cops, Rosa. 'Cuz you don't know shit!"

Mariela. Alonso felt the world tilt around him. *Mariela.* "Is she all right?"

Rodolfo snorted. "Oh, sure, she's fine. What do *you* think, Alonso?"

Rosa felt dizzy, a little sick. Mariela. A slender girl with a cascade of black hair, round-faced like Rodolfo's mother. She must be about nineteen now. Dragged from a cell and raped by a cop.

"My uncle's in prison," Rodolfo said. "With the political prisoners."

"With the terrorists?"

"They're not terrorists!" Rodolfo shoved Alonso's chest, lightly. "You know who's taking care of my sister? A doctor from the Party. She didn't even know Mariela, and she isn't charging us anything!" His voice grew quiet and he cocked his head. "You know what the Party does to rapists?"

The two boys stared at each other.

"Okay, *hermano*." Alonso shook his friend's shoulder gently. "Okay. But don't you get involved."

"I'm not stupid, Alonso." Rodolfo stood up. "But they're the only ones doing shit to change things."

"You can change things without killing anybody," Alonso said. "Look at Rosa's father."

Rodolfo laughed. "If you think that, you're dumber than I thought."

"Rodolfo—" Alonso began.

"Aw, shit, 'mano, just forget it!" Suddenly, Rodolfo was wheeling on his heel. "I gotta go. See ya some other time, okay?"

Alonso reached for him. "*Hermano*, we came here to see you—"

Rodolfo dodged. "I got stuff to do." He paused, his eyes on Alonso, pleading. "I gotta go, okay?"

A thin figure in loose jeans, he was in the road for just a moment. Then he turned down a narrow path between some shacks and disappeared.

·THREE·

Alonso lay in his bed, watching the bedroom grow pale with the dawn. Gustavo wheezed by his side. Across the room, the girls' hair traced black and feathery veins against a white pillowcase. The neighbor's rooster crowed—*kikirikiki!*—and somewhere outside a radio switched on. Electric guitars chimed as a band belted out a *música chicha* hit. *I'm small, but I get up early, I'm poor, so I get up early. . . .*

Alonso stretched his toes, looked out the window at a milky gray sky, and muttered a little prayer for sunshine. Today was the Cesip anniversary, the big party, and Rosa was coming. She hadn't been able to come to the clinic last Saturday, but she'd be here today, she'd promised. Alonso yawned and swung his feet over the side of the bed.

To work, to work, if you're poor you get up early. . . .

From the kitchen came the low murmur of his parents' voices. A spoon clinked, stirring sugar into coffee. Still yawning, Alonso pulled on his jeans.

The kitchen was warm, and smelled of morning. Of steaming coffee and bread fresh off the baker's cart. Alonso kissed his father, who was already dressed in his brown security guard uniform. He kissed his mother, and she wrapped her arms around his neck.

"Mamá!"

"Brush your hair before you get the porridge," she said. "You're all spiky."

Alonso padded across the cement floor and out to the backyard, a dusty rectangle three meters deep. His mother had been up early, watering the plants. Droplets of water still clung to the tomatoes. The cement patio, where they stored the water barrels and laundry basins, was brown with damp.

Alonso dipped a jug into a barrel and filled a basin. He steeled himself, staring into the tiny orange pool. He imagined himself a cliff diver, plunging into the sea. Then he held his breath, shut his eyes, and dunked. Sputtering and gasping, he surfaced and grabbed a towel.

Someday there'd be running water and hot showers, *someday, someday, someday*. He toweled off, brushed his hair, and ran inside.

His father was dipping his bread, sopping up the last of his coffee. His mother held out a coin for the porridge. Alonso grabbed a pot and headed for the *comedor* to pick up their breakfast rations. In the living room, his parents' bed was already made.

"Put on a sweater," his mother called softly.

"Ay, woman, let the boy be," his father mumbled.

Alonso was closing the front door when he saw the note. A folded sheet of blue-lined paper, wedged against the little panel of glass. He wriggled it out and shook it open.

Magdalena Rios: The Party unleashes the People's wrath on corrupt revisionist scum who castrate the revolutionary potential of the People. You have betrayed the People. You will be annihilated. Long live the People's War! Long live the Guiding Thought of Chairman Gonzalo!

Alonso didn't get it, at first. *What?* he thought. And, *Why?* Then he read the note again and his fingers grew cold.

The door opened. "Alonso, what is it?"

Alonso dropped the pot and handed his father the note.

It took his father a long time to read it. Lips moving, eyes narrowed. All those long words and Senderista slogans. Alonso waited. When his father folded the note and went back inside, Alonso slipped in behind him.

His mother was still in the kitchen, rinsing coffee cups in the basin. She frowned a little when she saw them, and Alonso's father gave her the note.

Her hands began to shake as she read. She crossed herself, kissed her thumb. Alonso stepped forward, but his father pushed him aside.

"Little dove," he murmured. He sat her down, holding her arms as though she might fall over. "We have to tell the police."

She shook her head. "If we take one side, the other will come after us."

Alonso leaned against the wall, his heart thudding. That wasn't his mother's voice, shaking that way.

"But Magda . . ." Alonso's father sank on his heels. "Magda, this is a death threat."

The kitchen was silent. Alonso could hear another *chicha* band, wailing from the neighbor's radio.

"Magda, *please*."

"They're just trying to frighten me." Chin rising, she tossed her hair back. "This isn't the first note."

"What?"

She turned to Alonso. "Go get the porridge, Alonso."

Alonso didn't move.

"There was another note?" Alonso's father shook her arm. "When? What did it say?"

"A few days ago." Her mouth snapped shut. "It said I had to resign."

"Then you have to."

"I knew you'd say that!" She twisted her arm from his hand. "And you know that as soon as I'm out the Mothers' Club will do exactly what Sendero wants. Turn the Cesip into a People's Hospital. And then the government will shut us down." Her voice turned brittle. "All the better for the revolution, no? The Cesip just cushions our misery. Isn't that what the comrades say?"

Alonso's father slid backward onto a chair. "Ay, Magda," he murmured. "Why do you have to be so stubborn?"

Suddenly she was shrieking. "How can you even ask me that? I lost two children before we had the Cesip!" Both hands flew to her mouth, covering it. Tears spilled silently down her cheeks.

Next door, the neighbor's rooster crowed.

"*Magda.*" Alonso's father leaned toward her, his voice low.

"Babies die. That's just the way it is. You still have four children to raise."

With one careful finger, she wiped the tears from beneath her eyes. "Ay, Tomás." She took his hand. "Please. We can handle this. We can organize a neighborhood watch. Pablo's getting me a bodyguard—"

"Pablo?" Alonso's father sounded bewildered. "You told *Pablo* about the other note?" He stood with a sudden upward jerk. "You told him and not me?"

"I was going to tell you . . ." She broke off. "It's not like that!"

"No?" Savagely, he swung around and shoved past Alonso. The front door slammed. Gustavo began to wail.

"*¡Ay, carajo!*"

Alonso stared. His mother never cursed. "*Carajo*, Alonso," she snapped. "Do something about your brother!"

She snatched the note and carried it over to the little propane stove. Alonso stepped uncertainly toward Gustavo's cries, watching as his mother struck a match and held the paper to the flame.

That's evidence, he thought.

The note flamed and fell, curling to black on the enamel surface of the stove. Alonso turned and ran for the front door. His father was fifty meters away, striding past the Cesip. "Papá!" Alonso sprinted down the road. "Papá, what are you doing?"

His father stopped. "I have to go to work."

"But—"

"She'll have to resign. She can do it tomorrow."

"But Mamá doesn't want—"

"*¡Carajo!*" His father grabbed him by the shoulders and shook him. "I don't care what she wants! They'll kill her!"

Alonso tried not to wince as his father's fingers drilled into him. "I'll take care of her, Papá. Today. At the anniversary."

His father's lips twisted into a mocking smile.

Aw, fuck him! Alonso thought. *He's always the same—*

But his father yanked him forward into a hug so tight it squeezed the air from Alonso's lungs. "There'll be a big crowd," his father muttered. "They won't come after her today." He gave Alonso a gentle shake. Then he turned and strode down the road. Alonso watched until he was a brown stick figure, disappearing into the distance.

When Alonso got home, his mother was sitting at the kitchen table. Gustavo, the baby of the family, sat on her lap, sucking his thumb. "Go get the porridge," she commanded. Her gaze, dry-eyed and cold, held his. "And Alonso, I want this to be a day of celebration. So not a word. Do you understand?"

"*Sí*, Mamá." Alonso nodded. "I won't say anything."

Hefting Gustavo onto her hip, his mother stood up to fetch a pan of milk that sat warming on the stove. Alonso slipped into the bedroom and pulled a wooden box from under his bed.

His treasure box. He lifted the lid. On top lay a picture of Rosa, and beneath that, everything else he'd cared to save from his fifteen years on the planet. Ticket stubs from an Alianza soccer game. A first-aid certificate from the Cesip. A San Martín de Porres medal from Padre Manuel. A little green car that had belonged to Emilio, one of his two baby brothers who had died. Green had been Emilio's favorite color.

Alonso reached into the box and pulled out a pocketknife. Then he went outside. The pot still lay where it had fallen, overturned in the dust.

□ □ □

TENTH ANNIVERSARY! A white banner stretched across the Cesip, with big blue letters to match the clinic's walls. Loudspeakers pounded *chicha* music, and a crowd of dancing, laughing, shouting neighbors jammed the front lot.

Alonso stood beside his mother, gnawing kernels off an ear of corn. She smiled absently, listening as a woman rattled on and on about her daughter's *quinceañera*. The cake. The dress. The forty-seven guests. The lavish fifteenth birthday party had put the family in debt. It was important to share every detail.

A car engine hummed somewhere down the hill. Alonso spun around to look, but the crowd surrounded him, too thick to see through. He groped for the knife in his pocket.

Corrupt revisionist scum . . . You have betrayed the People. . . .

Stroking the knife's smooth plastic shell, Alonso pressed closer to his mother and wished, for the hundredth time, that she were someone else. Someone kind, but anonymous. Serving soup in the *comedor*, maybe, or helping out with the latrine brigade. Why did she have to be such a big shot? People had been kissing her all afternoon. A photographer had taken her picture. A reporter from *Radioprogramas* had interviewed her. Everyone had news to share. A healthy baby. A son graduating from high school. How was he supposed to keep her safe when she kept kissing complete strangers?

And she was no help at all. She was glowing, all made up in her white blouse, her red skirt, her good black shoes. She'd put on pink lipstick and mascara and forgotten all about the note!

Feeling his arm against hers, she held up a hand to halt the stream of details about the *quinceañera*. "Alonso." She kept her voice light, but her eyes fixed on his. "Why don't you do something useful? Go help Rosa with the children." Alonso shook his head. With an exasperated shrug, she turned away.

Let her. He'd promised to take care of her.

Finally he spotted the car. Dark blue and huge, with armored windows and diplomatic license plates. Two tall, fair-haired men emerged from the backseat, and Alonso relaxed. They were Dr. Pablo's gringos, come to join the celebration. A few weeks ago, they'd donated a new refrigerator and a truckload of laboratory equipment.

Alonso followed his mother through the crowd. "Welcome, *señores*." She shook the gringos' hands with great ceremony, then turned to Alonso. "*Hijo*, go get them some *chicha morada*. They must be thirsty after their long drive."

He started to protest, but the look in her eye silenced him.

The gringos smiled down at her like friendly giants. Dr. Pablo had his arm across her shoulder. And Padre Manuel was approaching, a welcoming smile crinkling the corners of his eyes. What could the Senderistas do? Alonso slipped through the crowd and ran to the *comedor*.

Rosa met him at the door. "I need some *chicha* for the gringos," he panted.

"I haven't seen you all day," she complained. "We gave the kids lunch." She pointed at a nearby table. Livia, Diana, and

Gustavo sat eating. His mother's friend Señorita Ana waved, her polished fingernails fluttering like rose petals. Rosa's mother was cutting Diana's meat. She looked up, blond and gorgeous, and gave Alonso such a warm smile that on any other day he would have stopped to bask in it.

But not today. He splashed *chicha*, splattering the table. Rosa clucked at him. "Here, let me." She poured two glasses and followed him out.

His mother was explaining to the Americans how the new equipment would make it easier to vaccinate the kids in Salvador. The gringos nodded and smiled, baring rows of impossibly straight white teeth.

"Here you are, *señor*." Alonso shoved a glass at the taller American.

The gringo peered into the purple depths. Alonso tried to give the other glass to the shorter American, but the man shooed him away. For a moment their hands danced, Alonso trying to advance the glass while the man tried to ward it off. Finally Alonso glanced at his mother and shrugged.

Dr. Pablo laughed. "I put some Coca-Cola in the refrigerator," he said. "How does that sound?"

The Americans babbled with relief. "*Sí, sí*. Coca-Cola." Sheepishly, the taller gringo handed his glass back to Alonso. "*Gracias*," he said.

Alonso grinned at the accent, then caught his mother's glare. He raised his eyebrows innocently, and Rosa snorted, choking on a laugh. His mother grabbed them both by the arms. "We'll get it," she snapped. "You two come with me."

Silently, she led them across the lot, weaving through the crowd and into the Cesip. Her heels clicked on the cement.

Suddenly she burst out laughing. "Did you see that tall one?"

"The way he looked at the *chicha*—"

"As if something might crawl out of it and bite him," Rosa finished. "And that other one . . ." She waved her hands in a slapstick imitation of the American's effort to fend off the *chicha*. Alonso and his mother bent double, laughing.

Finally his mother wiped her eyes. "Ay, *Señor*. Rosa, your father warned me, but I forgot. The gringos are still panicking about the cholera epidemic. Come on." Nearing the laboratory, she patted her skirt pocket. "Ay, *no*. I gave the keys to Ana." She tried the laboratory door and then peered down the hallway. The back door stood open, spilling sunlight onto the cement floor. "Alonso, go see if you can find Señorita Ana. Otherwise, Dr. Pablo has keys."

Still laughing, Alonso loped through the lobby. The Americans must think Salvador grew Superman bacteria. Nothing survives in *chicha morada*, which you boil for hours. But maybe gringos didn't know that.

He hopped down the front steps and paused, blinking in the sunshine. People didn't step aside for him the way they did for his mother. Five men blocked his way. "Excuse me," he said.

They were arguing about whether the last President was worse than this one. "At least we had enough to eat," one declared. Two or three other men shouted him down.

"Excuse me," Alonso repeated. They ignored him, so he shrugged and shoved his way through. He went on shoving, pushing through dozens of happy and unyielding neighbors.

Señorita Ana wasn't in the *comedor*. Alonso circled around the edge of the crowd, looking for Dr. Pablo and his gringos. They weren't hard to find. The gringos towered over everyone else, so pale they seemed lit by a spotlight.

"Dr. Pablo, the lab's locked." Alonso coughed as a red car rattled past, spinning up a cloud of dust. "We need your keys."

Dr. Pablo reached into his pocket, watching the car. It stopped fifty meters below them. The driver leaned out, and a woman at the edge of the crowd pointed at the Cesip. "Were you expecting anyone else from the embassy?"

One of the gringos shook his head. "No, Doctor. Just us."

The car rolled down the hill, and Alonso felt a prickle, like soda fizz on the back of his neck. "Who could it be?"

Padre Manuel smiled as the car slid out of sight behind the Cesip. "Probably journalists. I was expecting a few more."

Dr. Pablo tugged a set of keys from his pocket and frowned. "These are my car keys. I must have left the others in my car." He turned to the Americans. "Why not come along? We'll have a look at the lab. You won't recognize it."

Jabbering about vaccine cold chains and germ cultures, the four men strolled to Dr. Pablo's Toyota. Alonso bounced nervously after them. *Come on*, he thought. How long could it take to unlock a car door? To root around in a glove compartment?

"Here we go." Dr. Pablo finally unbent his long body from within the car. He was holding up a ring of keys when a faint scream drifted toward them. *"MAGDA!"*

Alonso whipped around. The Cesip's front door stood open,

a shadowy rectangle in a blue wall. Hundreds of people crowded in front of it, drinking *chicha* and eating grilled chicken. Children darted in and out of a forest of adult legs. At the center of the crowd, a few couples pressed together, trying to dance.

Alonso strained to listen. He heard throbbing loudspeakers. Friendly shouts. *Carajo*, he thought. *I'm going nuts.*

He couldn't wait for the day to be over.

He was reaching for Dr. Pablo's keys when he heard the scream again. "MAGDA!" This time he recognized the voice.

Rosa.

In two steps, he was flying. Flying toward that shadowy doorway. His heart seemed to race ahead of him, plunging through the doorway and—

"Hey, watch out, kid!" With a dull thud, Alonso slammed into a fat man holding a glass of *chicha*. He dodged, seeking a path. An uneven line of people blocked his way. "I've got to get through," he panted. "My *mamá* . . ."

The fat man laughed. Enraged, Alonso hurled him aside. The man lunged, but Alonso slid into the crowd. Another scream rose above the noise and Alonso's heart clenched like a fist.

You will be annihilated.

"MOVE!" He shoved past a man in a white shirt. A woman in green blocked his way. An elbow jabbed him. He tripped over someone's leg, fell toward shoes and dust. Legs everywhere, a thicket of them. He pulled himself upright and bucked forward, squeezing between chests and backs. He had to get through. Shoulders slammed against him. The screams from the Cesip became one long wailing shriek.

A gunshot cracked, and now Alonso began to scream. To scream and to punch, opening a tunnel with his fists. Face after face fell back, startled, fearful. The way was opening. The screams from the Cesip went on and on and—

He was free. The blue wall rose before him. White-faced, Rosa lurched through the doorway.

"Where is she?" Alonso shouted. Two loud pops exploded in the Cesip. "Where's my mother?"

Rosa stumbled down to him. "No, Alonso!"

He shoved her away and ran up the steps.

In a single pounding heartbeat, he saw it all. The lobby's benches, lined up like coffins. Four shadows standing in the hall. At their feet, a twitching heap of red and white. Legs askew, she struggled to rise. The smallest shadow bent, aiming a pistol.

"NO!" Alonso hurled forward, but as the gunshot echoed up the corridor someone grabbed him from behind. Twisting, flailing, Alonso felt himself pulled from the building. "Let me go!" he screamed. "I said I'd take care of her!"

Grim, wordless, Padre Manuel dragged him outside. Behind them, a wave of people was trying to flee. Another wave was pushing forward to see what was happening. Somewhere in that choppy sea of bodies Rosa screamed. *Do something! Papi, do something!*

"Hold him!" Padre Manuel shouted. A dozen hands grabbed Alonso, tearing at his shirt. Arms tangled around his waist as Padre Manuel raced back to the doorway. Then he turned around, waving madly. "Get back, get back, they've got dynamite!"

The crowd screamed and surged backward. Padre Manuel ran inside as a thunderous explosion blew. He sailed out on a rush of air.

Thrown to the ground, Alonso struggled to his feet. His head rang. His eyes were full of grit. *Mamá—*

Another explosion boomed, louder than the first. A blast of air punched him in the chest. He went down again, fingers fumbling in the dirt.

I said I'd take care of her—

The Cesip's blue walls shuddered. The air itself shivered. Then a wave of dust and smoke rolled over him, and everything went black.

▫FOUR▫

Rosa sat in the living room, listening to the music of the ocean. Wave after wave, thundering against the shore, tumbling the stones seaward in a long tinkling murmur. She listened until the growl of a truck, rumbling down the *Malecón*, drowned out the waves, and the police captain sitting before her coughed discreetly.

The captain, a plainclothes detective from DINCOTE, the antiterrorist police, was tapping a pencil against a little notepad. Another officer stood beside the sliding doors to the terrace, looking out at the morning mist. Mamá sat beside Rosa on the sofa. Papá stood and listened, paced, then stood again, jerked like a puppet between stillness and motion.

"Can you describe them?" The captain repeated his question.

"I didn't see their faces. They had on ski masks."

"Please try to understand," Mamá told the officer. "We're still in shock. Rosa had to be sedated again last night. . . ." Her voice trailed off.

The police captain, in his gray suit and scuffed shoes, seemed remarkably mild-mannered for a member of the fearsome DIN-COTE. "I understand, *señora*. But the sooner we do this, the fresher the details will be in her mind." Arms folded, he leaned back and stretched his legs. "You said there were four of them. Men or women?"

Rosa looked down at her hands, and was surprised to find them tightly clenched. When she opened her fingers, her nails left four tiny crescents on each palm.

"Rosa." Papá's hoarse voice broke through. "Just try to answer, so the officers can leave."

Rosa stared at him, blankly, and Papá swallowed and looked away. "One was short," she said finally. "She was a woman, I think."

"What was she wearing?"

"Clothes," Rosa said. She scratched her birthmark. "I don't know. Her shoes . . ." The shoes had clicked in the cement hallway. Women's shoes. Black pumps, like Magda's.

The officer waited.

"The others were taller. Men, I guess."

"How short was the woman?" The captain's voice probed at her, and Rosa knew then that his mild ways were a ruse. He was an expert at torture. All the DINCOTE officers were. Everyone said so. "Do you remember how short she was, Rosa?"

"Very. Shorter than Magda."

"And they came through the back door?"

They had come through the back door, four shadowy figures in black ski masks. Magda was heading toward the front door, muttering about how long Alonso was taking. Rosa waited by the lab, staring as four shadows stalked up the hall. Six sneakers padding and two shoes clicking. Then the shadow people pulled out guns. That was when Rosa started to scream, when . . . "They ran toward us and shot Magda. I ran away. I heard them shoot some more. . . ."

She fell silent. It was remarkable, she knew, how calm she looked. In her living room, with the sofa cushions yielding beneath her thighs. The waxy scent of Mamá's lipstick at her side. And, in her mind, the screams.

She should have run, not screamed.

"Did any of them say anything?"

Rosa shook her head. Only Magda had spoken.

"Okay." The police captain stood up, and Rosa felt a wave of relief so huge she thought she might just float away on it. The captain was scribbling something on his notepad. He tore off the sheet and handed it to Papá. "Call us if she remembers anything else," he said.

As the door closed, Papá looked at his watch. "We need to get ready." Rosa stood, but Papá shook his head. "No, Rosa. You stay home. Get some rest."

Stunned, Rosa slumped backward on the sofa. "Papá—"

He bent to kiss her forehead. "Verónica's here. And we'll ask your grandparents to come over again." With a close-lipped smile, he went to the bedroom.

Mamá put her arms around Rosa.

"Mamá," Rosa whispered. "I didn't go to the wake."

"You were in no condition yesterday," Mamá soothed. "Everyone understood." She cupped Rosa's chin in her hand. "Alonso understood," she said firmly.

"But I have to go to the funeral!" Rosa heard the edge of panic in her own voice, and struggled to master it. "Don't you see? I have to."

They were both silent for a moment, as Mamá searched her eyes and Rosa did her best not to look away. Finally, it seemed that Mamá did see, for she nodded. "Wait here," she said.

Rosa sat on the couch, feeling nauseous. Mist seemed to have seeped into the room. But that was impossible. It must be the tranquilizers.

She couldn't remember much about the night of Magda's death. After the explosions, everything was a breathless blur of screams and sirens until Mamá took her home and gave her a pill to make her sleep.

Yesterday was clearer. Verónica, the maid, had made soup, the only thing Rosa could swallow. Her grandparents had come over while Mamá and Papá went to Magda's wake. They'd brought Rosa's cousin, Gabriela.

It was Gabriela who had set the roller coaster going. A little hug was all it took, and Rosa was sobbing into Gabriela's neck, getting Gabriela's beautiful straight hair all wet and sticky. But then they'd watched a Cantinflas movie on television, and Rosa had begun laughing uproariously at the Mexican comedian's antics. The others had watched her with worried eyes, but she couldn't stop laughing. And then she had gone to bed, and that was when the voice began.

A whisper. Barely formed. *Rosa* . . . Quietly, drifting like mist. *Rosa* . . .

Rosa hadn't been able to tell if the voice was inside her bed-room or inside her head. She'd started crying again and couldn't stop, a windup doll streaming sobs and tears. And the whispers had gone on and on. Rosa had tried to get a grip, to pray on the rosary her grandmother had brought. Polished mahogany spheres on a silver chain, with a silver cross and a finely muscled Jesus in agony. She had wept her way through one Our Father and three Hail Marys, and finally Papá had given her a tranquilizer.

"Pablo." Mamá was in the bedroom. "I think she should come with us."

Hangers scraped on a closet rail. "She's not going back there," Papá said. "It's too dangerous."

"I don't think so. I think it'll help."

Rosa heard her father's abrupt refusal, her mother's soft reply. "She needs to go, *mi amor*. She—"

"*Carajo*, Charo!" His voice slashed across hers. "This could have been her funeral!" The closet door slammed. "God, what was I thinking?"

When Mamá spoke, after a long pause, her voice was careful, as if she were picking up broken glass. "They were after Magda, Pablo. Not Rosa."

In the silence that followed, Rosa suddenly knew. This wasn't up to her parents. They didn't know. They couldn't know why she had to go.

"Pablo, don't you think—?"

"NO!" he shouted. But Papá never shouted. Rosa got to her feet.

Dizziness darkened the room around her, but she forced herself to stand, swaying slightly, until it passed. In the bedroom, Papá was pulling on a white shirt. A dark suit lay on the bed.

"I am going to the funeral," Rosa announced. "I'll get dressed now." She turned and walked to her room.

In her closet hung a black gabardine skirt and a black silk blouse. She'd worn them last spring for the funeral of her grandfather's sister. Tía Mercedes had been ancient, the oldest living Alcázar. Fifteen years older than Rosa's grandfather, with wrinkles beyond counting and blue eyes gone silver with age.

She touched the skirt, smelled the light, toxic perfume of mothballs. No one was surprised when Tía Mercedes died. Sometimes they talked about her at family lunches. A bit nostalgic, maybe, but without real pain.

She turned from the closet to find her parents watching her. Papá sat down on the bed and began buttoning his cuffs. "*Mi amor,*" he began gently.

Rosa cut him off. "I am going to the funeral," she repeated. A chill was spreading inside her, sharp and clean, driving the clouds from her mind. "If you leave without me, I'll take a *micro* to Salvador."

Her father blinked. "You'll do as I say." Beneath the sharp edge of his voice, Rosa sensed his longing. He wanted her to thaw, to cry as she had the day before. He wanted to comfort her.

But she didn't want comfort. She didn't want him or anyone else to tell her that it wasn't her fault, that everything would be all right. She pulled the blouse from its hanger. "Don't try to stop me, Papá."

Her father stood up, his neck bright red.

"Enough, Pablo." Mamá broke in curtly. "Enough. Rosa's coming with us. Now come and finish dressing." Mamá turned and went back to their bedroom. Papá stood, stroking his moustache, but Rosa knew it was decided. Mamá rarely used that tone, but when she did, there was no appealing it.

As her father left the room, Rosa pulled off her sweatshirt and slipped into the black silk blouse.

□ □ □

They drove to Salvador in silence, Mamá sitting in the backseat with Rosa. As they approached the Cesip, she reached over and held Rosa's hand. Staring out the window, Rosa saw the blue walls. Still standing, but blackened and covered with dust. Part of the roof had caved in.

On top of Magda. Rosa shivered.

Two green trucks were parked in front of the Cesip, an armored troop carrier and a large flatbed with canvas enclosing the back. A group of men in olive drab stood behind the flatbed, long black rifles slung across their backs. A man inside the truck was shouting at them.

"Soldiers," Rosa whispered.

Her mother nodded. "The Army. Special Forces."

"Why?"

Papá answered. "Because when Sendero kills a community leader, they usually mean to take over the community themselves." His eyes caught Rosa's in the rearview mirror. "The war has come to Salvador."

Rosa turned to watch as the Toyota toiled up the hill. The man in the truck, who wore a beret and seemed to be in command, jumped out. He strode toward the wreckage of the Cesip with his men following.

The Toyota passed Alonso's house, with its flat roof and its black metal rebar stabbing the air, waiting for a second story to be built. A police car was parked out front, and two cops in camouflage flanked the front door.

At the top of the hill, outside the church, stood a big black hearse. Cars swarmed, trying to park, squeezing as close as they could to the churchyard's whitewashed walls. People were pouring from the cars and through the gate. Three children in dirty sweat suits watched, openmouthed.

They've probably never seen so many cars in their lives, Rosa thought.

A man slammed the door of a shiny gray sedan and approached the children. Pointing at his car, he spoke to them briefly. The children nodded and smiled and sat down on the car's rear bumper. They were bouncing with excitement, and the man looked satisfied as he walked into the churchyard.

Papá parked a meter from the children's dangling legs. "Let's go," he said.

"Hey, *señor*," one of the little boys called. "You want us to watch your car? For one *sol* we'll make sure nobody touches it!"

His sister jabbed him with her elbow. "Shut up, silly. That's Dr. Pablo. *Hola*, Dr. Pablo. Don't worry, we'll watch your car. For free."

"*Gracias, hijita*." Papá cleared his throat. Above the white collar, the blue knot of his tie, his Adam's apple jerked. Rosa watched as he tried to lock the door. The key jammed and he struggled with it, choking out a few words and then slamming his fist on the roof. He slumped over with a ragged cry. He was curling downward, arms folded across his chest, sobbing.

He'll fly apart in pieces, Rosa thought. She looked away. *He has to hold himself like that or bits of him will go flying. The way Magda did.*

Mamá was getting out on the other side of the car, pale and elegant in her black dress. When she saw Papá double over, her expression changed, darkening with a tenderness so intense it made Rosa's throat ache. She watched him for just an instant, and then gave the children a bright smile. "Thank you," she said. "That would be very kind."

The children beamed as Mamá took over. She handed Papá a handkerchief, laying one hand on his elbow and beckoning to Rosa with the other. Then, holding them both, she walked toward the church.

Mamá's hand felt good on Rosa's elbow. It didn't crowd her with feeling, just kept her steady as she walked her tightrope. One wrong step and they'd all go crashing down to the ground. But if they could just stay cool, if people would just not get so *emotional*, she'd keep her balance. She'd be fine.

At the gate, Rosa stopped, startled. Padre Manuel's churchyard was jam-packed with people. It looked like a carnival, a block party. People were waving signs and flags. Banners from two or three different political parties. Hand-lettered placards. THOU SHALT NOT KILL, one read. NEITHER WITH HUNGER NOR WITH BULLETS. Big black boxes hung from the churchyard walls. Loudspeakers, so the funeral Mass could be heard outside.

Mamá nudged Rosa and her father through the gate, and they picked their way along the edge of the churchyard. The noise of the crowd blurred and mixed up together. Every now and then a single voice rolled toward them. "Mario said he was coming, but . . ."

"It was dynamite. . . . They spent all night picking up her pieces. . . ."

Then, abruptly, hundreds of angry voices began chanting. "Sendero, murderers, go to hell!"

Not everyone shouted. In one corner, near the gate, a tall, gray-haired man was talking to some reporters. Rosa knew him from television. He was a senator.

"Who are all these people?" she asked her mother. Mamá was still holding her elbow as they squeezed along the wall, heading for the big wooden doors of the church. "Did they all know Magda?"

Mamá shook her head. "It was in the papers, on the news. Some people want to express solidarity." She looked at the tall senator, but said no more.

And some people want to be on television, Rosa thought.

A slender, bearded man approached, spreading his arms wide. A socialist congressman, one of her father's oldest friends, he gave Papá a fierce hug, then kissed Mamá and Rosa.

As he did so, one of the reporters mobbing the senator glanced in their direction. "It's her!" the reporter exclaimed. All the journalists turned to look. They gave an excited cry and swooped toward Rosa. Microphones aloft, they surrounded her and her parents, pinning them against the wall of the church.

Rosa shrank backward. "No interviews," Papá barked. The bearded congressman tried to talk to the reporters, but they clamored in protest. One began shouting questions. "Rosa! Did you see them? Can you identify the killers?" The other reporters took up the cry. "Rosa! Tell us what happened, Rosa!"

Rosa pressed against the wall, trying to melt into it. To become one of the pebbly little bumps under the whitewash. Papá was shouting at the reporters. Mamá's shoulders were stiff. A television camera was looming above them like a locomotive bearing down. Camera lenses blinked and shutters clicked. Rosa closed her eyes. *Oh, God,* she thought. *Please.*

Abruptly, the din seemed to lessen. She opened her eyes to see Padre Manuel standing on the steps of his church. He wore a white cassock, with a rope around his waist. A polished wooden cross hung from his neck. The Archbishop stood beside him, tall and slender and swathed in satin. The two gazed at the crowd, and as they did so, the silence became complete. Padre Manuel walked down the steps toward Rosa, nodding gently as the journalists fell back. His homely face was ravaged with grief, but as his eyes met hers, Rosa saw only love.

Oh, no, she thought desperately. *Don't look at me like that.* Her eyes stung as she tried to look away.

"Come inside, child," he said, taking her hands. The crowd stepped back, and Rosa walked into the church with Padre Manuel and the Archbishop.

Inside, the church was cool and shadowed, thick with a sweet musk of incense. A hush hung in the air, though hundreds of people crowded the benches. Padre Manuel led Rosa up the center aisle. Her neck burned under the stares. She kept her head down, trying to wipe away the tears. But they wouldn't stop. They just kept rolling down her cheeks and she kept smearing them away, her hands wet and nowhere to dry them. Not on the gabardine skirt. Not on the silk blouse.

In the front of the church, she sat down on a roughhewn wooden bench. A shining casket lay in the sanctuary before the altar. Across the aisle sat Tomás and his children, along with Señorita Ana, a few neighbors, and a group of nuns. The nuns wore skirts and blouses. Simple crosses and close-cropped gray hair.

Papá handed Rosa a handkerchief and slid his arm around her. It felt heavy on her shoulder.

Across the aisle, Tomás was staring straight ahead, his shoulders rigid. Diana was curled on his lap, sucking her thumb and looking younger than her four years. Livia was crying. She was just nine, but nobody was holding her. Sitting between her father and Señorita Ana, Livia cried alone, her feet not reaching the floor. *Somebody should hold her,* Rosa thought. *Livia needs someone to hold her.* But Señorita Ana was holding Gustavo. Her head was bowed, and her hair brushed his as she prayed and held him tight.

Rosa stared at Alonso's high-cheeked profile, and he turned to look at her. Blank-eyed, as if she were a stranger, and then with a twitch of recognition. But when she wiped her cheeks, trying to get rid of those stupid, endless tears, his expression froze. He turned back to Padre Manuel, who opened his Bible and began to read.

" 'I am the true vine, and my Father is the vine grower,' "
Padre Manuel said.

Rosa's thoughts flew to Alonso, to the way he had turned
from her. *He hates me*, she thought. She forced herself to listen
to Padre Manuel.

Alonso sat very still, watching the priest speak. *He hates me*,
Rosa thought again. The certainty made her heart grow very
still, as if it might simply stop beating. *Alonso hates me.*

" 'This is my commandment: love one another as I love you.
No one has greater love than this, to lay down one's life for one's
friends.' "

No wonder he hates me. His mother laid down her life for me.

Padre Manuel closed his Bible and looked up.

"One April morning, ten years ago," he said, "a young
mother climbed on a *micro* to take her baby to the Children's
Hospital in downtown Lima. The child was desperately ill, bled
so dry by dysentery that he cried without tears.

"When she finally reached the hospital, she found a young
pediatrician who had been on call the night before and was
about to go home. 'Do something,' she begged. And instead of
leaving, the doctor looked past all the causes for despair and
found reason for hope."

Papá's grip tightened on Rosa's shoulder. The priest looked
down at him, his sad eyes filled with the same love she had seen
on the church steps.

"Side by side, the doctor and the mother fought for the
baby's life. For two days, they held death at bay. And then the
child died."

Rosa felt her throat closing. She tried to listen, to breathe. Papá had told her about Magda's two babies who had died, both within a month of each other, but Magda herself never talked about them. Why was Padre Manuel talking about them now? How must Tomás feel, with the priest heaping sorrow upon sorrow?

Padre Manuel's voice rose. "Crucified though she was by grief, Magda turned to the doctor and said to him, 'I must bury my son. But when I am done, I will come back. And you will help me do something to stop all this dying.'

"A month later, the Cesip was born."

Rosa knew the rest of the story. How Papá began working with the Mothers' Club. How the families paid dues, held cook-outs, raised money any way they could. How a delegation of mothers from Salvador marched on the Ministry of Health to demand help. How the whole community worked together to build the Cesip. And when it was finished, Salvador had a real clinic, where children got checkups and vaccinations and saw doctors when they were sick, just like children in Miraflores or New York.

"The Cesip," Padre Manuel said with a desolate smile. "A little blue building where hope lived. And the babies stopped dying in Salvador."

Rosa understood what Padre Manuel was saying now. It was obvious. Magda's courage. Her faith. *But I'm afraid*, Rosa thought. *We're all afraid.*

Padre Manuel spoke on and on, his head bowed. Finally he raised his eyes and gazed at the congregation. "We have two commandments given to us, greater than all the rest. These two commandments are Magdalena's legacy: You shall love the Lord your God with all your heart, with all your soul, and with all your mind, and you shall love your neighbor as yourself!"

As the church rang with the priest's final words, the Archbishop stood, and Padre Manuel turned to the altar. The Eucharist seemed to Rosa to last for hours—the endless swaying line of mourners approaching to receive the Host, the flat wafer dry in her mouth, refusing to dissolve so she could swallow it. Throughout the long sacrament, the church remained nearly silent, save for a few sniffles and Livia's soft sobs. Finally Padre Manuel beckoned to the congregation, and eight men stepped forward to hoist the casket onto their shoulders. The Archbishop and Padre Manuel, followed by the altar boys with their crosses and incense, walked down the aisle from the church. The casket bearers followed, and then Tomás stood and led his family out.

Though Rosa's eyes never left Alonso, he did not look at her again.

▫FIVE▫

Alonso's foot connected and the ball flew. A black-and-white sphere, hurtling through the mist in the churchyard. The goal was an open mouth, waiting.

Arms raised, the priest flew straight up in the air. Like some kind of jump jet in a clerical collar. *Thwack!* Padre Manuel caught the ball and winced. For a moment he stood there, breathing hard and twirling the ball between his palms. Then he drop-kicked it back to Alonso.

The priest caught it every time. Those big hammy hands seemed to pop up in front of the ball no matter which way Alonso kicked it. Like Padre Manuel could read his mind or something. It drove Alonso nuts. But it felt good, too. Knowing that Padre Manuel would catch it no matter how hard he kicked.

He ran up to the ball, swung back his leg, and let fly.

Padre Manuel dived sideways. Tiny lines crinkled around his eyes when the ball slammed into his palms. *Ouch.*

Alonso could hear the kids somewhere behind him. Livia and Diana had some kind of doll game going. Gustavo was pushing a yellow dump truck down the church steps, laughing as it clattered to the ground.

Padre Manuel kicked the ball back.

Sometimes Alonso imagined Senderista heads flying through the air. He knew he shouldn't think that, not in a churchyard. Not in front of a priest. But it didn't matter. Mostly Alonso didn't think at all. He just kicked, as hard as he could.

"I have to go to Spain for a while," Padre Manuel said.

Alonso toed the ball, positioning it. Then he reared back and walloped, sending it rocketing into the goal. The net flared as the ball punched into it.

Padre Manuel was walking toward him. "I have to go back to Spain for a while," he said again.

Alonso looked past him at the ball, lying under a fold of netting. "You're leaving?"

"I'll be back. It's just for a couple of months."

"Why?" Alonso finally looked at the priest's sagging face.

Padre Manuel smiled wryly. "Orders. I've been ordered to go. I've got a flight the day after tomorrow."

"Tell them no." Alonso felt suddenly breathless. "Tell them you have to stay."

But the priest just shook his head. "I can't. I have no choice, Alonso."

Alonso didn't know what to say. She'd been dead only a week.

Padre Manuel read his mind, just like he did in the goal. "I know it seems wrong, *hijo*. But I'll be back in two months. Maybe I can find some way to help from there."

Alonso stared down at his feet. *Oh, yeah*, he thought. *Like you helped my mother.*

That's what he wanted to say. He wanted to say all sorts of things. Like, why did God let them kill her? Why'd you say that "love your neighbor" stuff at the funeral? Did you mean my mother loved her neighbors more than her family?

We needed her more than they did, he wanted to scream. *I needed her.* The words stuck in his throat. So he stood there like an idiot, staring at his feet. He needed new sneakers. On the hard cement, his soles felt thin, like socks.

"We have to go," he said finally.

"Alonso . . ." The priest hugged him awkwardly and Alonso's arms disobeyed him by reaching to return the embrace. "I'm sorry," Padre Manuel mumbled.

Fog seemed to rise in front of Alonso's eyes. He pulled away and headed blindly for the gate. Then he remembered the kids. Everywhere he went, they went, stuck to him like chewing gum on the bottom of his shoe.

Still not seeing very well, he strode back and picked up Gustavo. Torn so abruptly from his yellow truck, Gustavo began to kick and scream, stubby legs thrashing. "No, Wonzo! Down, DOWN! 'Tavo, STAY!"

"Shut up!" Alonso snapped. Cringing, Livia and Diana dropped their dolls. Padre Manuel crouched before them, his arms spread wide. He actually had tears in those spaniel-kicked-in-the-balls eyes of his. The girls clung to his neck as his arms enfolded them. He started kissing them, Livia and then Diana and then Livia again. His cheek was pressed to the top of Livia's head as Alonso strode off.

The girls could make it home by themselves. Just this once.

But as soon as he was through the gate they came charging after him, crying for him to wait.

□ □ □

The Sunday after Padre Manuel left, a priest came to say Mass. Alonso saw him at dawn, standing at the top of the hill. A portly man in a long black robe, pacing the length of the churchyard. His hands were clasped behind his back. Red swirls of graffiti covered the whitewashed wall.

When Alonso took the kids to Mass, he saw the usual slogans. *Long Live* this, and *Long Live* that. *The People's War* and *the Armed Struggle* and *Marxism-Leninism-Maoism-Gonzalo Thought*. And a new one. *Religion is the opium of the masses.*

When the priest in the black robe finished saying Mass, he locked the church's big wooden doors. He put a chain and a padlock on the churchyard gate.

Everyone knew what that meant. No more Mass. And no more soccer, either.

Watching from across the street with Gustavo in his arms, Alonso heard the padlock click. Then the priest scrunched into a little car and drove down the hill. He passed Alonso's house and the ruined Cesip and the *comedor* and the neighbors' shacks and finally all Alonso could see of him was the dust settling in the little car's wake. Then even that was gone.

They all acted kind of numb that afternoon. They sat on the bed in the living room, watching variety shows. The kids laughed at screaming comedians while Alonso's father drank a beer. Alonso leaned against the cool cement wall, yawning, eyes half open.

Gustavo and Diana had fallen asleep, and Alonso's father was onto his third beer, when a car came humming up the hill. Alonso glanced through the gauze curtains. A Toyota stopped outside their door.

Blue Toyota. Alonso sat up. *Dr. Pablo.* His mind raced as the engine cut off. He hadn't seen Rosa since the funeral.

She'd been crying that day, cheeks red and glistening, eyes pooled with tears. And when Alonso saw her trying to wipe away tears that wouldn't stop, he'd wanted to lay his own head on his knees and weep. He had turned from her then, feeling her eyes on him but afraid to look back. Afraid that he'd start crying, too. Terrified that if he started, he'd never stop.

Dr. Pablo was getting out of the car, a slow upward unfolding of that long body of his. Rosa would be getting out on the passenger side. Alonso stood and looked out the window.

"Sit down, Alonso." His father put his beer glass on top of the television, beside the empty bottles. "I'll handle this." He shouldered past Alonso and opened the front door.

Dr. Pablo stood at the bottom of the steps, squinting behind his soda-bottle glasses. Alonso peered through the window into the Toyota. The passenger seat was empty.

"*Buenas tardes*, Tomás." Dr. Pablo glanced at the window and smiled at Alonso. "I thought I'd see how you were all doing."

Alonso's father blocked the doorway like a goalkeeper.

"Tomás . . ." The doctor raised both hands and let them fall. "I'd like to help."

Alonso's father stepped outside and pulled the door closed.

Dr. Pablo was jiggling a key ring in his palm. "I know how you must feel—"

"Do you?" Alonso couldn't see his father, who spoke from the top step. "My wife gets killed trying to keep your clinic open. How you think I feel about that?"

"Tomás, I never . . . None of us expected . . ." The key ring moved faster, then the fingers closed over it. "Tomás, please. Hear me out. I have a friend—she specializes in trauma. Your kids need that kind of help."

"My *kids?*" In two short strides, Alonso's father had bull-dozed down to the street to face Dr. Pablo. "Don't you come near my kids!"

On the television, the laugh track exploded into hoots and cackles.

What his father said next, Alonso never knew. Dr. Pablo twitched as if he'd touched a live wire. He paled to the burned-out color of ashes. And then, breathing hard, he turned away. He got into his empty car. He slammed the door and drove out of Salvador.

He didn't come back.

The days sank down, one after another, into the Southern Hemisphere winter. Late June set the fog swirling beneath the streetlights. And still no one came. Alonso looked out the window whenever he heard a car, but no one came.

One, two, three. Sometimes Alonso counted them on his fingers. Rosa, Dr. Pablo, Padre Manuel. Gone, like his mother.

Yeah, he told himself. *You thought they'd come back for you?*

On a night when his father had the late shift at the parking lot, Alonso sat on the bed in the living room. The kids lay sprawled around him, Diana and Gustavo fast asleep in the television's silver glare. Gazing at the screen, Alonso felt his own fingers twitch as the cyborg fired. Brilliant flashes. Guns gripped in massive hands. Ropy muscles under taut skin. The cyborg's victims screamed and collapsed in agony.

Livia whimpered, her face ghoulish in the light of the screen. She inched closer to Alonso and hid her face against his leg.

Livia was having a hard time. Nine years old, and she'd gone back to wetting the bed. They'd taken her to a *curandero*, a shaman, to heal her of the *susto*, the fright she'd suffered when the Cesip blew up. He'd rolled an egg all over her, up and down her arms, her legs, her chest. Then he'd blown cigarette smoke in her face. But inside Livia, the *susto* was still growing, like the monsters in that movie about the aliens. She kept her face pressed to Alonso's thigh and didn't fall asleep till the credits started rolling.

The late news came on. A car bomb had gone off downtown. The camera zoomed in on shattered glass and a pool of blood. Alonso hit the power button and shifted Livia's head off his leg.

Feeling his way through the living room, he edged around the bed and past the refrigerator. Cold metal, smooth as ice beneath his fingertips. It was the old fridge from the Cesip. Dr. Pablo had sent it over when the gringos donated the new one. Stupid yellow thing. His mother had never even wanted it. She'd left it unplugged in the living room and kept her kerosene-powered one in the kitchen.

Alonso flipped on the backyard light. He peed in the latrine and then washed his hands and picked up a toothbrush. From a mirror, nailed to the brick wall, a *cholo* with a puffy black eye glared at him. Alonso touched the bruise and winced.

She probably had it coming. That's what Juan had said at school today.

Alonso had heard the whispers. Seen the chins, jutting at him. *Magda's son. You know . . .* The rumors. His mother had stolen that refrigerator. Skimmed funds from the Mothers' Club. *She had it coming.*

When Juan said it at school today Alonso was over the desk before he knew what he was doing. He remembered Juan going down. Remembered his own fist, slamming into purple lips. He didn't remember much else, but Juan had a lot more than a black eye when they were finished. The principal had sent them both home with notes, but it was worth it.

Alonso cocked his head at the ugly bruise. At the ugly black eyebrows above it. At his own flat *cholo* cheeks and arrowhead nose.

His hands started to tingle, jabbing pinpricks of rage. "*Cholodemierda.*" He felt a queasy pleasure, running the words together the way those rich white-boy *pitucos* did when they really wanted to piss you off. *Cholopieceofshit.* Ugly black-eyed brown-skinned . . . No wonder Rosa hadn't come back. She probably had some *pituco* boyfriend now. One with green eyes just like hers.

Abruptly nauseous, he threw down the toothbrush and stumbled inside. In his bedroom, he lay down and put the pillow over his head. As soon as he closed his eyes, the show began.

Four shadows in a corridor. A body twitching on cement. The smallest shadow bending. Point-blank. Gunshots, the Cesip exploding, then back to the four shadows. Like a video loop in his brain.

Out in the living room, the kids were breathing softly, sniffles and sighs in three-part harmony. Alonso rose, padded barefoot through the darkness and lay down beside them. The video in his head came back on. He was lying there, sweating, when someone's fist slammed into the front door.

Rising from the bed, Alonso felt his shoulders begin to shake. "Who is it?"

"Open the damn door!" His old man. Alonso fumbled with the latch.

"Who is it, Alonso?" Livia whimpered.

"Shhh," he replied. "It's just Papá. Go back to sleep."

With a naked screech of metal on metal, the latch slid back and the door swung inward. His father slouched beside the doorway, shirt untucked. "Papá, what happened? Are you all right?"

Shoving Alonso out of the way, his father stumbled through the living room and out to the latrine, leaving the back door open. Alonso heard soft drumming as liquid cascaded into the pit.

Livia sat up.

"Close your eyes, Livia," Alonso ordered. "Go to sleep." She lay down, but he knew her eyes were still open.

His father lurched back into the living room. "Get the kids in their own beds," he slurred, unbuckling his belt.

Alonso was bending to pick up Gustavo when his father grabbed his arm.

"Wha's that on your face?"

Alonso jerked his arm free and touched the bruise.

His father seized his arm again. "Wha' happened?"

"I got into a fight at school."

"At school?" His father's voice rose. "What've I told you about fighting at school?"

Alonso shrugged. "I beat up some kid. I got a note from the principal. You wanna see it?" Oh, sure. His father could barely read at the best of times. "I can read it for you if you want," Alonso drawled.

The slap came with blinding speed, crashing into the side of his head. "I don't need to see no note," his father snarled. Before Alonso could even raise a hand to defend himself, another blow sent him reeling to the floor. His ears filled with a high-pitched whining, as if a mosquito had gotten trapped inside his head. Dazed, he watched his father pull off his belt, wrap the end around his fist, and raise it.

"Papi, no!"

Livia's cry detained the arm, but only for an instant. Then the belt slashed across Alonso's shoulders. As he fumbled to his feet, his father grabbed him by the back of the neck and shoved him into the kitchen. Too shocked to react, Alonso felt himself thrown against the table, felt his father's rough hand push his shirt up. Then the belt came down again, the buckle thudding into his bare skin with such searing heat that he cried out. He tried to twist around, to fight back, but his father grabbed him by the neck and slammed him down. Once more, the belt tore into him.

"No, Papi, don't!" Livia stood in the doorway, her thin arms poking from a shapeless old nightgown. "Don't!"

As his father turned, Alonso twisted free and backed against the refrigerator, panting. Livia shrank from her father and with a gasp of fear Alonso stepped between them. "Shut up, Livia! Just shut up!"

His father grabbed him again and threw him back down on the table. The belt whistled through the air and crash-landed on his back. Livia wept, watching from the doorway, and the belt came down again.

Ay, Dios. Something in Alonso's throat, something he couldn't control, grunted each time the buckle landed. He pressed his cheek against the table. He clenched his teeth. He counted and lost track of the blows. But he didn't cry. He wouldn't. Not now. Not ever.

Suddenly his father dropped the belt. For a moment he stood over Alonso, breathing raggedly. Then, with a strangled cry, he staggered away.

Alonso slithered off the table and watched his father grope for the kitchen wall. His old man swayed a little, trying to brace himself. Then, pressing his forehead to the wall, he sank to his knees. "Ay, no, Magda." Hands pressed to the wall, he rocked, thudding his head into the cement. "Ay, no, Magda."

Alonso forced Livia out of the kitchen, back to the living room, but there was no escaping the sound of those moans. Those soft thuds. "Ay, no, Magda. No." It went on for hours. Finally, as a bleak gray light appeared in the front window, their father quieted. Slumped on the bed in the living room, Alonso tried to lie down, but his back seemed to rip in a dozen places. Tears sprang to his eyes.

There was nothing for it but to get up. He wasn't going to lie there sniveling, that was for sure. The *comedor* would open soon, and Señorita Ana would be working the breakfast shift. Maybe she'd have something for his back. Wincing, in slow motion, Alonso pulled on his sneakers and opened the front door.

A slender boy, his head a mass of dark curls, sat on the step. "Rodolfo?"

Rodolfo jumped up and hugged him, and Alonso wasn't sure if tears sprang to his eyes because his back hurt so bad or because he was so damned glad to see his friend.

They stepped back and looked at each other, Alonso wiping his eyes.

Rodolfo grinned. "You look like shit, *hermano*." And then they were both laughing and slapping each other on the shoulders, and it didn't matter if it hurt.

"Come on," Alonso said. "I was going to the *comedor*."

"*Mmmm*," Rodolfo said slyly. "Porridge."

Laughing, Alonso dragged him down the hill. "Sorry," he said. "It's the best I can do."

"That's okay. How you been? I mean, aside from . . . what happened to you, anyway?"

Alonso suddenly felt proud of his wounds. "Remember Juan, at school?"

"That little rat? Always kissing up to the teachers?"

"Yeah, him. He shot off his mouth about my mother, so I beat the crap out of him. He gave me a black eye"—Alonso touched the bruise gingerly—"but you should see him. Then my old man comes home last night, pissing beer—'mano, you should've smelled him—and beats the crap out of *me* for fighting in school."

Rodolfo shook his head sympathetically, and all at once Alonso felt tired and deflated. "You didn't come to the funeral."

"I couldn't get off work." Scuffing dust with his toe, Rodolfo dodged Alonso's eyes. "I'm sorry, *'mano*. About your mother. I'm really sorry."

Alonso nodded. Everyone was sorry. No one ever knew what to say next. They said sorry, you nodded, and then what?

Rodolfo threw his arm around Alonso's neck and dragged him down the street in a chokehold. Before he could stop himself, Alonso was laughing and punching Rodolfo in the ribs. "*Carajo, hermano.*" Rodolfo loosened his hold. "It's good to see you." He threw his arm across Alonso's shoulder, and together they walked to the *comedor*.

Rodolfo spent the morning with him and the kids, eating breakfast with them while Alonso's father snored in the bedroom. At lunchtime Rodolfo bought some *empanadas* from the bakery man with the tricycle cart. By then Alonso's back was so stiff that every move hurt. But the morning mist had lifted and Rodolfo convinced him to take the kids up the rocky dune above Salvador.

They had a picnic up there. Rodolfo played hide-and-seek with Gustavo and Diana. He stumbled blindly, pretending not to see them as they hid behind rocks too small to hide a guinea pig. Their shouts of laughter rang across the dune. Rodolfo even got a smile out of Livia, holding her hand as they climbed the hill, teasing her gently. He called her "Your Highness" and handed her dusty rocks that he swore were diamonds. Soon her lap was piled high with them and she was laughing in a way Alonso had not seen since the day before their mother died.

Finally, as the kids sat eating their *empanadas,* Rodolfo flopped down beside Alonso. "Let me see your back," he said.

Alonso shook his head. "Don't worry about it." He breathed in deeply. Even with the clouds, it felt clean and beautiful up here. No noise, no garbage. Down the rocky dune, Salvador was a thicket of huts, crowned by the white blossom that was Padre Manuel's church.

"Padre Manuel left," Alonso said. "Went back to Spain."

Rodolfo snorted. "That's the last we'll see of him," he said. He looked at Alonso. "Let me see your back, *hermano.*"

Alonso glanced at the kids. They were busy eating, looking down at Salvador and marveling at how small the shacks looked from up here. He turned sideways and lifted his sweatshirt. Rodolfo gave a soft whistle and gently pulled the shirt back down.

"He really laid into you."

"He was drunk." Alonso felt suddenly defensive. "He isn't really like that. It's just . . ." Remembering the sound of his father crying, his voice trailed off. "It's just because he was drunk."

"You tellin' me?" Rodolfo sidearmed a stone down the hillside. "You remember my old man?"

Alonso nodded.

"There's no excuse for it," Rodolfo spat. "Gettin' so drunk you beat up your own kids."

"My old man's not like yours," Alonso snapped. "Quit preaching. You sound like Padre Manuel."

Rodolfo faced him, his thin cheeks an angry red. "Forget Padre Manuel! He's gone, no? I'm just saying there's no excuse for what your old man did to you. Don't get so soft-headed you forget that."

Alonso shrugged, and Rodolfo called Livia over. "Don't bring her into it," Alonso protested.

Rodolfo ignored him, and before Alonso could stop him, he reached over and pulled the shirt up. Livia gave a little moan, but Rodolfo took her by the hands and pulled her so that she stood facing him.

"Livia, you know your brother's hurt and you know how it happened."

Livia nodded, biting her lip.

"Now don't cry. This isn't the time to be a crybaby. You need to be a warrior queen, okay?"

Livia nodded again, and Rodolfo smiled at her. Alonso could see hero worship rising in his sister's pinched little face.

"Now listen," Rodolfo commanded. "I'm gonna buy an ointment. I want you to put it on Alonso's back every morning till he's better. But you gotta get up early, 'cuz we don't want Diana and Gustavo to see this, right? It would scare them too much."

Livia stood a little straighter. She was being distinguished from the younger children. "They'd be scared," she agreed.

"But not you," Rodolfo said. "You can do this."

"Yes, I can."

Rodolfo smiled, and Livia beamed as she sat down beside him.

"Where are you getting the money to buy me stuff?" Alonso demanded.

"Oh, I'm a working man, now," Rodolfo replied airily. "I work in a factory. We make blankets."

"What about school?"

"There are more important things, Alonso." Rodolfo lay back on the ground, squirming a little on the rocks and looking up at the high, gray sky. "I know it doesn't seem like it, 'mano, but this is a good time to be alive." He spoke with a conviction as simple as it was absolute.

Alonso snorted skeptically, but Rodolfo said no more.

▫ SIX ▫

A white-jacketed waiter slipped through the crowd, and Rosa snatched a tiny *empanada* from his tray. He swirled away, hands grabbing at him, and Rosa watched as the tray emptied and the waiter disappeared into the kitchen.

She wore black. So did her parents. They were still in mourning. But it was her grandmother's seventieth birthday, and the Alcázar mansion was a jumble of laughter and color and smoke. Women in red and green and blue, in silk and satin, perched like tropical birds at the edges of chairs and sofas. Their men cast a smoky shadow around the bar, talking politics and laughing. In the kitchen blenders roared, crushing ice for *pisco* sours.

Rosa bit into her *empanada*. Powdered sugar and pastry and spicy meat filling. The tastes merged and suddenly it wasn't just the *empanada* she was tasting but the bakery man she was seeing, pedaling his three-wheeled cart up the dusty hill into Salvador. Ay, *Mamá*, Alonso had said. *Couldn't we just get some empanadas off the cart?* And Magda had arched her eyebrows and laughed. Given Alonso money for a bus ride and an *empanada*.

He hadn't even looked at her at the funeral. But who could blame him? He hated her. He had the right. A month later and she still hadn't seen him. Still hadn't told him the truth.

She hadn't told anyone. Not the cops nor her parents and certainly not her psychiatrist, Andrea, who sat so patiently every week, waiting to hear what had really happened inside the Cesip. Andrea didn't need to know. But Alonso—

"Rosa!" An age-spotted claw gripped her wrist. "You didn't say hello!"

Rosa blinked. "*Hola*, Tía." She bent to kiss her great-aunt's cheek.

"You've grown so tall and pretty." Tía Virginia's thumb caressed Rosa's birthmark. "You're nearly as beautiful as your mother." She turned to Tía Cecilia. "Doesn't Rosa look just lovely?"

Rosa forced a smile. Tía Virginia was always nice to her now. And to Mamá and Papá as well. No nasty gossip anymore, no talk of Salvador and all the *cholos* there. Tía Virginia had read about Magda in the newspaper. She knew what had happened inside the Cesip. Everyone did.

Or thought they did.

With a smile, Tía Virginia released Rosa and shifted her weight back toward Tía Cecilia. She had just lowered her voice—*Of course he's got money, Ceci, he's a Jew*—when the lights flickered and the whole room seemed to sigh in dismay. "Oh, no . . ." The lights came back on, but Rosa's grandmother wasn't fooled.

"Light that candle," she ordered a waiter.

Just as the waiter flicked on a lighter, the house shuttered into darkness. In the kitchen, the blender fell silent.

A blackout.

Rosa stumbled, bumping over Tía Cecilia's ankles. She nearly fell, righted herself. She felt her way to the wall and grabbed the edge of a bookshelf. Out on the street, gunfire popped. Warning shots from the cops at the bank on the corner.

Around Rosa, curses rippled. *Damned Senderistas!* The waiter went on lighting candles, and a mirror-crusted crucifix became a mosaic of reflected flames.

Rosa clung to the bookshelf like a shipwreck victim clinging to a raft. Trying to stave off panic, to take deep breaths the way Andrea had taught her to. Breathe in. Breathe out. Breathe deep. But it was all coming back. That heartbeat like a galloping pony. That cold feeling in her hands, as though she'd plunged them into a bucket of ice water. Her legs hardening to pillars. It was all coming back, she was seeing it all again. . . .

They had waited by the lab. They had laughed at the fearful gringos and their Coca-Cola. Finally Magda had gone to look for Alonso, *ay-ay-aying* about how long he was taking. Rosa had stayed by the lab, so when the back door opened and the Senderistas stepped in, she saw them first. They pulled out pistols and she screamed.

Screamed, but then froze in panic. Like a little kid, lying stock-still in bed because if you don't move the monsters won't get you.

Magda had already reached the lobby. She was nearly out the front door. But when Rosa screamed, she wheeled and came running back. Rosa still couldn't move. *"Santa María,"* Magda had said. And then, with a little shove, "Run to your papá, Rosa. Run!"

Rosa had screamed again, and stumbled. Magda had stepped toward her attackers, hands outstretched as if in welcome. And as the first gunshot thundered, Rosa had finally begun to run. The shot had echoed through the corridor. In its wake, Rosa had heard a soft sound. A little grunt that must have been Magda when that first bullet hit her.

Run, Rosa. Run to your papá.

Her cheeks were wet. If only she hadn't seen them. If only she had gone, instead of Magda, to find Alonso. If only she had run. If only . . . If only, if only . . .

The candles flickered around the room, and a tall shadow edged through the crowd. Ski masks. Pistols pulled from beneath jackets.

"Rosa . . ." Papá pried Rosa's fingers from the bookshelf. "Let go, *amor.*" He enfolded her clammy hand in his.

Beyond him, in the darkness, everyone stood subdued, gulping their drinks like children finishing their milk. "I guess the party's over," Rosa's grandmother said sadly.

Mamá replied, soothing. "This won't last long." Her gaze found Rosa. "The lights will come back on."

And they did, a few minutes later, flooding the room with color and laughter and cries of relief.

Papá's brow furrowed. "Are you okay?"

"Sí, Papá." Rosa pulled her hand free and wiped her cheeks. She wanted air, fresh air. "I just need to go to the bathroom."

"Do you feel nauseous?" He gripped her arm.

"*No*, Papá." She rolled her eyes at him, a sixteen-year-old rolling her eyes at her father, she knew just how to do that, to look like she was the same as everyone else. "I just have to go to the bathroom." She turned and he let her go. She felt his eyes follow her as she slid past her cousins, her aunts and uncles. Then she rounded the corner, out of sight, and opened the front door.

Air. Rosa sucked in a thirsty lungful, then another. The spotlight, glaring through the mist, turned the patio a sickly yellow.

Rosa sat down on a bench beside a tile and terra-cotta fountain. Beyond the high cement wall that edged the patio, she could hear her grandfather's *guachimán*, standing guard and blowing his whistle. As the mournful hoot died, she heard the electrified wires humming like bees through the bougainvillea that topped the wall.

It had always seemed so enormous, that wall. Once, when Rosa was little, and stupid and fearless, she had ventured beyond it to paint a cement lamppost blue. All the way around and as high as she could reach, a blue the color of the sky. She had felt so happy with herself, and with the blue paint she'd found in her grandfather's garage.

The lamppost was dirty and faded now. They'd passed it tonight on their way to the party.

It's still beautiful, Rosa. That blue.

It was the same blue as the Cesip. Rosa trailed a finger through the fountain's shadowy little pool, and listened to the whisper in her head.

Sometimes Rosa thought the whisper was the Virgin. But then she always laughed at herself. Santa María, talking to her? She wasn't really crazy if she could laugh at herself.

You could go out again, Rosa. Outside the wall.

I could go to Salvador, Rosa thought.

But her father wouldn't take her. There was no point in even asking.

Impatiently, she flicked a forefinger against the water, sending drops flying. Inside the house, someone was plucking a guitar. Rosa heard her mother's lilting soprano. *I remember the day I met you. I remember the afternoon.*

They'd be dancing soon, if they weren't already.

The front door opened and a fruity smell of lip gloss drifted down the walk. Rosa's cousin Gabriela picked her way over the patio and grimaced at the bench. "Is that wet?"

Rosa shook her head and slid sideways to make room. "You're not dancing?"

"To that?" Gabriela grabbed her throat as if she'd swallowed poison. "Fico would kill me if I asked."

"Where is he?"

"Out back, smoking a cigarette." She sighed and sat down. "I wish he didn't smoke."

"Is it like kissing an ashtray?"

Gabriela giggled. "Not really."

"It was nice of him to come. I mean, a family party and all."

Gabriela tossed back her hair, a long curtain of it, glossy and brown and enviably straight. "What are you doing out here all by yourself?"

"Did my father send you out to ask that?"

Gabriela shrugged. "He wondered where you were, is all."

"I was thinking of taking a walk."

"Are you kidding? Why?"

Rosa didn't know why. It was the wall, maybe. Or the cement post. Or the *empanada*. She turned to her cousin. "Would you come with me to Salvador? To see Magda's family?"

"What?" Gabriela's eyes rounded, darkened. "Rosa, what are you talking about? You can't go back there."

Rosa could practically taste her fear. Sour and sharp, like Papá's.

"My father will never go back," she said.

"Can you blame him?" Gabriela shook her head reproachfully. "You're his only child. He almost lost you."

Rosa felt tears pricking her eyes. Abruptly, without meaning to, without even wanting to, she felt sad for her father. Sad, in a deep-as-the-ocean way. All those years. All that talk of solidarity. All of it gone, like Magda.

She swallowed. Her throat ached.

"Ay, *prima*." Gabriela leaned over and rubbed Rosa's arms. "Why don't you come inside? It's freezing out here." She stood, hunching her shoulders against the mist. "I dressed all wrong for tonight."

Rosa stared into the pool. Where the fountain hit the water, dark ripples spread outward.

Gabriela's voice rose. "It's too tight on me, isn't it? This dress."

Startled, Rosa looked up. "Ay, Gabriela, don't be ridiculous."

"Do I look fat?" Gabriela tugged at her dress, a sleeveless sheath the color of communion wine. Gabriela was overacting, smoothing the dress with fretful little pats.

Like a *tía*. She looked just like a *tía*.

Rosa laughed in spite of herself, and Gabriela laughed, too. Then she took Rosa's hands and Rosa let herself be pulled, up and out of the mist and back into her grandparents' house.

· SEVEN ·

A singsong tinkle of shattering glass pierced the darkness. Alonso heard his father raging and sat up. Livia and Diana shot up in their bed, and Diana began to cry.

"Shhh." Livia put her arms around her little sister. "Shhh. It's just Papi, Diana. Shhh."

The shouted curses sounded distant, as if their father were yelling out a window.

The old man had gotten fired on Monday. He'd shown up drunk at the parking lot where he worked as a security guard. Not the kind of man you wanted guarding the Mercedes. Now he walked the streets, an *ambulante* like so many others. Selling toothpaste and marionettes and little plastic fans people could stick on their dashboards. Chasing after cars begging people to buy. He'd stumbled through the door a few hours ago, stinking of beer and vomit. His feet swollen and his face crumpled like a brown paper bag.

Alonso's toes curled on the cold cement as he padded across the floor.

In the living room, sheets and blankets lay coiled across the bed. Alonso's father stood shouting out the open window, hands clenching the iron bars that cut the nighttime mist into stripes. At his feet, below the window, lay a rock and a scattering of broken glass.

Alonso heard Livia creep from the bedroom. Felt her hand, a silky little bag of bones, slip into his.

With a last, savage curse, their father slammed the window shut. Another shard of glass tinkled, broke free, and fell. Livia pulled free as he turned and dropped into bed, stepping to his side to pull a blanket over to him. Then she bent in the shadows to pick a scrap of paper from the floor.

It had entered the house wrapped around the stone that crashed through their front window, and it had two words written on it.

Magda ladrón. Magda thief.

Alonso read without flinching. Livia looked up at him, her thin face pinched, her eyes big and sad. Too sad for nine-year-old eyes.

"Come on," he said. "You want to sleep with me and Gustavo?"

But Livia shook her head and crawled into bed with Diana, who had fallen back to sleep easily, the way she always did.

Alonso lay in his bed, listening to the sounds of the darkened house. Diana's sighs were slow and steady, Livia's uneven and wakeful. Gustavo's breathing sounded raspy, full of rattles and gurgles. Out in the living room, their father began to snore.

Magda ladrón.

The words had begun appearing on Salvador's walls a week ago. Red scribbles that didn't say a thing about the People's War or Chairman Gonzalo. Just *Magda ladrón*. Magda thief. And beneath the words, sometimes, a crude picture of a refrigerator.

Alonso tucked the blanket under Gustavo's chin. Another sleepless night lay waiting. Another night replaying the video of the Cesip, exploding with his mother inside. Blown to smithereens. And why? Because she wouldn't let Sendero use the clinic? Because when the gringos donated the new refrigerator, Dr. Pablo gave her the old one? Why? It made no sense. The Senderistas said they wanted to help poor people. They said they hated rich people. So why did they kill his mother?

Eyes open, Alonso stared at the darkness. Just once, he'd like to meet one of them. One Senderista. Meet him and ask him why.

And then, he figured, he'd kill the son of a bitch.

□ □ □

Señorita Ana came by the next morning while they were eating breakfast. She knocked on the door and they all jumped. Nobody stopped by much anymore.

Carrying Gustavo, who'd been sitting on his lap slurping porridge, Alonso's father let her in. She followed him into the kitchen and kissed them all good morning. Her jeans were perfectly blue, and there was just a sprinkling of dust on her shiny black pumps.

"Coffee?"

She nodded, so Alonso got up to make her a cup. When she sat down, Diana clambered onto her lap.

"I can do a somersault," Diana announced proudly.

"Really?" Señorita Ana's voice rose a little.

Diana nodded. "You want to see?"

Alonso's father grunted at her to finish her breakfast, or Diana might have gone tumbling past their feet. Señorita Ana would never have said no. Alonso smiled at her as he handed her the coffee.

She had been his mother's best friend, one of the three or four women who'd worked hardest to set up the Cesip and keep it going. After the murder, she had offered to watch Gustavo and Diana while he and Livia went to school.

Señorita Ana took a tiny, careful sip. Then she looked at Alonso with a sad smile. "Alonso, will you please take the children outside? There's something I need to tell your father."

Alonso sighed, but he took the kids outside, and after a little while Señorita Ana came out and said good-bye. She said she and her father were leaving Salvador. They had decided to go back to Oxapampa, where they'd come from a long, long time ago. She cried a little as she hugged them, but they all, even Diana, were dry-eyed when she left. Alonso figured they were getting to be experts at saying good-bye.

Things were quiet, then, for a few days. His father came home after dark each night, tired but carrying a great stillness around with him, smelling of sweat and exhaust fumes instead of beer. He sat with the kids on the bed and watched television. Gustavo clambered over him, bored with the game shows and movies. The two girls snuggled beside him and made much of him. Two fussy little women, jumping up to get him juice or soup or anything else he might want.

He made Alonso do his homework at the kitchen table, and

he put the kids to bed himself. Alonso and his father stepped around each other warily, like two dogs that don't want to fight but are afraid to let the other dog know it. His father's expression was grim and unapologetic when their eyes accidentally met. *Maybe I deserved the belt,* Alonso thought. *Leaving her alone to die that way.*

His father woke him early one morning. "Go get breakfast," he said, reaching to pick up Gustavo. The little boy muttered sleepily, then opened his eyes with an outraged wail.

Alonso pulled on his sneakers and left for the morning rations, letting the door slam behind him. Mist blurred the shacks across the street. A dog barked aimlessly on somebody's roof. Radios blared, salsa down the hill and *Radioprogramas* the next block up. Yawning, Alonso almost walked right past the graffiti, the line of thick red letters that turned his house into a billboard.

Magda ladrón. Salvador te repudia. Magda thief. Salvador repudiates you.

Alonso stopped, his mouth half open. He tried to catch his breath but couldn't. *Mamá,* he thought.

And then the wave slammed into him. A pain that emptied his lungs and drained his gut and left him barely able to stand. He'd had dysentery when he was a kid, and it had nearly killed him and that's what this felt like, like his mother's death was hollowing him out and might someday kill him.

Señora Méndez from the top of the block walked by. Alonso was gasping like a beached fish, but she passed him without a word. She didn't look at him, or at the red letters on the wall. She stared down, stepping carefully, as if the familiar street were a steep and narrow footpath.

Alonso stood there a long time. Then he walked up the steps and went back inside.

The kids were watching television. They didn't look up as Alonso passed. His father was out back, shaving in front of the mirror. One cheek covered in white lather, the other scraped down to smooth brown skin. Razor in hand, he paused in mid-stroke. His reflected eyes met Alonso's, and then he began shaving the other side of his face. Alonso went to the bedroom and lay down. He was never getting up.

Cheeks glistening, his father came in a few minutes later and sat down on the bed. Alonso shied away, but all his father did was place a hand on Alonso's head and smile. A wry, bitter smile that lifted only one corner of his mouth.

"Papá . . ." A knot rose in Alonso's throat, and he turned to face the wall.

"I saw it."

"Why? Why'd they do that?" Alonso felt his throat close. "Why?"

For a moment his father didn't reply. Then he stood up. "We're leaving," he said. "My cousin Lucho left me the key to his place in San Juan. Go get breakfast and we'll pack."

It didn't take long. They didn't have much, really. The television set. Towels and blankets. Two old dressers with sticky drawers. Alonso's treasure box. Alonso himself had to pull the box from under his bed. Everyone else, even Gustavo, knew better than to touch it.

The last thing they packed were the family pictures, wrapping them in old shirts and placing them in a box. Alonso's father stood for a long time, staring at a photo Padre Manuel had taken last summer.

The family was standing in the church doorway after Gustavo's baptism. Gustavo was grinning in his father's arms. His mother stood beside them, a protective hand on Gustavo's fat brown leg. Flanking them were the godparents, Dr. Pablo and his wife, Señora Charo. The rest of them, Alonso, Livia, Diana, and Rosa, stood in front of their parents, holding hands.

Alonso remembered that suit, how he'd hated the tie. He remembered how excited Livia had been about her ruffled little dress. And he remembered how Rosa had dazzled him, her skin tanned dark from the beach, her lips a frosty pink. It was the first time he'd ever seen her wear lipstick. The first time he'd ever really thought about what Rosa looked like.

There was a honk outside the door. His father's friend from up the street, Señor Jaime, had come by with his truck. A big open truck with wooden sides. Señor Jaime lowered the tailgate and swore at the red words on the wall. Alonso shrugged.

The hardest things to move were the stove and the old refrigerator. But his father and Señor Jaime were strong, and Alonso was almost sixteen. He was getting strong, too.

They left the Cesip refrigerator behind.

When everything was packed and his father was padlocking the front door, Alonso lifted the girls up into the truck bed and vaulted aboard. Señor Jaime tied the tailgate with a piece of rope and started the truck rolling down the hill.

Alonso stood up as they passed the Cesip. Someone had painted graffiti on the wall. *Magda ladrón* again. A couple of soldiers were painting over the words, using the wrong blue and making the Cesip look like a badly patched shirt. A dozen more soldiers loitered around, cradling their guns. One of them waved at Alonso, and Alonso waved back, though he didn't like the soldiers. The way they always stopped you to ask for your I.D., as if you didn't have the right to walk down your own street. Their faces always hard and suspicious.

The truck bumped down the hill. Dust boiled from under the wheels, turning the air behind them brown. Alonso tasted diesel. As they reached the highway and the tires rolled onto the asphalt, he looked back at Salvador. On the hill above them, at the very top, where the shacks ended and the dunes began, he thought he saw a shimmer of white that was Padre Manuel's church.

But that was silly. You couldn't see the church from this far away.

□ □ □

A stream of kids in gray and white uniforms poured through the schoolyard gate. The high schoolers strutted, masters of their universe. The grade schoolers tumbled ecstatically, racing to mothers and soccer and freedom. Alonso's gaze bounced across the blur of black heads. No Livia. Not yet. She had to let that wild herd of school kids gallop past before she'd even step from her classroom.

Livia's new school, the María Auxiliadora School, was built of cinderblocks and mortar, dank and rough and unfinished.

Named for Holy Mary, Helper of Christians, but ugly enough to be the devil's work. No glass on the windows, no electricity. Not even a decent latrine. Just a stinking open hole in the ground.

Gustavo wriggled and fretted, but Alonso held him tight. A month after catching cold, Gustavo was still coughing. Last night his wheezing had kept Alonso awake for hours.

"When's she coming, Alonso?" Diana hopped up and down and rubbed her arms. "I'm cold."

"Well, I'm cold, too," Alonso snapped. But he had to wait for Livia, for the same reason he had to stay home with the kids instead of going to this piss-poor school. San Juan had a lunatic, a guy everybody called *Pishtaco*. Supposedly he had yellow eyes, but he wasn't a real *pishtaco*. Real *pishtacos* had blue eyes. They lived in the mountains and sliced open *campesino* farmers to steal their body fat. San Juan's *Pishtaco* was just a rapist who liked young girls.

Their new home—Tío Lucho's old shack—was a single room with a dirt floor. It was so small that Alonso's father had sold one of their beds. Now Alonso slept with the kids in the double bed. His father slept in the girls' old bed. The kitchen table stood opposite, by the gas stove and the kerosene-powered refrigerator. The television sat unused on the floor. Electrical pylons perched on the hills behind the shack, but here in San Juan nobody had electricity.

A cluster of teenaged girls flounced through the schoolyard gate. They glanced sideways, checking Alonso out. He ignored them. In the doorway, a cowering little stick finally appeared.

My little flower, Alonso thought bitterly. That's what his mother used to call Livia. But she was a wilting little flower now. Last night she'd wet the bed again. She'd been up, crying in the darkness, when their father staggered in.

Alonso could still feel the stripes on his back. Could still see the belt, hanging like a dead snake from his father's hand. His shirt still stuck to him, the wounded skin tearing in minute rips each time the fabric shifted.

"You take care of your sister," his father had hissed.

The schoolyard was empty now, and Diana ran to Livia and tugged at her book bag until, with a reluctant smile, Livia surrendered it. Diana proudly slung it onto her own back as they left the schoolyard.

Chin tucked into her chest, eyes downcast, Livia fell in step beside Alonso. They marched silently up the dirt road, and Diana prattled about the ducks she'd seen in the market.

"*Quack, quack, quack*— Look!" With a squeal of joy, Diana broke off her monologue. "Look, Alonso, it's Rodolfo! And Mariela!" Hooting with delight, she darted ahead to the shack.

They stood by the front door, waiting. Rodolfo was wire and bone topped with a mop of curls, but his sister Mariela had a round face framed by straight black hair. She had a macramé handbag slung from her shoulder, and a big shirt covered her belly like cheesecloth over rising dough. Alonso tried not to stare.

"Wide 'Dolfo, wide 'Dolfo," Gustavo pleaded.

"*Ya, ya.*" Alonso put him down and Gustavo ran to Rodolfo, who swung off his backpack and in almost the same motion swung Gustavo onto his shoulders.

Watching, Alonso felt something inside himself ease.

San Juan was supposed to be their refuge. Where they'd be safe, if no one knew they were here. But Rodolfo lived only a few kilometers away. It had been easy to slip out. To jog over to Canto Grande. To think, *To hell with my old man.*

Mariela stepped toward them with a huge smile. "Alonsito!"

"*Hola,* Mariela." Alonso dug into his pocket for the key. "How've you been?" Then, mortified, he felt his face flame. What was she supposed to answer? *Oh, just great, aside from getting raped.* He stammered. "I mean, how's . . . ?"

She squeezed his hand.

Mariela. Standing this close, he could smell her hair. So sweet, so clean. Like flowers, maybe, or freshly cut apples. When he was a little kid he used to sniff around her like a hungry dog. And once, when he was ten and she fourteen, he had deliberately stumbled into her. Trying to fake a fall, to dive into that fragrant black river. Mariela had tilted her head with a teasing smile, tucked a shining lock behind one ear. And then, to Alonso's unending wonder, she had leaned forward and kissed him on the mouth.

Mariela bent to kiss Livia now, and Livia touched that rounded belly. "Are you having a baby?"

"Shut up, Livia!" Alonso gave Livia's shoulder a light shove.

Mariela nodded. "Yes, I am," she said.

"Is it a boy or a girl?"

Alonso felt like smacking her, but Mariela just shrugged. "I don't know."

"It's a girl," Rodolfo predicted, jiggling Gustavo on his shoulders. "A warrior queen, just like Livia."

Livia turned rosy, and Diana started babbling about how she was a queen, too. Alonso stepped around her and unlocked the padlock on the shack's front door. It was just a sheet of plywood with latches screwed into it. "Come on in," he mumbled.

"I can't stay," Mariela said sadly. "But I wanted to give you this." She reached into her bag and pulled out a little gift wrapped in red paper. Stepping closer to Alonso, she pressed it into his hand. It felt soft, beneath the crackling paper. "Happy birthday, Alonsito."

He stared down at the shiny red square, and Rodolfo laughed incredulously. "What, did you forget your own birthday?"

"Open it," Mariela urged. Chattering with excitement, Livia and Diana crowded close as Alonso tugged the package open. Inside lay a blue scarf, downy soft. Tiny hairs stuck from it like fuzz from the skin of a peach.

"She's worried about you catching cold, 'mano," Rodolfo teased.

"Somebody has to," Mariela retorted.

Alonso wrapped the scarf around his neck, and Mariela reached up to straighten it. "I wish I could stay." She kissed his cheek again, then laid a hand on her stomach and stepped back. "But I better go. I'll be late for class."

Alonso was thinking, Gracias, Mariela. He was thinking it with all his might, but for some reason he couldn't speak. So he just nodded, and she gave his hand one last squeeze. Then she kissed the kids and headed down the street.

From behind, her curves looked just right, the way a nineteen-year-old girl ought to look. No belly. Just a girl who wanted to be a teacher, heading off to class.

Rodolfo threw his backpack into the shack. "Duck," he warned Gustavo as he stepped through the doorway. Laughing, Gustavo reached up a triumphant little hand and patted the cardboard ceiling. "'Tavo BIG," he announced.

"Oh, me too, me too," Diana begged.

"You're too fat," Alonso said. Diana's lower lip poked out, but Alonso crossed the shack to the back door and stepped outside. The scarf felt warm around his neck, and he was wishing down to his very bones that Mariela had stayed.

The shack's backyard was a few square meters of dirt, walled in by adobe and bisected with clothesline. In one corner stood three barrels of water and some washbasins. Wet shirts and pants and underwear drooped over the line. Water dripped from them with an uneven *pit-pat*, *pit-pat*, dotting the ground with tiny pools of mud.

With a sick wave of despair, Alonso grabbed his father's shirt. Water oozed out. He squeezed, but it was hopeless. The shirt would never dry by nightfall. He'd screwed up again.

"New shirt?" Rodolfo leaned against the doorjamb, mimicking a detergent commercial. "No, I washed it with Ña Pancha!"

Alonso slapped the shirt away.

Rodolfo's laughter cut off. "Oh, come on, *hermano*, it's not all that bad."

"No?" Alonso snapped. He had told Rosa he wanted to be a doctor, and here he was, washing underwear instead of going to school. "At least you've got a job! How'd you get off, anyway?"

"I got someone to cover for me," Rodolfo said. "It's not every day your best friend turns sixteen."

Alonso stared sullenly back at him.

"Livia, Diana," Rodolfo roared. "Ready?"

"Ready!"

Rodolfo grabbed Alonso's arm. "Now quit fussing about your laundry and shut your eyes."

Grumbling, Alonso closed his eyes and let Rodolfo drag him inside.

When he opened them, he saw Gustavo sitting at the table, a cone-shaped party hat on his head and a half-moon grin splitting his face. Before him lay a plate of *alfajor* cookies filled with sweet, sticky *manjar blanco*. Another plate held chicken and avocado sandwiches. The girls had set five places. Beside one of them sat another gift, wrapped in the same shiny red paper.

The girls and Rodolfo burst into song. "Happy Birthday," sung in a slow, dirgelike English that even Alonso could tell was horrendously mangled. Then, switching to up-tempo Spanish, they clapped in time while Gustavo pounded the table, wildly out of sync.

"*Gracias* to my mother for the sandwiches and *alfajores*," Rodolfo said when they finished.

Alonso's eyes stung. "What are you doing? You can't afford all this!"

Diana and Livia took him by the hands and dragged him to the head of the table. "Okay, okay," he growled. "But no hat!"

"Don't worry," Rodolfo laughed. "I could only afford three hats." He sat down, reaching for a sandwich. Gustavo bit into an *alfajor*, grinning through the crumbs, and Alonso finally smiled. *To hell with my old man*, he thought again. He'd done the right thing, telling his best friend where they lived.

Rodolfo turned the radio to a *chicha* station and sang along.

Diana joined in, her mouth full, and soon even Livia was singing. The pile of *alfajores* dwindled.

"Go on." Rodolfo slid the gift closer to Alonso. "Open your present."

Alonso shook his head. "This is too much, *'mano.*" He pulled the gift into his lap and tore off the wrapping paper. A small book, red with gold lettering. *The Little Red Book of Mao Tse-tung.* He looked blankly at Rodolfo. "What is it?"

"Well, I figured you got bored, sitting around all day. Here, give it to me."

"Sitting around? You try washing clothes all morning!"

Rodolfo leafed through the tiny pages and began to read. "'The world is yours, as well as ours, but in the last analysis, it is yours. You young people, full of vigor and vitality, are in the bloom of life, like the sun at eight or nine in the morning. Our hope is placed on you.'" He closed the book and gave it back to Alonso. "Happy birthday."

Alonso snorted. "Boy, is he in for a shock, if his hope is placed on me. Who is this guy, anyway?"

Rodolfo raised his eyebrows. "What do they teach you in school, *hermano?*"

"I don't go to school, remember?"

"Mao, Chairman Mao!"

"You mean the Chinese guy?" Alonso frowned. "Like Gonzalo Thought Mao? What do you mean, giving me that crap!" He threw the book down on the table, but before he could say anything more, the front door swung open.

"Papi!" Diana slid from her chair. Their father stood framed against the light, a canvas bag slung from his shoulder. His gaze traveled from the table to the cookies to Gustavo's hat. It settled on Rodolfo.

Rodolfo stood up. "*Buenas tardes*, Señor Tomás."

"*Buenas tardes.*" His father took off his jacket and tossed it on the bed. "*Ya, ya*, Diana," he muttered, bending to kiss her. Gustavo waved both hands, and Livia picked up an *alfajor* and carried it to her father.

"Here, Papi, Rodolfo brought these for Alonso's birthday."

His father accepted the cookie but didn't eat it. "Where's my shirt, Alonso?"

"On the line."

"Well, help me get it down." His father jerked his head at the back door.

Dry-mouthed, Alonso followed him outside. His father closed the plywood door and leaned against it, arms folded. Alonso looked down. "Your shirt's not dry," he muttered.

"What's he doing here?"

"He brought over some stuff for my birthday."

"How'd he find us?"

Backing nervously into a wet undershirt, Alonso replied. "I told him."

His father rubbed his chin. "You left the kids alone and went to tell him?"

Alonso nodded, bouncing a little on his heels, every nerve strung tight.

"How stupid can you be? *Carajo*, Alonso, we came here to be safe."

Alonso flushed. "Rodolfo won't tell anybody."

"You know your problem? You think you're smarter than everybody else." His father shook his head, disgusted. "Your mother was such a fool for you."

Fists clenched, Alonso stepped forward. "Don't talk about her that way!"

His father sneered. "What, now you're going to fight me? Save it for the Senderistas. Maybe you'll get luckier next time." With a derisive snort, he turned and went into the shack.

Trembling with rage, Alonso heard the front door slam. He heard Rodolfo inside, speaking quietly to the kids. Overhead, the sky began to darken. And still Alonso stood there, his mind thrashing like a hooked fish. His father was right. He was an idiot, risking their safety the way he had. No, his father was the idiot. He'd brought them to this stinking slum. They came here to be safe? What about that yellow-eyed lunatic, *Pishtaco*? None of this was Alonso's fault. His mother had left them in this mess. That love your neighbor stuff was bullshit. The Cesip was finished. What had his father said? She was a fool. She'd died for nothing. Nobody could explain it to him. Nobody could say why they'd killed her. What'd she die for? Why'd they kill her? *For nothing*, he thought. *Nada.*

The back door opened and Livia stepped out.

"Alonso," she whispered. She held out a small package wrapped in brown paper. "Papi left this."

Alonso shook his head, but she placed it in his hand. Slowly, unwillingly, he began to tear off the wrapping, handing brown shreds to Livia. Finally he had it open. It was a radio, a little black radio with an earphone so he could listen at night when the kids were asleep. The radio he'd been asking for since he was twelve.

For a moment he gripped it, his finger on the dial. Then, with a savage curse, he hurled it against the adobe wall. The plastic cover split apart. Pieces of metal-studded green cardboard fell into the dust. He stomped them, over and over, feeling plastic snap beneath his sole. He swore viciously at two batteries that refused to buckle. Finally, he kicked them across the yard, where they settled under a dripping pair of jeans.

When there was nothing left of the radio but tiny shards, black and green and silvery in the dirt, he looked at his sister. She was trying not to cry, biting her lip. Her lost expression fanned his anger to a blaze again. Roughly, he shoved her toward the door. "Go inside, Livia. Get the kids ready for bed. And you, too."

"But it's early—"

"Just do it!" It was all he could do to stand there and not slap that look off her face.

The door closed behind her, and Alonso began to tear the laundry off the line, damp T-shirts and underpants and trousers. He wanted to throw the clothes down, to grind them into the dirt like he had the radio. Instead he put them in a plastic basin and carried them inside. Rodolfo was sitting cross-legged on the double bed, with the kids gathered around him.

"You better go," Alonso said. "It's almost dark."

Rodolfo shook his head. "I'm staying," he replied. "I'll catch a *micro* to work in the morning."

Alonso started to argue, but he recognized the look in

Rodolfo's eye. It was Rodolfo's superhero look. The look said Rodolfo knew all about drunken fathers. He was sticking around to better Alonso's odds.

Alonso shrugged. "Fine. Give the kids the soup that's in the fridge." He pulled on his jacket and stepped out to the street, ignoring Gustavo's wail of protest. *Wonzo staaay. . . .* Alonso slammed the door.

Wet fog was sinking down, and the stink of San Juan rose to greet it. Smoke and rotting garbage. Piss and shit. That was San Juan. No Cesip latrine brigades here, going around making sure everyone got a cement toilet, a pit, and a bag of lime.

Alonso zipped up his jacket.

A kerosene lamp flickered inside the bodega on the corner, where a little girl stood behind the bars. Her little brother sat on the counter, sucking his fingers. *Pishtaco* or no, this girl looked younger than Livia, and here she was baby-sitting and working the store. Their eyes met briefly. Neither said anything as Alonso walked on. In the shack next door, a radio blared *chicha* music while two angry voices cursed at each other. Mingled with their quarrel were a baby's breathless cries. A trio of young men watched him from a corner, shoulders hunched against the damp.

The dirt road followed the curve of the hill, a pale stripe between unbroken lines of shacks. Alonso walked in the middle of the road. Lanterns flicked shards of light through the *esteras* and voices drifted through the walls. Radios played, trombones blasting salsa and Luís Miguel singing about his broken heart again. Laughter, quarrels. The groans and sighs of couples making love. Alonso walked on and on till his feet hurt and the angry voices in his head finally shut up.

It was nearly ten when he returned home. The familiar rasp of Gustavo's nighttime wheezing rippled through the shack. The kerosene lamp threw uneven pools of light and shadow around the room. Rodolfo sat at the table, reading the little red book he'd given Alonso.

"Listen to this," Rodolfo said. "'A revolution is not a dinner party, or writing an essay, or painting a picture, or doing embroidery,'" he read. "'It cannot be so refined, so leisurely and gentle, so temperate, kind, courteous, restrained and magnanimous. A revolution is an insurrection, an act of violence by which one class overthrows another.'" He grinned at Alonso, dazed, like he'd just seen the Virgin. "*Hermano*, you've got to read this. Peru's gonna change—"

"Shut up!" Alonso could barely speak. "*Carajo*, Rodolfo!" They stared at each other and then, his voice failing him, Alonso tried to unzip his jacket.

Not Rodolfo, he thought. His fingers turned clumsy and the zipper slipped off track. "Things *were* changing," he whispered hoarsely. "The Cesip was changing things."

"*The Cesip was changing things?* Like what?" Rodolfo closed the little red book and gave a scoffing laugh. "Nothing was changing, 'mano. Your mother was a fool for the bourgeoisie. Don't you be."

Alonso lunged across the table and threw Rodolfo from his chair. They fell to the ground, Alonso on top, grabbing Rodolfo's arms, feeling thin sinews straining against him. Rodolfo wriggled, every muscle moving. It was like trying to hold down a nest of snakes. Then, slithering, Rodolfo slid from beneath. Alonso's head hit the dirt, and Rodolfo's knee, bony and hard, sank into his gut. His nostrils flared. Alonso was drawing back his arm to throw a punch when a frightened cry rang from the bed.

"Alonso!" It was Livia. "Alonso, Gustavo can't breathe!"

Alonso threw Rodolfo off and ran to the bed. Gustavo lay on his back, eyes wide, sucking in air as fast as he could. Rodolfo came to the bedside, holding the lamp aloft.

Alonso pulled up Gustavo's sweatshirt as his brother heaved another breath. *Look at the chest, between the ribs*, Dr. Pablo had said. *That's where you see if the child is in danger.*

The brown skin of Gustavo's chest clenched inward, sucked down between his ribs. "Go to the avenue and get a taxi," Alonso muttered. "We've got to get him to the hospital." He pulled the blanket around Gustavo. "Breathe, *hermanito*, just breathe," he begged. Diana woke up and began to cry.

Rodolfo was staring at Gustavo. "His lips are blue," he whispered.

"Would you just go and get the damned taxi!"

"No." Rodolfo's voice was decisive. "There's no time. I know a doctor. Diana, Livia, get your shoes on." He grabbed the blanket and wrapped Gustavo in it. "Hurry!"

Alonso threw open the door and they tore from the house into a nightmare of mist. Gustavo was coughing, coughing and not stopping, wheezing and grunting in an awful struggle for air. They raced through dark streets, block after block. San Juan's huts gave way to little cement houses, the dirt to asphalt, the darkness to streetlights. Still they ran, nearly sobbing with exhaustion. Finally Rodolfo stopped in front of a darkened house and banged his fist on the door. From the flat roof above them, a dog the size of a Volkswagen began to bark.

Nobody's home, Alonso thought, panicking. *Nobody's home!* Then a light came on and a little barred hatch in the door opened.

Eyes peered out. A woman's voice spoke sharply. "Who?" The dog went on roaring, its jaws snapping above their heads.

"Dr. Vargas, I'm Mariela's brother. Please—this baby can't breathe."

The eyes framed in the hatch glanced at the bundle in Rodolfo's arms. Then the face withdrew and the hatch shut with a click. A latch screeched, locks clicked, a security bar creaked upward. Finally the door opened. A woman in pink pajamas reached out and took Gustavo into her arms. "Sit right here." She gestured at a bench just inside the door. Then she switched off the light and disappeared with Gustavo into another room.

Panting, Alonso sat down on the bench and pressed his fists between his knees. Gustavo would be all right. The doctor in the pink pajamas would save him.

Livia sat beside him, leaning her head on his arm, and Diana crawled into his lap. He felt like a tree, giving shelter to a pair of frightened sparrows. "Shhh," he whispered. "He'll be okay." Rodolfo closed the elaborate array of latches and locks, then sat down and put his head in his hands.

They waited in a darkness eased by the glow of streetlights through the curtain. On the roof, the dog barked. It sounded muffled, more bored than savage.

Slowly, the quivering inside Alonso stilled. Diana's sobs died off. When the dog shut up, her eyes closed and her head flopped backward. A thin black line crossed her cheek, a lock of hair she'd been sucking. Alonso tugged it from her mouth and slid his finger through it, separating the strands so they wouldn't knot.

Finally, a door opened and the doctor came out. A stethoscope hung from her neck, black and shiny atop her pink flannel. Alonso huddled with his sisters on the bench, too frightened to speak.

The doctor's gaze came to rest on him. "He's your brother?"

"Sí, Doctora," Alonso whispered.

She nodded. "It was an asthma attack. He's all right now."

Swallowing hard, Alonso hugged Diana so tight that she woke up with a sleepy cry of protest. Then he laughed, shakily, and looked up at the doctor. Behind her, fluorescent light streamed from the room where she had saved Gustavo. She yawned, and jabbed her fingers at her hair.

They'd gotten her out of bed, in her pink pajamas. "Gracias," Alonso said.

"De nada. I gave him a cortisone shot. I have a bronchodilator for you, in case this happens again. Put your sister down and come here so I can show you how to use it. What's your name?"

"Alonso, Doctora." He stood, feeling a surge of panic. "But Doctora, I don't have any—"

The doctor put her hand on his shoulder, holding him steady. For a moment Alonso remembered how that felt. Feeling anchored. "It's okay, Alonso." The doctor's voice was soft. "Come."

It was nearly midnight when they reached their own street. Gustavo lay bundled in the blanket, asleep in Alonso's arms. Alonso kicked the door open. In their panic, they had left it unlocked, and their father was not yet home.

When all three kids were in bed, Alonso took Rodolfo by the arm and led him to the table. They stared into the tear-shaped flame of the kerosene lamp.

"Was she the doctor you told me about?" Alonso asked. "The one you said helped, after Mariela got raped?"

Rodolfo didn't answer.

"The one from the Party?"

"I go to the prison on Saturdays," Rodolfo murmured. "To visit my uncle. Come with me. You'll see."

Alonso stood in silence, chewing his lip.

Go *visit* those bastards? No.

But a morbid curiosity gnawed at him. What kind of people would kill a person like his mother? And why?

The lamp's flame, caught by a current of air, flared and then grew dim.

▫EIGHT▫

"Are you coming to the movies tonight? Fico and Javier are coming, and so is Sara." Gabriela sounded wildly upbeat, like an announcer in a radio ad.

Cradling the telephone against her shoulder, Rosa peered into the refrigerator. Verónica, the maid, had cooked a pot of stew before going home for the weekend. Rosa slid it out of the way and reached for a plate of cheese.

"I don't know," she said, closing the refrigerator with her hip. "I don't feel like going out." She lifted a roll from a bag of bread.

"Come on, Rosa," Gabriela wheedled. "My *mamá's* picking us up after."

Lucky you, Rosa thought. Gabriela wouldn't have to ride a *micro*, stuffed in with all those *cholos*. She slapped cheese onto the roll as Gabriela made one last try. "We can invite Jano, too, if you want."

"Oh, *please*, Gabriela." Jano was a thin boy with crinkly brown hair and a reputation for being the smartest kid in class. "He's such a jerk."

"No, he's not!" Gabriela's voice turned sharp with indignation.

"He's conceited and he's a know-it-all." Jano had a languid way of raising his hand when no one else had an answer. As if he were doing everyone a favor but was himself slightly bored by the whole affair.

"But he likes you!"

"Why should I care?" Rosa bit into her sandwich.

Gabriela surrendered. "Fine," she retorted. "Suit yourself."

"*Chau.*" Rosa slammed down the phone.

The remains of breakfast still covered the dining room table. A glass pitcher with orange pulp stuck to the bottom. The bruised-looking skin of a cherimoya. The morning paper, pulled into sections.

On Verónica's days off, Papá usually insisted they all clean up after themselves. But this morning he'd rushed out after breakfast, dragging Mamá with him. The furniture store was having a big sale, and Papá wanted a new sofa.

Papá kept busy these days. Working his private practice, teaching at the university. And now he was remodeling.

Rosa grabbed *El Comercio*'s entertainment section and headed for the living room. She sank down on the sofa, bit into her sandwich, and opened the paper. Beyond the balcony, the bottle recycling man was pedaling by. "*Botellas*," he called. "*Botellas, bo-taaay-ahs.*" His nasal bray drifted down the *Malecón*.

Rosa was reading about the warring actors in a Brazilian soap opera when the phone rang. Probably Gabriela again. She'd been buzzing around Rosa like a stubborn mosquito for weeks, apparently not offended when Rosa swatted her. The phone rang again, and Rosa decided to let the answering machine pick up.

She resisted until the fourth ring. "*Alo.*"

"Rosa?" It was a boy, his voice tentative.

"Alonso!" Rosa was dumbstruck, and so, apparently, was Alonso. The line remained silent, buzzing slightly. "Where are you calling from?"

"Canto Grande. The phone company office."

"You're in Canto Grande? Are you with Rodolfo?"

"Not right now."

"How is he? I mean, how are *you*?" *Don't be an idiot*, she thought, tossing *El Comercio* to the floor. *Don't blow it.* She curled her legs under her, drawing her body as close as possible to the phone.

"He's . . . I'm okay. We're both okay. How are you?"

"Okay, I guess." He'd called her! They hadn't spoken in three months, almost to the day. But he'd called her! "How are the kids?"

"So-so. Gustavo has asthma. And Livia . . . she doesn't eat much."

"Oh, I'm so sorry to hear that." *Trite*, Rosa thought desperately. *Like a pituca. Next you'll be asking—*

"Rosa—" He broke off.

"Are you really okay?"

"I don't know. It's . . . we moved. A month ago. We're not in Salvador anymore. Did you know that?"

Rosa felt a downward plunge, like an elevator dropping too fast. "No." He had moved a month ago and she hadn't even known. "Where do you live?"

"I'm not supposed to tell anyone," Alonso said miserably.

"Alonso!"

There was a moment's silence. "We're in San Juan, in my uncle's place. They went back to the mountains. Rosa, don't tell anyone," he begged. "Please don't tell your father. Promise me!"

"Alonso, have you been threatened?"

"Just promise me." She could hear voices in the background, the bustle of the phone company office.

"I promise. But what about school?"

"I'm not going. Livia goes. It's down the street from the house. The María Auxiliadora School. It's a dump," he said acidly. "I'm not missing anything. Rosa, is your father going to rebuild the Cesip?"

"What?" Rosa was flabbergasted. "He . . ." She sat up straight. *Of course he will,* she thought. *He has to.* That's what she wanted to tell Alonso. *He has to. Because that's who we are. Not just school and Miraflores and Mamá's family. We're also Salvador and the Cesip and Alonso's family.*

"I don't know," she said at last. The receiver felt slick in her palm.

"So he isn't."

"I said I don't know!"

"Well, why should he?" Alonso's voice was bitter. "Lima's full of *cholos* for him to experiment on."

"What a horrible thing to say."

"I've got to go."

She couldn't let him go, not now, not so angrily. "Alonso, can I come see you? I could take a *micro.*"

Alonso laughed. A nasty, mocking laugh she had never heard before. "To San Juan? Are you nuts?"

"Then come see me. Come to my apartment." She heard herself begging, hated the pleading note in her voice. But she'd lose him if he hung up now. She'd lose him and never find him again. From San Juan they'd move somewhere else and then he'd be gone forever. Just another of the six million dark faces crowding the shantytowns. "Please, Alonso."

That laugh again. "The doorman wouldn't let me past your front door, Rosa." There was a click, and the line went dead.

Rosa stared at the receiver and then slammed it down. A cry tore from her throat. He was gone.

Pulling on a jacket, she ran downstairs, past the doorman and across the *Malecón*. A little park stretched between the road and the cliffs. Grass, mostly, and a few flowers wilting in the salt air. Beyond the cliffs, the sea moved, dark and shadowy against the cold pallor of the horizon.

Rosa sat at the edge of the park, near the cliff, hugging her knees to her chest. She'd blown it. Alonso had called her—he had called her, he hadn't hated her too much to call—but she'd blown it anyway. Said the wrong things. Not reached out of her world into his, his world that was obviously falling apart. She had failed him.

She wept. Stupid, useless tears. She hated crying, hated herself for crying. And still she cried.

After a time she felt, rather than saw, someone watching her. At the edge of the park, a steep trail led down the slope of the cliff. A few shacks clung there, a tiny shantytown stowed away among the apartment buildings of the *Malecón*. A barefoot child in filthy shorts had climbed the path to stare at her.

Wiping her cheeks, Rosa smiled. A little girl. The thin, fragile kind, like Livia, looking as if she might blow away in a stiff breeze. The little girl peered at Rosa, then scampered down the trail. Like a rabbit, disappearing down a hole.

I guess that makes me the fox, Rosa thought.

Isn't that what Alonso had really been saying? *You're not like me, Rosa. We don't belong together.* He had laughed at the very thought of it.

Rosa felt a sob rise in her chest. *No,* she thought. *No.* She put her hands between her knees and squeezed so hard that it hurt. That can't be right.

Everything was wrong now because she hadn't run, she'd stood there frozen like an idiot. That had gotten Magda killed and everything had fallen apart but that didn't mean Alonso was right. They *did* belong together. Or they had belonged together. It could have been. There had been a moment, there had been years, when they belonged together. It hadn't been impossible, even if it was now.

Footsteps fell over the grass behind her. *Ay, Dios,* Rosa thought wearily. Just leave me alone.

"Rosa?" Papá sat down at her side. "Are you okay?"

Staring out at the sea, Rosa nodded. She had nothing to say to him, this shell that had once held her father.

Papá had once believed it was possible. Had driven into a shantytown every Thursday and Saturday for ten years. Rosa had watched him save a little girl's life once. A little *chola.*

A man had raced into the Cesip, shouting for help, carrying a screeching child with a hideously blistered face. Everyone in the Cesip had stared in panic, even Magda. But not Papá. He'd taken the child into his arms. He'd called for one of the medical students, and they'd disappeared into the examining room. When they'd emerged, the child was quiet, her head swathed in gauze. Papá took the child and the father to the hospital, and Rosa ended up spending the night at Magda's house.

She'd seen the child around Salvador from time to time. A little girl, named Sonia. After she got out of the hospital, Papá found a plastic surgeon to help her. She ended up with horrible scars and a bald patch, but Papá said she'd be able to eat and talk and live a fairly normal life. He said she was lucky to be alive, that it was a blessing her eyes had been spared.

Papá had once believed.

"Ay, Rosita," Papá murmured.

She could feel him, his tall, familiar body. The clean smell of his aftershave. That shadow of gray was the sweater she'd given him for Christmas.

For a moment, neither of them said anything. Then she looked at him.

He touched her cheek. "I know it feels like nothing will ever be okay again."

Rosa looked away. "It feels like we just . . . abandoned them," she said. "All of them." A thin line of breakers appeared on the ocean, cutting white streaks across the gray.

He took a deep breath and let it out slowly. "In a way we did. But I don't know what to do." He lifted her hand and rubbed it against his cheek. His skin felt smooth, cool. He'd shaved this morning, the way he always did, even on Saturdays. "You have your mother's hands."

Rosa heard the smile in his voice. "You think Tomás says that about Livia's hands?"

Papá dropped her hand. "You don't have to feel guilty you're alive."

Rosa shrugged. It was what her shrink told her. It was what everyone told her. But if she weren't alive then maybe Magda wouldn't be dead. "What about Alonso, Papá? And Livia and Diana and Gustavo? Who's taking care of them?"

"They still have their father. Tomás is a good man. It's just . . . he's different from Magda. He thought the Cesip took her away from his family too much." Papá gave a short, surprised laugh. "And look how right he turned out to be."

His laugh dying to a sigh, Papá took off his glasses and pulled a handkerchief from his pocket. "They moved. I didn't want to tell you. It just seemed like more bad news." He began to wipe the lenses carefully. "Sendero was trying to justify—oh, Lord. At first it was just rumors, talk. Ana told me about it before she left." Rosa turned to face him and he nodded. "Ana left, too. She got a death threat." He put his glasses back on and grimaced. "I went to Salvador last week. There's graffiti everywhere. It says Magda stole that old refrigerator. You know, after the Americans donated the new one."

Rosa gasped. "How can they say that? Who would believe it?"

"It's easy to lie when people are frightened."

Shocked, Rosa stuttered. Stealing an old refrigerator couldn't justify killing someone. But Papá just shook his head. "Magda ladrón," he said. "Can you imagine?"

"Nobody could believe Magda was a thief."

"I don't know," he said. "I guess Tomás felt they were in danger." He paused. "No one seems to know where they went."

Rosa spread her fingers through the grass and tore up a handful. After watching her in silence for a moment her father went on. "Padre Manuel's trying to work out some way to help them. Maybe get them asylum in Spain. I don't know what he'll do when I tell him they're gone."

Rosa opened her hand, letting the tiny green blades blow off her palm. It was easy, keeping secrets. "Is Padre Manuel ever coming back?"

"I think so."

Promises, promises, Rosa thought. She watched a trio of pelicans glide above the waves.

"His order is afraid for him," Papá said. "They don't want him to come back."

An image came to Rosa's mind. Alonso, dialing the phone in a crowded public office. The tentative strain in his voice when he heard hers. *He sounded so alone,* Rosa thought. *So absolutely alone.* She put her head down on her knees. "Isn't there anything we can do?" she whispered.

Her father put his arm around her shoulders.

"Papá?" Rosa turned to him. "Don't you even *want* to do something? Magda always said—"

"I know, I know. *You can always do something.*" Papá's fingers twitched over his moustache. "But what can I do? Ana's gone, and she was the only one—the *only* one—in the Mothers' Club who wanted to rebuild. What am I supposed to do? Help the Army turn the Cesip into a civic action project?"

"Would that be so bad?"

"It wouldn't be the Cesip!" Her father's vehemence startled her. "It would belong to the Army, not to the people who live there! Magda died trying to prevent that!"

"So instead there's no Cesip at all," Rosa muttered. "She died trying to prevent that, too."

"Rosa, things are not as simple as you seem to think."

"I don't think they're simple!" She jumped to her feet. "You think I . . ."

Blinded by tears, she turned to leave, but her father stood and held her by the arms. "Rosa, please."

"You think I don't understand, but I do," Rosa cried, her voice shrill. "I just don't see things the way you do!" She wiped her eyes. "What I don't understand is you! How you . . . why you just want to give up and do nothing!"

Papá gazed down at her, his eyes tired, the color of weak tea. Rosa tried to look away but couldn't. She clenched her jaw. "You're wrong," she said. "I do understand."

"We can only do so much, Rosa."

"So that's it? We tried, but they're *cholos*, so good-bye? Was that what Mamá did when everyone in her family turned against her for marrying you?"

Her father's hands tightened and he gave her a violent shake. "My God, Rosa! Do you want to see me dead, too? You think that would even the score so you could look Alonso in the face again?"

Rosa stiffened, and her father winced, his voice now hoarse. "Ay, Rosa. Why do you have to make this so much harder than it already is?"

Rosa felt the tears, once again. But she blinked, and shook her head and clenched her teeth and refused, absolutely refused, this time, to cry. "Is that what you want, Papá? For me to make it *easier*?"

Papá's hands fell from her arms. "Rosa, we *have* to go on. We just—" He turned toward the ocean. "We have to move on."

Rosa took a deep breath, fighting the airless feeling in her chest. "What do you want me to do then? Forget about them?"

"Not forget." Papá shut his eyes. "Just . . . keep on living." He leaned toward her, pleading. "Can't we do that? Isn't that what Magda would have wanted?"

Rosa looked at him, dull-eyed. Magda was dead and Alonso was gone and Papá was never going back. That was just the way the world was.

Finally she nodded. Together they turned, her father at her side, not touching her. They crossed the street in silence, and as the doorman swung open the door, Rosa spoke. "I'll try, Papá."

She'd move on. Because Papá was right. It was what Magda would have wanted.

·NINE·

Alonso placed two steaming cups of coffee on the table. A faint light, gray like winter, squeezed through the gaps where the *estera* walls didn't quite meet the cardboard roof. The kids were still asleep, curled up in the double bed at the other side of the shack.

Dipping a spoon into his coffee, Alonso watched the sugar melt to a grainy swirl. His father sat opposite him and, with narrowed eyes, sipped. Outside the shack, San Juan was silent, a rare predawn stillness.

"I have to go to the market today," Alonso said.

His father dug into his pocket and dropped a few coins on the tabletop.

"But that . . ." Alonso broke off. *Isn't enough,* he thought. It never was. And today was Saturday. His father would come home late with nothing in his pocket.

Alonso took a gulp of coffee. His mother never let him drink coffee. But if they drank it without milk, they could afford it.

Come see me, Rosa had begged.

The phone call had been a disaster. He'd been cruel and

she'd been stupid. As if she could come to San Juan, with that *Pishtaco* running loose. As if he could visit her apartment. He'd painted enough buildings in Miraflores to know that unless he was there to work, the doorman would throw him out on his can. Or the maid would leave him standing in the hallway. Or the neighbors would clutch their handbags, watching him suspiciously. *Pitucas de mierda.*

His father stood. "I'll be home late."

Surprise, surprise, Alonso thought.

"Alonso."

Sideways, out of the corner of his eye, Alonso glanced up at his father.

"No running off. Stay with the kids."

Alonso looked back down into his cup.

His father had found the kids alone while Alonso was calling Rosa. He hadn't been drunk this time. If anything, he'd seemed almost sorry about the belt. But he'd given it to Alonso anyway. Like he had no choice anymore.

"Well." His father pushed his chair close to the table. A tidy gesture. The kind of gesture Alonso's mother had drilled into them all. "See you later."

Alonso was putting the cups away when a thump sounded at the door. He spoke quietly. "Who?"

A choked voice, outside. "Alonso?"

Fumbling, Alonso undid the lock.

Rodolfo stood damp-haired in the mist. Hands in his pockets, eyes red and swollen. Beside him stood a sharp-eyed girl with a narrow brown face.

"Alonso . . ." Rodolfo's hands came out of his pockets. "Mariela . . ." His voice broke and he began blinking rapidly.

Alonso felt a frisson in his stomach. Felt a sudden urge to leave. To back away. Out the backyard and over the wall.

"May we come in?" The girl's voice was silky soft. A surprise, coming from that hawklike face.

Dumb with fear, Alonso let them pass. He kept his mind blank as he locked the door, slipping the curved shackle into the cold metal case. He didn't look at them as they sat, chair legs scoring the dirt floor.

"The Army took over the teachers' college," the girl said.

Mariela's pregnant, Alonso thought. He pulled two enameled cups from the shelf and opened the thermos. Poured steaming water and pried open the instant coffee. *She's pregnant. They can't touch her.* Round and round went the coffee spoon. Behind him, Rodolfo began to cry.

"They arrested some students." The girl stood and heaped three spoonfuls of sugar into one of the cups, then carried it to Rodolfo. "Took them in for"—her eyes flashed like black diamonds—"what they call interrogation."

Alonso's heart punched against his ribs. Interrogation. The day the Hulk had almost got him. What his father had said. *You know what they'll do to you if they arrest you?*

They'd kick you? Electrocute you? Stick things inside you? Alonso didn't know, didn't want to know. He stared at the bed. Gustavo lay hunched, facedown with his butt in the air. But now Rodolfo had sniffed, wiped his nose on his sleeve. Had curled his hands around the cup and was speaking.

The soldiers had taken Mariela in with the rest. Interrogated her, and then released her. She'd made it home before the hemorrhage started. Rodolfo had run for a taxi, but the driver had taken one look at all that blood and driven off. Mariela had screamed, with her mother pressing towels between her legs, for what seemed like a long time. Finally she had stopped. She'd lain quietly, her eyelids fluttering. And then, like an engine shutting off, she had stopped breathing.

Alonso listened in disbelief.

Rodolfo curled his body over the table and wept.

"We came from the wake," the girl said. She rubbed Rodolfo's back, gently, and Alonso bit back the ache in his own throat. The tears that if they began to fall would drown them all. He sat in front of Rodolfo, unable to move.

Finally Rodolfo's sobs subsided. The girl stopped rubbing his back. "Rodolfo's mother would be grateful if you went to the wake," she told Alonso.

"But I—"

"I'll stay with your sisters and brother."

Rodolfo looked up with a watery hiccup, rubbing his fists over his eyes. "She's Victoria," he muttered. "A friend"—his jaw muscles worked—"of Mariela's."

"It's all right, Alonso." The girl smiled. "I have four brothers." She glanced at the bed, where Diana was sitting up, tousle-haired and wide-eyed. "And two little sisters."

"Alonso?" Diana's voice was a whisper.

"I'm Victoria." The girl crossed to the bed and held out her arms. "A friend of Mariela's." Uncertainly, Diana clambered into her arms, then wrapped her legs around Victoria's waist. "We'll be fine," the girl told Alonso. "Won't we, Diana?"

Rodolfo opened the door. Still mist, but San Juan was beginning to awaken. A few boys ran by, kicking a soccer ball. Up the street, the market was coming to life. A man heaved sacks of potatoes from a tricycle cart. Two cops watched him, lounging against a sign.

"Fucking cops." Rodolfo sounded more tired than angry.

Alonso stepped to his side and stared at the cops. They wore green uniforms, had Uzis slung from their shoulders.

Terroristas, he thought. With or without uniforms. "Let's go," he said.

o o o

San Tadeo's, where Mariela lay, was a one-room chapel in the farthest, poorest corner of Canto Grande. A few backless wooden benches lined the walls. A single wreath of flowers hung from an easel beside the coffin. A few people waited around the edges of the room. That's what wakes were for. The wait until the final moment in the cemetery, when the coffin slid into darkness and the funeral niche was plastered over forever.

As Alonso entered the chapel, his eyes found Rodolfo's mother. Wearing a shapeless black sweater, her face rubbery with weeping. She looked as if she might collapse into a shadowy heap. But a woman stood beside her, keeping a hand under Señora Domitila's elbow, and Alonso realized with a start that it was Dr. Vargas. The doctor in the pink pajamas, who had saved Gustavo. As Alonso approached, she gave him a sad smile.

He bent to kiss Señora Domitila's cheek. She put a hand

on his forearm and, instinctively, he hardened the muscle, brac-
ing her.

"Come," she murmured, broken-voiced. *"Mi Marielita."*

Willing himself to keep pace with Señora Domitila, Alonso
darted a glance behind him. Rodolfo had gone to sit on one of
the benches. Dr. Vargas sat beside him. A few men clumped
round the doorway, their black pants too short, white socks
showing at the cuffs.

The coffin lay open, and as they drew near Señora Domitila
grasped the rim. Her knuckles yellowed as she peered in.

Alonso forced himself to look down.

Mariela.

Hands carefully folded around a rosary. A round face, waxen
now. And that hair. Black hair like a river. Sweet, and smelling
of flowers. Ay, Mariela.

If he opened his mouth, would words come out? Or just mist?
Mist that dampened their hair and wet the dust. Everything sank
like death into the ground.

Alonso wanted to speak, but his feet backed him away, leaving Rodolfo's mother alone, clinging to the coffin and weeping. A
woman approached—Alonso recognized her as one of Rodolfo's
aunts—and from the wall beside Rodolfo, Dr. Vargas rose. She
waved a hand at Alonso. Come, the hand said. Sit with him.

Unable to refuse, Alonso sat at Rodolfo's side as Dr. Vargas
returned to her post beside Señora Domitila. The three women
clustered by the coffin. Waiting.

"I'm sorry," Alonso muttered.

Rodolfo nodded.

They sat for a long time. Outside the chapel, dawn brightened to morning. An occasional truck rumbled past. Voices. Life. Finally Dr. Vargas sat down once more, her hand on Rodolfo's shoulder.

"You should go," she murmured. "Your uncle will want to see you."

Rodolfo cleared his throat and turned to Alonso, wraithlike in his grief. "You coming?"

"Where?"

"The prison."

Dr. Vargas touched Alonso's elbow. "Things will make more sense there."

To the prison? Alonso stiffened. *More sense?* Was there a why for any of this? For his mother, for Mariela?

You'll never know, he thought. *If you don't go, you'll never know.*

Suddenly feeling tired, Alonso nodded. And then he stood.

□ □ □

They waited in line for an hour, outside a high perimeter wall topped by razor wire. Most of the visitors were women. Wives and girlfriends and mothers, laden with baskets of food. Alonso bounced a little, nervous. Rodolfo stood mute and still. The strip-search was terrifying, the guards' fingers as cold and hard as their eyes. A guard in a beige uniform handed them prison passes without even looking at them.

Pulling his sweatshirt over his head, Alonso stepped from

the guardhouse onto the prison grounds. A sidewalk led between freestanding cellblocks. Crazily curved buildings, four and five stories high, the barred windows pocking them with square holes. The prison had about a dozen cellblocks, some unpainted cement, others painted red or dirty yellow. The paint stopped halfway up the facade, as if it had run out in mid-job. Everything reeked of sweat and fear. Of piss and shit. Of rotting food and hot oil that's been used a thousand times till it stinks like poison. The sky was a narrow avenue of gray, light-years away.

"Come on," Rodolfo said.

Alonso followed him between the cellblocks. A hand reached through the bars, fingers outstretched. "*Papito*," the man murmured. He had a scar on his right cheek, an old scar like a thick white worm. His tongue slipped out, passing slowly over his lips. "Mmm."

Rodolfo grabbed Alonso's shirt and pulled him to the center of the sidewalk. Gasping, Alonso bumped his head into a bucket. Hung from a string, it seemed to have dropped from the sky. From a window on the fourth floor, a prisoner cried out. "A piece of bread, pal!" The man jiggled the string, making the bucket dance. "Bread! Put it in the bucket!"

Rodolfo shoved him forward. "Don't stop," he said. "Don't look at them."

"*¡Carajo!*" Alonso swore. "Don't they even feed these guys?" It was a horror movie, not a prison.

Rodolfo shrugged. "If you call rice water food." He quickened his pace.

Alonso tried not to look, but it was impossible. They were

everywhere. Men in dirty T-shirts and torn pants. Men crowding the bars, men hooting at the boys, men lying on bare cement floors. Men shouting, laughing, fighting, crying, begging.

"There." Rodolfo pointed. "Pavilion 4."

Pavilion 4, the high-security Senderista cellblock, was set apart from the rest, surrounded by a chain-link fence. A few meters inside the fence, a gate with iron bars led into the cellblock itself. Guards with machine guns stood by the gate.

Alonso and Rodolfo stepped up to the fence and flashed the passes they'd gotten in the guardhouse. A cop let them in and led them across the cracked cement patio. Beside the gate leaned a sergeant, one black-booted foot jacked up against the wall. He was picking his teeth, scraping a thumbnail along his gums. The boys waited, holding out their passes, and finally he spat. He looked at the slips of paper, then at the boys, then at the passes again. Alonso overcame an urge to start bouncing.

Behind the gate, just inside the cellblock, stood several men in red sweaters, holding wooden staffs. *Senderistas*, Alonso thought. One of them, a short, hefty man, muttered something to the sergeant, who handed him the passes. The Senderista glanced at the passes and then at the boys, and then he nodded. The sergeant nodded, too, and one of the cops unlocked the gate.

I'm here, Alonso thought.

He had come, almost in a daze, his throat full of what had happened to Mariela. Cloudy and aching and confused. But as the gate clanged shut behind him, he felt a moment of panic. He thought of his mother and tried to explain. *It's because of Mariela. And Dr. Vargas. She saved Gustavo's life.*

But that wasn't all, and his mother would know it. She always knew.

I want to know, he told her. I want to know why.

Rodolfo shook hands with the hefty Senderista in the red sweater. "*Buenos días*, comrade."

"*Buenos días*," the Senderista said. He shook Alonso's hand. "Morning assembly is about to start."

Ahead of them lay a broad lobby. Red banners hung like tapestries all around, and on a far wall a painted army of workers and *campesinos* seemed to march out of a mural. They carried red flags with hammers and sickles, had popping muscles and square jaws. Leading them strode a man in a gray suit, a stout man in spectacles. He held a book in one hand.

Alonso walked to the middle of the lobby. "Isn't that . . . ?"

For the first time that morning, Rodolfo smiled. "Chairman Gonzalo."

Above the mural were carefully lettered words. WELCOME TO THE SHINING TRENCH OF COMBAT.

"How could they paint that? This is a prison!"

Rodolfo's smile spread into a grin.

"I don't get it."

Rodolfo pointed back to the entrance, through the black bars to the stink and cries and grasping fingers. "The old Peru." He pointed at the mural. "The People's War." Finally he pointed at the ground. "The New Peru. Right here. Right now."

"Oh, come on, Rodolfo. Don't be an idiot."

"In here, the Party's in charge," Rodolfo insisted. "The guys in red sweaters? They're all EGP. People's Guerrilla Army. The comrades can't get out of the cellblock, but the cops can't get in."

Alonso snorted. "Yeah, right, wooden sticks against machine guns."

"The comrades can defend themselves, 'mano," Rodolfo said darkly. "Like I said, they're EGP." He jutted his chin at the short Senderista who'd shaken their hands. "Who you think's gonna fight better, Comrade Arturo or some fat slob of a cop?" Rodolfo spat in contempt. Then he cocked his head at the bubbly puddle on the floor. He smeared his foot over it, rubbing carefully till it was gone.

"I don't believe it," Alonso said.

"Look." Rodolfo pointed at the red banners and flags. Some had hammers and sickles, others cryptic initials, as if the Senderistas spoke in code. "You think the cops would leave those up if they could get in here and take them down?"

Alonso read from a gold-lettered banner. "'Whoever has an army has power. War decides everything.'"

"Come on," Rodolfo said. He led Alonso through a corridor lined with cells. Halfway down the hall, a doorway opened onto a crowded exercise yard. Men, women, and children waited in silence around two closely ranked lines of prisoners. Alonso could hear them all breathing, like one colossal body with a hundred heads.

Rodolfo pointed at four gigantic heads painted on the brick walls of the courtyard. "The Four Swords of Communism," he whispered. He pointed to each portrait in turn. "Marx. Lenin. Chairman Mao. Chairman Gonzalo."

"Shhh!" A woman froze them with a disapproving glare.

The prisoners in the courtyard threw back their shoulders and began to sing.

Workers, peasants, break your chains.
Raise the flag of the People's War.

The crowd started to sing and Rodolfo joined in, his voice high and clear.

Everything is an illusion, everything but power.
Rifles in hand, we storm heaven's tower.

A shiver crept along Alonso's scalp. Trapped by the high walls, the anthem rang like church bells.

The song ended, and a prisoner stepped forward. "Long live Chairman Gonzalo, leader of the Party of the Revolution," the prisoner shouted. "For his masterful leadership and his position as the continuation of Marx, Lenin, and Chairman Mao Tse-tung!" He was out of breath when he finally finished. The two lines of prisoners took up the chant and shouted it back, pumping their fists in the air. When they were finished another man began to shout, and once again his comrades chanted back at him.

The chants dragged on and on. Everyone seemed to want a turn. Alonso was yawning when the prisoners finally broke ranks and the visitors surged toward them. A moment of chaos ensued, a confused tangle of outstretched arms. Then, with embraces and cries of delight, the mass sorted itself out into families.

"This way," Rodolfo said, pushing through the crowd. At the edge of the exercise yard, a man in wire-framed glasses sat at a table. Chairman Mao ballooned, fat-faced and solemn, on the wall behind him.

Rodolfo pulled two bags of rice from his backpack. He handed them to the man, who tossed them into a basket beside the table. Then, with a smile, the man wrote Rodolfo's name on a list. Rodolfo stepped away and others approached. An old lady in a black dress handed over a bag of sugar. Two women hefted a sack of potatoes. A blushing little boy placed a pouch of powdered milk on the table.

They all gave something. And they all looked poor. Like maybe that powdered milk was all they had.

Rodolfo went off to find his uncle. Señor Ernesto was standing in the middle of the courtyard, talking to a young man. When he saw Rodolfo he broke off and held open his arms.

He looked just like Rodolfo's mother, broad-chested and moon-faced, but thinner than Alonso remembered. He hugged Rodolfo for a long time. Then he pushed his nephew back, gripping Rodolfo's shoulders. "We carry our lives in our fingertips, hijo. ¿Ya?"

Rodolfo nodded. "Our lives belong to the Party," he replied in a husky whisper.

"Is your mother okay?"

Rodolfo shrugged. "Comrade Micaela is with her."

Alonso looked away, blinking. The Senderistas already knew about Mariela. Even here in prison, they knew. *The Party has a thousand eyes and a thousand ears.* That's what they always said.

Señor Ernesto shook Alonso's hand. "It's good to see you again, Alonso."

"I'm sorry about Mariela," Alonso said. He tried to remember what his mother had taught him, what you were supposed to say. My *most sincere* . . . Something like that. The neighbors in Salvador had said it to him, the day of the funeral.

Sincere hadn't lasted very long. "I'm sorry," he mumbled.

Rodolfo's uncle nodded, gripping Alonso's hand. "Alonso, Comrade Felipe would like to meet you." Señor Ernesto spoke as if Alonso should know who Comrade Felipe was. Rodolfo whistled softly.

Señor Ernesto explained. The highest-ranking Party member ever taken alive. Captured after a gun battle that left him lame. The political-military commander of the cadres in the Shining Trench of Combat.

Buffeted by the crowd, Alonso listened in a stupor.

"He's our leader, Alonso," Señor Ernesto said. "It's an honor. Rodolfo hasn't even met him yet."

"He knows Chairman Gonzalo," Rodolfo said. "Personally." He shook his head, incredulous.

"Why does he want to see me?" Alonso asked.

"I guess he'll tell you that," Señor Ernesto replied. "Comrade Victor will take you."

The young man Señor Ernesto had been talking to stepped forward. He gestured for Alonso to follow.

Alonso ignored him. "Rodolfo . . ." This wasn't part of the deal.

Rodolfo gave him a slight smile. Alonso shook his head, but Rodolfo tipped his head toward the young man. Go on, he was saying. Please.

"Go on, Alonso," Señor Ernesto barked. "He's waiting for you!"

Dazed, Alonso turned to follow the young man. People backed up to let them pass. Comrade Victor stepped into the cellblock and Alonso followed.

What am I doing? He could hear his feet, that squishy sneaker noise padding down the long corridor. His mind returned to his mother. *I need to know,* he told her. *I need to know why.*

The doors to the cells were open, and he slowed down to look. If his mother's murderers ever got caught, this was where they'd end up.

He saw bare cement rooms, each with four or five pallets on the floor and a plastic bucket in the corner. The occasional portrait of Chairman Gonzalo. Red flags on the walls. One man sat on a pallet, reading a little red book like the one Rodolfo had given Alonso for his birthday.

Alonso thought of Dr. Vargas, wearing those pink pajamas as she saved Gustavo's life.

Comrade Victor's footsteps receded down the corridor. Alonso paused at the open door of another cell. Stripped to the waist, a man was doing pushups on the floor. His lean arms pumped like pistons as his body rose and fell. Dozens of angry red circles puckered the skin on his back. Scars, like the holes burning cigarettes leave on a tablecloth.

Interrogation, Alonso thought. He thought of Mariela. Pregnant. Strapped to a table. Screaming. Slammed by a wave of nausea, he stumbled to the next cell. He grabbed cold iron and stood, hanging from the bars, till the nausea passed.

Comrade Victor's footsteps stopped. He turned, waiting for Alonso.

Alonso walked slowly to the end of the corridor.

Comrade Victor tapped his fingernails on the bars of a cell. "Comrade." He spoke in a low, almost reverential voice. "It's the Ríos boy."

The Ríos boy. His mother's name, not his father's. To the Senderistas, he was his mother's son.

"Send him in," came the quiet reply.

Comrade Victor nodded to Alonso.

The cell was large, with a big barred window and a view of the exercise yard. It had a single bed, not four or five floor pallets like the other cells. A table and two chairs stood by the wall. Beside the window, a man sat in an upholstered easy chair. Five-star luxury.

The man in the chair spoke again, in the same quiet voice. "That will be all, comrade. Thank you."

The young man backed silently from the cell and the man in the chair stood up. His face was skeletal, carved into jaw, cheek-bones, brows. As if prison were shaving him down to bone. The sunken gray eyes were cool as they surveyed Alonso.

Alonso met them, red-faced. When his feet betrayed him, rocking him back on his heels, he willed them into stillness. *I am not afraid*, he thought. *He thinks I am but I'm not. I just want a gun.*

He imagined the weight of it, his fingers curled around the cold metal.

Comrade Felipe held out his hand. "*Buenos días*, Alonso. Welcome."

Baffled, Alonso didn't move. The hand was a skeleton's

hand, bones with a bit of sinew. The gray eyes held a speculative look. Nothing would surprise them, but they were waiting to see what Alonso would do.

Alonso stuck out his own hand and Comrade Felipe shook it firmly before limping to the table. Wincing, he lowered himself into one of the wooden chairs and gestured for Alonso to sit in the other.

Alonso perched at the edge of his chair, feet jiggling.

"Alonso, it's good to meet you. I was very glad to learn you'd come to visit our Shining Trench of Combat." The thin lips curled up. A slight, ironic smile.

"I came for Rodolfo. And because Dr. Vargas saved my brother's life."

Comrade Felipe nodded. "You felt you owed the Party a debt of gratitude."

Gratitude! Unsure of how to respond, Alonso looked out the window. A little band, drummers wearing ponchos and a man with a wooden pan flute, played a marching tune.

"That must be a confusing thing to feel," Comrade Felipe went on. "A brother saved, a mother executed. It's a difficult equation to balance out."

"I can balance it fine," Alonso snapped. "I'd like to kill the bastards who shot my mother."

Comrade Felipe tapped his fingers on the tabletop. "You should save your rage for the revisionist scum who used your mother. They're the ones who signed her death warrant."

"What are you talking about?"

"Alonso, do you know why the Party executed your mother?"

The word he used was *ajusticiar,* an execution in the cause of justice.

"Because . . ." Alonso shook his head. "She said Sendero wanted her to resign. She wouldn't let them use the Cesip."

"The Party needed her help in convincing the Mothers' Club."

"She was afraid the government would shut them down."

Comrade Felipe shrugged. "We all have to make sacrifices, Alonso. What matters is that we gave your mother several chances." He shook his head regretfully. "She was a daughter of the People, but sadly misled."

"By who?"

Comrade Felipe sighed and shifted his bad leg. "Bourgeois reformists. Revisionist scum." He grimaced, as if a cockroach had scuttled across the floor. "They convinced her there was a peaceful path for the People's struggle, a path that didn't lead through war. All lies. As long as hunger, misery, and exploitation exist, war is inevitable." He looked closely at Alonso. "Forgive me for saying this, Alonso, but your mother was an opportunist."

Alonso jumped to his feet and slammed his fist on the table. "Don't insult my mother!" he shouted. "Don't EVER insult her!"

Footsteps came running down the hall. Comrade Felipe held up a hand. His gaze never left Alonso's. "Sit down," he said softly. "And never, ever shout in here." He spoke slowly, each word crisp, a command. "Sit down."

Alonso glared back at those cold gray eyes. "Don't insult her," he repeated sullenly. He sat.

"I'm not talking about that ridiculous business of the refrigerator."

"She didn't want it! Dr. Pablo made her take it!" His anger surged again, half lifting him from his seat. He was driftwood, tossed on waves of rage.

"Of course." Comrade Felipe pursed his lips. "She would have made a fine cadre." He shook his head with a sigh. "Ay, Alonso. Without the Party, these grassroots leaders always go astray." His voice turned fierce. "Do you really think saving a few children will make a difference? What kind of future awaits those children? Do you want your sisters to be maids? Do you want your brother to be an *ambulante*? Or do you want him to be a free man who can look any man in the eye as his equal?"

Against his will, an image sprang into Alonso's mind. Gustavo as a proud young man, with his father's black eyes and high cheekbones, but without that brooding look of defeat. Never having to even think about running through traffic to sell some *pituca* a tube of toothpaste.

His head had sprung a leak. Comrade Felipe's words were seeping in. He tried to stop the flow.

My mother, he thought. *Mamá*.

She buttons his sweater and hands him a cardboard sign. It's small, just the right size. She reads it for him. "Every child deserves to be healthy."

The Mothers' Club is going to march on the Ministry of Health. They're going to tell the Minister to pay for the Cesip's roof.

Alonso is going along. Six years old, and strutting. Ready to march and wave his sign.

"Be brave," she says, helping him up the steps of the micro. "You're going to do something important today."

Alonso stared down at the table. "You haven't told me why you killed my mother."

"Alonso, if the bourgeoisie can cushion the People's misery, spend a few *soles* buying them off without really changing anything, don't you think they will? Your mother played right into that. She became what we call a useful fool. A chain around the neck of the People. So we had no choice. We had to execute her." That word again. *Ajusticiar*. They had executed his mother with justice.

Alonso's throat constricted. "You don't know shit about her!" Oh, for a gun. A gun! He'd spray-paint this whole fucking cellblock with blood. "You people murdered my mother!"

"We did not murder her! If a rotten class system makes war inevitable, whom do you blame for that war? The bourgeoisie who benefit from the system? Or the People who fight to overthrow it?" Comrade Felipe jabbed a slender finger at Alonso. "You know what they did to Mariela. Why did they do that?"

"How the hell should I know?" Alonso stood up, feeling acid sear his throat. "I've got to go."

"Don't be a child. You're old enough to understand." Comrade Felipe stood and faced him. "We kill to make things change. They kill so things will stay the same."

Alonso turned away. Go, he told his feet.

"*Hijo*." Comrade Felipe touched his shoulder. "I know it's hard. I know it better than you imagine."

Go to hell, Alonso thought.

"Look at me, *hijo*." The hand stayed on his shoulder, feather-light.

For a moment Alonso didn't move, his back to the Senderista and every muscle tense. Then, slowly, unwillingly, he obeyed. Turning, he found himself looking into gray eyes that now seemed almost tender.

"My father was a Navy admiral," Comrade Felipe said softly. "At the end of his career, he was put in charge of one of the Emergency Zones. His men slaughtered thousands of *campesinos*. If they'd caught me, they'd have killed me, too." A sad half-smile curved Comrade Felipe's lips. "My father was never bad to me. He loved me, and I loved him." The Senderista nodded, his eyes on Alonso's. "And he loved Peru. He believed in Peru!" Comrade Felipe rested a hand on the tabletop. "When he retired, the Party executed him."

Alonso gasped. "Your father!"

"It was necessary. That doesn't mean I don't mourn him. Can't you see the difference?" Alonso didn't reply, and Comrade Felipe leaned against the table, wincing. "Many people can't. My mother has never come here to visit me."

A photograph hung on the wall above Comrade Felipe's head. Dozens of children in spotless white shirts and red bandanas, running toward the photographer. They looked Chinese. Little round faces, with open mouths and the untainted glee of the very young.

Alonso looked from the photo to Comrade Felipe. "Do you have brothers?"

"Only one. He lives in the United States, and no, he's never visited me either." Comrade Felipe chuckled, as if it were funny, the idea that his brother might visit him in jail. "You know, Alonso, we communists see revolutionary violence as the universal law for taking power. But Peruvians die every day, and not because of the People's War. They die for the simple reason that they're poor. After we triumph—and it's inevitable, we *will* triumph—there will be no rich or poor, no hunger, and instead of one Cesip there will be thousands." Squinting with effort, he straightened up to look at Alonso face-to-face. "I'm willing to pay any price to bring that about. The question is, are you?"

Alonso looked at him, the back of his neck prickling.

"When you're ready to say yes—and you will say yes, Alonso, because I can see the warrior in you—the Party will be honored to receive you." Comrade Felipe smiled, and then looked at his watch. "I'm afraid you have a funeral to go to." He extended his hand, and after a heartbeat of hesitation Alonso shook it. "Please give my most sincere condolences to Mariela's mother."

Alonso walked to the doorway. "Comrade Felipe?"

"Yes, Alonso."

"What's Chairman Gonzalo like?" Rodolfo would want to know. He wanted to give Rodolfo something. Something good, on this terrible day.

Comrade Felipe smiled. "He's a very nice man. Courteous. Gentle." He laughed. "The kind of man my mother would like."

·TEN·

"Smoke?"

Rosa held a hand to her ear. "What?" The band was blasting away and kids were swarming the pub's dance floor, singing and laughing and shouting along. "What did you say?"

In the smoky half-darkness, she saw Jano grin. A thin boy with crinkly brown hair. The smartest boy in her class. "I SAID"—Jano shook a cigarette from the pack and extended it over the table toward her—"SMOKE?"

Rosa shook her head. "No, thanks."

"WHAT?"

"I SAID—"

But Jano winked, teasing now. He kept the cigarette for himself and slipped the pack into his pocket. Then he snapped a match and lit up, his narrow face eerie in the glow. "HAVING FUN?"

Rosa nodded. "GREAT." She took a sip of beer.

Jano slid his chair closer to hers, jutting his jaw to blow a puff of smoke.

He practices that, Rosa thought. She imagined Jano in front of a mirror. Cigarette in hand, eyebrows shaping those ironic arcs.

Abruptly, he stubbed out his cigarette. "Come on."

"Where?"

He grabbed her wrist. "Time for you to dance."

"But I—"

Jano's back was already turned. He pulled her across the dance floor, using his elbows to nudge open a space near Gabriela and Fico.

Fico was red-faced, already drunk. He bumped against Gabriela's chest and Gabriela laughed. She winked at Rosa as she shoved him away.

Rosa started to move her shoulders, stepping sideways, trying to keep time to the music. Her feet kept sticking to the floor, to dried-up spills. She felt like she was dancing on flypaper.

Jano shuffled, his white high-tops barely moving.

He's too cool to dance, Rosa thought. She blew a lock of hair from her face and watched the high-tops step closer. Jano slipped his arms around her waist.

He was bony, his arms as thin as his face.

If he grew his hair longer, Rosa thought, *he'd look a lot like Rodolfo*. All bones and curls. Though his colors are all wrong. All light where Rodolfo's dark. And Alonso's even darker. Black hair, black eyes . . .

Alonso smiled at her, those black eyes filling with light.

No. Rosa blinked. I can't. Not here. Not now.

But Alonso was already there. He was laughing, talking, bouncing at her side. Rosa tried to look away, but there he was again, riding the *micro* in his paint-spattered jeans, his fingers entwined with hers. Wading into the crowd of boys to save that little Ayacuchano. Hugging Rodolfo.

Gunshots. Alonso. Arms flailing as Padre Manuel dragged him from the Cesip. Wrapped in octopus tentacles, screaming. And the dynamite blew and the Cesip spat dust and glass and bits of cement and Papá fell on her trying to cover her while Alonso went on screaming. . . .

Rosa took a deep breath. She stretched out an arm, groping. As if she might find him there. As if he might be reaching for her, somewhere in the darkness.

But it was Jano's back she touched, and his shirt, sticking to his skin. The pub was smoke, was red and green and white lights, murky above the stage. Beer and sweat and perfume and cigarettes. The smells made Rosa nauseous and she leaned, breathless, against Jano.

And Jano, misunderstanding, pressed her to his chest.

His long fingers traveled down her back. His hips began to swivel, and he rubbed himself against her.

"Jano . . ." Rosa pulled away.

Jano grinned, slipped backward, and went on dancing. Moving now, really dancing, not just watching. His eyes, gray like the winter sky, never left hers.

He liked her. Jano the classroom ironist, with eyes like chrome. Rosa looked away, and they danced, bumping and swaying and sweating, until the band finally took a break.

Canned music came on. Fico was kissing Gabriela. When Jano slid his arm over Rosa's shoulders and led her back to the table, Gabriela dragged Fico after them.

"ISN'T THIS GREAT?" she screamed in Rosa's ear.

Rosa nodded. *I shouldn't have come,* she thought.

The beer had been sitting on the table while they danced, a half-empty pitcher and four plastic cups. Rosa took a gulp. It was warm. She took a second gulp, then a third. She wanted to drink the whole thing. Then Jano could refill her cup and she'd drink that, too. She knew, from dribbling rum into Cokes with Gabriela at family parties, that if she kept drinking, the edges of her mind would blur and she'd be able to start laughing.

On the fifth gulp, her stomach twisted shut and the beer stuck in her throat. *Now what?* Rosa imagined spitting beer onto the scratched wooden table. Her eyes began to water and she swallowed hard. Her hand was trembling when she put the cup down.

At least she hadn't spat up on Gabriela's cute little black dress. Or on Jano's gleaming white high-tops. A hysterical giggle rose in her throat, and she swallowed that, too.

It was important to act normal.

Jano reached across the table and tapped her shoulder. Rosa, wondering, stood and let him take her hand. They squeezed between chairs and tables and clusters of giggling girls, and finally they were at the back door and outside.

Another damp night, the mist twinkling like tiny stars beneath the streetlights. Parked cars sat nose to tail in the narrow lane behind the pub. Jano climbed onto the hood of a big gray Ford and lit another cigarette. "You looked like you needed some air." He patted the hood.

He was nicer than she'd thought. He noticed stuff she wouldn't have expected. Rosa slid up beside him.

"This is great." Jano propped a foot against the bumper and blew smoke, sending it swirling above him. His hands reached skyward. "THIS IS GREAT!"

A few cars down, three boys turned and laughed. "No kidding, man," one of them shouted. He held up a cup of beer in salute.

"You don't have to yell out here," Rosa said. "I can hear you."

Jano's arm came down around her shoulder. "You know how long I wanted to ask you out?"

Rosa slid her hands beneath her thighs. She'd kiss Jano tonight. Alonso would never know. Never care.

Jano tapped her leg. "Guess how long."

She tried to make her voice bright. "Three weeks?"

"Three *years*. You never noticed, did you? I always figured there was somebody else." Jano took a long and satisfied drag on his cigarette.

Rosa's eyes stung. Ay, *Dios*, she thought. *I hate myself.*

"Rosa?"

She was leaking again. Leaking all over herself.

"Hey, why the tears?" Jano pulled her closer. "What's wrong?"

"Ah." She took a deep sniff. "Nothing."

He laid a finger alongside her chin and turned her face toward his. "Hey."

Magda's dead, Rosa thought. *Magda's dead and Alonso's gone and you're nicer than I thought.*

"You can tell me, you know."

Yeah, sure. Rosa wiped her eyes. "Sorry."

"It might help to talk about it."

Rosa shook her head with a broken laugh. "That's what we pay the shrink for."

"You're seeing a shrink?"

"Yeah."

"Because of what happened?"

"Uh-huh."

"It must have been rough."

Rosa nodded.

"Shit." Jano flicked away his cigarette and wrapped both arms around her. "It's okay. I understand."

Rosa felt like a cardboard dummy, something left standing outside a store. There would be fold marks where she bent, leaning awkwardly against Jano.

"So." He took hold of her shoulders and pressed her away so he could look in her eyes. "You want to go out with me?"

Rosa slid her gaze sideways. "Maybe."

Jano smiled. "It's not a trick question, you know." He cupped her chin in his palm and kissed her.

Rosa felt lips. She felt an open mouth and teeth and a strange, wet tongue. Jano pressed into her and she gasped. "Jano . . ."

Breathless, she slid from the car. "I can't. . . ." She stumbled, and the sidewalk moved beneath her. "I just can't. . . ."

Jano followed, his voice high and boyish. "Rosa, what is it?"

"Nothing. . . ." The sidewalk wouldn't stop moving.

Jano grabbed her arm and jerked her to a halt. "There is somebody else, isn't there?"

"No." She was going to throw up; she had to get away or she was going to throw up right here on somebody's car. . . .

"Then what is it? What's wrong?"

"There's nobody else." Her voice rose, and the three boys down the lane fell silent. "There's nobody!"

Rosa, it's all right. You can still—

"Shut up," she shrilled, putting her hands over her ears. "Just shut up, oh please shut up."

The whisper was becoming relentless. Soft, but relentless. It would never stop, never go away. *Rosa, you can still do something. You can help.*

"Stop it!" Rosa screamed. She stumbled backward, against a car, and felt herself sliding downward, hands over her ears, though that was stupid, she'd need to stick her hands inside her brain and squeeze it like a wet sponge before the voice would ever stop, ever let her go. . . .

Rosa, you can't forget. You don't want to forget.

"I do, I do!"

"*Carajo*, Rosa, what's the matter with you?"

"Hey, man, chill out!" The three boys were trotting toward them, running. "Leave her alone!"

Jano whipped around to face them. "Fuck off!" One of the boys shoved him, and Jano shoved back and Rosa collapsed, sobbing, against a gritty black tire. It was all her fault, it was always her fault, she should go to confession and tell the priest that it was all her fault, everything. . . .

"STOP IT!" Gabriela came screaming from the back of the pub. "What is WRONG with you guys?"

Fico followed, swaying. "Come on, guys, just back off."

Gabriela fell to her knees, her arms around Rosa. "What did you *do* to her, Jano?"

"I didn't do anything, I swear! She just started—"

"Well, what do you expect? You start a fight and you think that won't make her—*ay, prima,* don't cry." Gabriela stroked Rosa's hair. "Don't cry. Shhh."

The press of Gabriela's fingers was real. Gabriela's lycra dress was real, the cool skin of her arms. All of it real, real, not just in her head. Rosa took a sodden breath. Gabriela was real.

"It's okay, *amor.*" Gabriela lifted her chin. "I can't believe you, Jano."

Jano sounded defeated. "I didn't do anything. She just started losing it. And then these guys—"

"Hey, man, don't blame us!"

"It wasn't them." Rosa mumbled into Gabriela's chest. "I'm sorry."

"Don't you be sorry," Gabriela snapped. "You ought to know better, Jano."

"No," Rosa insisted. Fico handed her a handkerchief and she dabbed her eyes with it and then thought, *Ay, mierda,* and blew.

Clearing her nose seemed to clear her mind. She stood up, leaning against Gabriela, and Gabriela stood, too, on shimmery brown legs with a tear at the knee.

"You got a run," Rosa murmured. "I'm sorry."

Gabriela looked down at her knee. *"Mierda."*

"Sorry." Rosa looked at Jano. Thin and slumped and fearful,

standing beside a black car with his hands in his pockets. "Sometimes it just comes over me."

Jano nodded.

"Fico, get a cab." Gabriela kept an arm around Rosa. "I'm taking her home."

"No, Gabriela. . . ." Rosa shook her head. "I'm sorry. It's okay."

"Fico, go."

Fico slapped Jano on the shoulder and they walked down the lane toward the corner. The three boys wandered off. *Una loca,* one of them muttered.

"He's right," Rosa said. She felt drained, exhausted. "I am crazy."

"No, you're not. You're just sad." Gabriela looked down at her stockings and cursed again. "These were brand-new."

"I'm sorry."

"Rosa, would you *please* stop saying you're sorry? It's just a run, okay?"

Rosa shivered. "I'm sorry about Jano, too."

"*Ya,* well, he'll survive."

"He'll never ask me out again."

Gabriela laughed. "Yes, he will. You'd be amazed."

With a sigh, Rosa leaned against the car. "I ruined your evening."

"If you say sorry again I'll smack you."

A weak chuckle rose from Rosa's stomach. She was hopeless, a disaster, but Gabriela would never admit it. "Don't tell my father, okay?" She dabbed at her eyes, hoping the mascara hadn't turned her into a goblin. "He fusses too much."

Papá wanted things to be normal. That's what he'd said to Mamá last night, his voice tired and snappish. *Let's just try to be normal, okay?* And Mamá's gentle reply, always trying to smooth things, to make things right once more. *Sí, amor, sí.*

"We're trying to be normal at home," she told Gabriela. The thought struck her as outrageously funny, and she started to laugh.

To her relief, Gabriela laughed with her. "Normal, huh?" Inside the pub, the band started up again, thundering out their biggest hit. "Listen." Gabriela cocked her head. "They're singing 'The Towers.'"

One terrorist, two terrorists, were balancing on a bombed-out tower . . .

Gabriela laughed again. "Normal. Right."

▫ELEVEN▫

The suds were disappearing, tiny bubbles popping one by one. The bar of laundry soap had thinned to a disk. Alonso plunged Livia's blouse into the water. Holding it under, he scrubbed, then pulled it out and scrubbed some more.

In. Rub a bit. Out. Rub a bit. *Carajo*, he hated doing laundry. Nothing to look at but dust and walls and the frayed stripes of the laundry line. Nothing to think about but stuff he wanted to forget.

In. Mariela.

Out. Mamá.

In. *Mariela* . . . Rodolfo had cried at the funeral, surrounded by a dozen somber young men and women. He hadn't seemed to care if his comrades saw the tears running down. The young men had kept their arms around him. The young women had circled Rodolfo's mother, bearing her up. Rodolfo's little brothers had flitted between people's legs, scared and lost. Rodolfo's father wasn't there, though. Didn't even bother to show up.

Ay, Mariela.

Now for the sheets. They billowed upward on the water, ballooning as he punched them down.

Every Saturday for the past month, he'd gone to the prison with Rodolfo. Not sure why, but going anyway, like a drunk going back to a bar. After morning assembly, with the hymns and the chants, the visitors would gather in a cell filled with wooden benches. They'd sit facing a cracked green chalkboard while one of the prisoners talked about the Party and the People's War. The Senderistas called it an *Escuela Popular*. A People's School, right there in the prison.

Alonso grabbed the laundry brush. One of the sheets had a stain where Gustavo had spat up. He scrubbed, and the stain faded to a reddish brown.

Last week, he'd sat again with Comrade Felipe at the little wooden table. They'd sipped coffee while the comrades chanted in the mist outside the window. Comrade Felipe had reminisced about going to the highlands as a young man. About joining Chairman Gonzalo and turning the rocky mountain-scape around Ayacucho into a liberated zone.

How that man could talk. He painted pictures, every word a brushstroke.

We all worked together, Alonso. All the campesinos and all the cadres, together. No one goes hungry in a Liberated Zone. We were up before dawn to plow, and all the campesinos came to help. Practically barefoot, most of them, and, carajo, it's cold up there. They brought thirty teams of oxen. Have you ever seen an ox? Enormous brutes with tongues as big as towels. They're like bulldozers with hooves. . . . We put red flags around the field and started plowing. When the sun came up, it was like an orchard in springtime, the wind flapping all those red flags. . . .

Alonso scrubbed and scrubbed. His knuckles stung in the cold water. He saw that rocky field. Oxen like bulldozers and an orchard of red flags.

They can't stop us, Alonso. We'll pay our quota of blood, and the People's War will triumph. It's a law of history.

Alonso hauled the sheets from the basin, wringing as he pulled. Streams of water gushed down.

Now Rodolfo wanted him to come out at night. That's how you got started in the Party. A couple of cans of paint, a few scribbles on a wall, and you were a Senderista. Livia could lock the door behind him. Their old man would never know. He never stumbled in before two or three in the morning anymore.

What did his mother used to say? *Do something.* Don't just sit around feeling sad.

Diana sat chattering in the doorway, a bald and ancient Barbie doll in her hand. She rolled one of Gustavo's toy cars and sent the Barbie hopping after it. "Buy from me, *señor*," the Barbie wheedled. "Don't be mean. Buy from me." Like an *ambulante*.

What kind of future do you want for your sisters, Alonso?

Shit, his sisters! He'd forgotten Livia!

He dropped the sheets into the basin, sending water surging over the sides. "Come on," he cried, wiping his hands on his jeans. Gustavo was napping inside on the double bed. He started to whine as Alonso snatched him and ran out the door. Shushing him impatiently, Alonso looked up and down the street.

Shacks. The market. An old man pedaling a tricycle cart. No kids in gray uniforms. Alonso cursed. School must have let out half an hour ago. Where the hell was Livia? A colic of fear bit his gut, and he told himself not to be an idiot. The *Pishtaco* wouldn't wander around in broad daylight.

Only they said it had been morning, the last time he grabbed a girl.

Alonso began to run. Gustavo bounced in his arms, whimpering sleepily. Diana trotted behind, still prattling with her Barbie.

Ahead of them, the outer walls of the María Auxiliadora School jutted into the road. Beside the schoolyard gate, Alonso could see two people leaning against the wall. One taller than the other. "LIVIA!"

The smaller figure stepped away from the wall and watched him approach.

"Livia, get over here! Get away from . . ." Pressing his hand against the stitch in his side, Alonso slowed to a stop. Livia's lips were smeared with chocolate. The person standing next to her was a young woman, not a yellow-eyed *Pishtaco*. Alonso panted and stared. She had short hair and a gap between her two front teeth. She was smiling, but Alonso recognized her. She was the somber, hawk-faced young woman who'd stayed with the kids the day of Mariela's wake.

"Alonso, Victoria found me here." Livia spoke stickily, her mouth full of chocolate. "She's—"

"Hello, Alonso." Victoria held out her hand. Alonso shifted Gustavo to his left arm and shook it, carefully. A tiny hand, on the most delicate wrist he'd ever seen. He could easily have encircled it between his thumb and his forefinger.

"I was coming to see you, Alonso," Victoria said. "And I saw Livia crying."

"I told her about the *Pishtaco*," Livia said. "But she wasn't scared."

Diana butted up to Livia. "Can I have some chocolate?"

Gustavo started to squirm. "Me too, me too."

Livia looked at the tiny square of chocolate in her hand. She tried to snap it in two, but squashed it instead.

Victoria laughed. "Finish your chocolate, Livia."

Diana yelped in outrage. "But I want—"

"AH!" Glaring, Victoria held up one finger. Diana's mouth snapped shut.

Balancing her backpack on her hip, Victoria unzipped the front pocket. With a dramatic flourish, she pulled out two more chocolates.

Diana jumped up and down, grabbing for the chocolate. Still jumping, she peeled off the waxy white wrapper and shoved the whole square into her mouth. Victoria unwrapped Gustavo's chocolate and handed it to him.

"What do you say, Diana?" Livia spoke primly, her tongue darting out to lick her lips.

Diana mumbled through melting chocolate. "*Gracias.*"

With a sigh, Alonso shifted Gustavo back onto his right hip. "Come on, then," he muttered.

Livia slipped her hand into Victoria's as they walked to the shack.

"I have to finish the laundry," Alonso said. He walked out the back door, leaving Victoria besieged by the kids. Diana wanted to show her Barbie's car, Livia the tattered baby doll, Gustavo his favorite yellow truck. Alonso could hear them. The kids babbling, Victoria laughing. Her laugh was surprisingly low-pitched for such a tiny person.

He stuck his hands into the basin and started pulling out the sheets.

The back door swung open. "Let me help," Victoria said. She slid off her backpack and placed it carefully beside the door.

"I can handle it." Alonso's face burned as he stared at the tangle of sheets. Bad enough that she found him doing laundry. Now she'd see him turning purple.

Slender hands slid into the water. They hauled out a length of sheet and began twisting. A string of muscle popped up across her forearm.

Alonso sighed and twisted.

They wrung out the sheets, water dripping everywhere, and hung them over the line like narrow white tents. Victoria shook her head. "They'll never dry by night," she said.

Women knew that sort of thing. Though it probably didn't take a genius. It was just that Alonso never seemed to do things in the right order. To wash the clothes after breakfast. After dressing the kids. *After* getting Livia to school but *before* cleaning up from breakfast. And definitely before heading back to the *comedor* to pick up lunch. He still couldn't get it right.

Alonso dumped the water in a corner of the yard, then tossed the basin onto the counter. It spun for an instant and stopped.

"Alonso." She stood beside him, that little hand on his forearm. "I need to ask you a favor." Her grip tightened. "I need you to hold on to something for Rodolfo."

Gently, he pulled his arm free and looked at the wall surrounding the yard.

"You don't have to do anything with it," she went on. "Don't tell Rodolfo you have it. Don't tell him anything, even that I was here."

Alonso kept his eyes on the wall. Made of adobe bricks, the wall was just dried mud, cracked and filthy and poor.

"In a couple of weeks, he'll ask you. *Do you have a package for me?* And then you give it to him." Her voice lightened. "That's all."

Alonso's gaze traveled up the wall. It was topped with poor man's razor wire, jagged pieces of broken glass stuck in the mud. The walls shut out the sky, all but a tiny jailbird's rectangle of gray.

Victoria stepped away from him and he heard her unzip the backpack. Maybe it was a gun.

She held it before him. A rectangular package, wrapped in brown paper and taped up like a gift. Alonso took it from her. He could feel, from the shape and the heft of it, that it held paper. Lots of sheets of paper.

He looked up and saw that little gap between her front teeth. She was smiling again. Hawkish, but smiling.

She stayed with them for a couple of hours, playing with the kids while he chopped vegetables for the night's soup. She kissed his cheek when she left. Murmured, too low for the kids to hear, "*Gracias*, comrade."

Alonso put the package at the bottom of his box, the wooden one with all his treasures.

□ □ □

After that, saying no to graffiti didn't seem to make much sense. He and Rodolfo met up on Saturday nights in Lima's crummiest shantytowns, the ones with no electricity and no lights. Misty, unlit darkness became their best friend. Alonso never knew beforehand where they were going. He just went where Rodolfo told him to go. Finally, one Wednesday night, Rodolfo asked him. *Do you have a package for me?* Neither of them mentioned Victoria. Inside the brown paper they found five hundred fliers announcing the upcoming *paro armado*, the strike that would bring the revolution to Lima for a day. They wallpapered San Juan with the fliers, racing each other around corners with a bucket of homemade flour-and-water paste. They were almost finished when they bumped into a pair of drunks. The drunks lunged at them, but the boys sprinted off, laughing and invincible.

That was how Alonso felt. Like nothing could stop him now. Striding down a dark street for the fourth Saturday in a row, he scanned the shadows like a cyborg. Left to right, right to left. He could almost hear the beeping in his head.

Only this was real. A kid with paint in his backpack, walking down a dark street at eleven o'clock at night. His old man's belt was happy hour compared to what the cops would do if they caught him.

Rodolfo stood at the next corner, a slender shadow leaning against a bodega. Alonso's muscles sprang to life as he broke into a jog. Every cell awake, as if he were back on the soccer field, bouncing between the goalposts. *Just try me*, he thought. History was on their side. A thousand Cesips, nobody hungry, and orchards of red flags blossoming in the sunlight.

Rodolfo drew him into the shadows as a car emerged from a side street. The car had a little red light on the dashboard and a rubber TAXI sign, the kind cab drivers spit on to make them stick to the windshield. The taxi stopped beside them, sputtering.

"Get in back and don't look at the driver," Rodolfo said in a low voice.

Alonso opened the door and climbed in, shoving his backpack under the seat in front of him. Without a word, the driver pulled out, bumping through the ruts until they reached the avenue. He shifted gears and hit the gas. *Micros* rumbled by. Cars darted like minnows from one lane to the other. The driver followed the expressway around Lima and turned onto the Panamerican Highway.

This was familiar territory. Alonso felt a shock of recognition when the taxi pulled onto a sandy shoulder. "One hour," the driver muttered. The boys tumbled from the car.

"This is Salvador!" Alonso exclaimed. Spinning up grit, the taxi lunged in front of a passing truck.

"*Ya*. Let's go. We don't have much time." Rodolfo began to trot away.

Alonso didn't move and Rodolfo paused a few meters off. "C'mon," he said impatiently.

"Tell me where we're going."

"You know I can't—"

"I don't care. Tell me now."

Rodolfo grinned. "To church, *hermano*."

"You want me to spray paint Padre Manuel's church?"

The grin slipped from Rodolfo's face. "It's not his church," he snapped. "He's gone. What difference does it make?"

"No," Alonso muttered. He shook his head. "Unh-unh."

"Why not?"

"He was my friend!"

"Some friend," Rodolfo snapped. "He got your mother killed and then he took off. He used her, Alonso, and what did he ever give you? Or your family? *Religion is the opium of the masses,* remember?"

That's what the Senderistas said. People who believed in God were like *drogadictos,* running away from reality. Praying was not all that different from rolling cocaine paste into a cigarette and lighting up.

Rodolfo stuck his hands in his pockets. "Come on, Alonso." There was an edge to his voice, to the way he tilted his head.

Feed those dying of hunger, because if you haven't fed them, you've killed them. That's what Padre Manuel always said.

People die for the simple reason that they're poor. Comrade Felipe.

Do something. Alonso could hear her, the way she always said it. Hopeful, but a little exasperated.

"Let's go," he said, and started to jog up the hill.

"This way," Rodolfo said. "The Special Forces might be at the Cesip."

They ran along the highway and up a narrow lane. Sneakers thudding, past houses and bodegas and shacks. Up, up, up. They passed the shack where Rodolfo had lived, and a narrow alley that led to Señorita Ana's old house.

Finally they stood in front of the whitewashed churchyard wall. Rodolfo looked down the road at the Cesip. "Looks like it's all clear," he said softly.

Alonso was peering through the wrought-iron gate. Padre Manuel's churchyard lay buried under a layer of sand and dust. Five months of it, blown down from the hills. What had he said? *I'll be back in two months.*

Alonso kicked savagely at the gate.

"Hey!" Rodolfo grabbed his shoulder and pulled him away. "Quiet!"

"Quiet yourself!" His head humming with anger, Alonso unzipped his backpack and tossed Rodolfo a can of spray paint. Then he pulled one out for himself, shook it till it rattled, and popped off the lid. Grimly, he fired an arc of red paint onto Padre Manuel's wall.

Long live the People's War!

"What are you doing?" Rodolfo asked.

"Sending a message," Alonso snapped.

Rodolfo shook his head. "Well, write this instead: 'Long live the Armed Strike!' Only write it big."

Alonso started writing, his anger shooting out with the paint. It felt good. He was leaving a mark. "Next Wednesday," he murmured. "It's almost here."

"Ya, 'mano, we're gonna shut Lima down. I wish I could be here to see it."

"What do you mean?"

"I'll tell you later." Rodolfo started spraying, the paint hissing gently. "Get back to work."

Alonso flinched at Rodolfo's tone, but he let it pass and shook the can again. He was spraying huge letters now, stretching as high as his arm could reach. Big, big, big. He wanted the

Special Forces to see it from the bottom of the hill. He wanted everyone to see it.

Someday they'd understand. He was on the right side of history now.

Rodolfo was still spraying when Alonso finished and stepped back to view his work. *¡Viva el paro armado!* he read. At the bottom of each letter, wet paint dribbled down like a streak of blood.

A rumble sounded at his back and he whipped around. Far below, a truck was climbing the hill, headlights bouncing yellow beams off the Cesip's walls. Alonso froze. "Rodolfo!" he hissed. "Special Forces!" Dropping the can with a clatter, he broke into a run.

The truck began to roar up the hill. They'd been spotted.

Alonso sped along the wall toward the narrow lane they'd come up. Rodolfo ran in the opposite direction, slipping behind a row of houses. The truck screamed to a halt, and as Alonso raced down the lane, he heard shouts and thudding feet.

Halfway down the block, he slipped into a narrow passageway. It was a tight squeeze. Bricks scraped him as he struggled through, gritting his teeth. At the end of the passage stood another wall, and beyond it Señorita Ana's old house.

Footsteps and shouts. Louder now. Behind him, a beam of light bobbed down the lane, brighter and brighter. The soldiers were nearing the passageway.

Oh God, please . . . Alonso grasped for a handhold and pulled himself up. His fingers and toes found the familiar notches. A brick stuck out here. Mortar didn't fill that gap. A crummy wall, easy to climb. In an instant he was up it, blessing the lazy mason who'd built it.

Shards of broken glass stuck from the top of the wall, but there was a bare patch, just space enough for one hand, one knee. . . . Cautiously, he pulled himself up and jumped, landing with a thump on the hard dirt of the backyard.

Panting, he ducked beneath the laundry line and crawled to the darkest corner of the yard. Huddled behind the water barrels, he listened.

"Over here!"

"No, down here!"

"Where the fuck did he go? Look over there, you idiot!"

The shouts receded down the hill. They hadn't noticed the passageway. The hammering in Alonso's chest slowed down.

One, he thought. He was alive. *Two*. He wouldn't move. *Three*. He'd stay here, counting until he reached two thousand. *Four* . . . He'd miss the pickup, but the soldiers wouldn't catch him. *Five* . . . They wouldn't do to him what they'd done to Mariela. . . . Alonso swallowed and listened again. In the silence, a light patter of feet, up by the church. A single pair of sneakers, not a pounding crowd of Army boots. A boy, running.

Past the church now, toward the lane. More slowly now, cautiously. Heading straight for the soldiers.

Alonso raced to the wall, scraping his fingers as he clambered up. At the top, he crouched, scanning the lane. He saw Rodolfo at the top of the hill. Straightening, he peered around Señora Castro's house, and his heart seized. Right there, just around the corner. Fanning out, rifles ready. Soldiers as silent as sharks. In a moment Rodolfo would cross the corner, and they'd devour him.

Without thinking, Alonso ran along the edge of the wall toward the soldiers, barely avoiding the sharp points of glass. A shard pierced his sneaker, slicing the side of his foot. He hissed in pain, teetering sideways before regaining his balance. He had to reach the edge of the wall, draw off the soldiers, before Rodolfo hit the corner.

When he was close enough for the soldiers to see him, Alonso cursed above their heads.

Ten bodies froze. Ten faces looked up. And for one terrifying instant, one of them stared into Alonso's eyes.

A face like a tank, big and pitiless.

Alonso turned and ran.

He was back at the passageway, slithering down the wall. Squeezing through. He emerged into the lane just as three soldiers rounded the corner.

A shout went up and Alonso raced back up the hill toward the church. His feet flying, he flanked around the church to the back, where the dunes rose against a clouded night sky. Just two dunes away was Villa María, another shantytown. It was bigger than Salvador. He'd lose the soldiers there.

He broke from the church's shelter and started up the dune. Ahead of him, a dark figure charged up the sand. Slender, and moving too fast to be one of those soldiers in their black boots. Alonso tore after it, watching as it crested the hill and disappeared.

Footsteps pounded behind him as he reached the top of the dune. With a mighty shove of his feet, he leaped over the crest.

He allowed his body to fall on the rocky slope, hardly feeling the blow, and rolled part of the way down the other side. Then he righted himself and went on running. Rodolfo was still ahead of him, halfway up the next dune.

Alonso pelted after him, slipping and sliding, running harder than he had ever run.

Shouts behind him. *Take him down!*

A rifle cracked, searing through the darkness. *Zing!* A rock near his foot burst into fragments.

Terrified, his mind frozen into a slow-motion nightmare, Alonso reached the top of the second dune. Once more he shoved off into space, leaping and rolling and clambering back to his feet.

Please God please God please God . . .

He could see Villa María now, the shantytown's ragged edge beckoning. Shacks, scattered up the side of the dune. Alonso nearly wept with relief as he slid into their embrace. His lungs were screaming.

Rodolfo broke from the shadows. "Keep running," he panted.

More shouts from the dune, growing muffled as the soldiers neared the shacks and began to fan out.

The boys ran, gasping for air. Their feet slapped clumsily against the dirt. On and on, until they reached Villa María's one paved road.

Alonso slowed when his cut foot hit the pavement, but Rodolfo hissed at him to speed up. He sucked in a sobbing gasp and made one last, desperate effort to run flat out. A stitch sliced into his side.

Several blocks ahead stood a dance hall where bands played

música chicha all night long. Alonso dashed around the corner of the building and collapsed against the wall. The cement seemed to pulsate with the rhythm of the keyboards inside.

"Come on," Rodolfo wheezed. He grabbed Alonso's arm and dragged him to a row of narrow wooden outhouses. As they stepped into the last one, the stench of the pit rolled over them. Rodolfo latched the door. Someone was pissing a few doors up.

"Why"—Alonso gasped, nearly gagging—"do we have to hide in here?"

With a choked gurgle, Rodolfo bent double, laughing.

There was nowhere to sit. Just a hole in the ground with two cement footprints on either side of it. Weak with relief, Alonso slid to the ground and started to laugh.

"Shit, *hermano*! That's disgusting! Get up!" Rodolfo broke off, breathless with laughter, and Alonso stumbled to his feet.

They laughed, then swore, then laughed some more. Finally they were able to breathe.

"We'll never make it to the pickup in time," Alonso said.

"For a minute there, I didn't think I'd make it, period." Rodolfo turned sober. "Was that you cursing on that wall?"

"I didn't know how else to warn you," Alonso said.

"Shoot. I was about to jump into their arms when they heard you and started yelling." Rodolfo put his ear to the outhouse door. "Shhh. Listen."

Their neighbor in the other latrine had returned to the dance hall. Guitars, bass, keyboards . . . the singer was belting as loud as he could. *I'm lookin' for a new life in this city where everything's money and nothin' is pretty. . . .*

"You think it's safe?"

"We better wait, just in case. I want to talk to you, anyway." Rodolfo's voice dropped. "Alonso, I'm catching a bus to Huaraz in the morning."

"What?" Rodolfo's words hit like a sucker punch to the jaw. "You're leaving?"

"I'm joining the EGP. I'm gonna be a *guerrilla*, Alonso." Even whispering, there was no mistaking that brassy edge of pride.

"But . . . what about your mother? Your brothers?"

"They'll be okay. The Party takes care of its own." Rodolfo paused. "Come with me, Alonso. The Party wants you."

"Wants me?"

Rodolfo nodded, grinning, his teeth gleaming in the shadowy booth.

For an instant, Alonso's heart fluttered wildly, like a wounded bird trying to fly. To be a *guerrilla*! To go to the mountains and fight! To be free!

He stepped toward Rodolfo—

And Livia's face popped in front of him. Terrified and half starved, like she always looked these days. That *susto*, that cannibal fear, staring out of her eyes. And now Diana, fat and stupid. Gustavo, coughing, clueless about everything. Even his old man was there in that stinking outhouse. Drunk. Drunk and raging. Drunk and snoring. Drunk, drunk, drunk. Alonso slumped against the wall.

"I can't," he groaned. "I can't."

"Why not?" Rodolfo sounded incredulous. "Do you realize what I'm telling you? It's not just me asking, Alonso. Understand? The Party is asking!"

And you will say yes, Alonso, because I can see the warrior in you.

Alonso closed his eyes. "I can't—I can't . . ." He gritted his teeth. "Rodolfo, I can't just leave, with my father the way he is."

"The Party will look after your family."

"My father hates the Party as much as he hates me."

Rodolfo's whisper came back, a fierce hiss in the darkness. "Do you know what the Party does to drunks like your father?"

"I don't want them to touch my father!"

"Are you crazy? You're scared to leave because of what he might do, and then you tell me you don't want anyone to stop him? That's the stupidest thing I ever heard!" Rodolfo spoke in an icy whisper. "This is it, Alonso. Your chance to do something with your life. Don't you want to fight?"

Oh, yes. More than anything in the world. He had never held a rifle, much less fired one, but he knew just how it would feel. Cold, smooth metal. The soft squeeze of the trigger. The explosive blast. And relief, oh, the relief it would bring to the anger that never quite stopped hissing and humming and boiling over inside him. The thought of it filled him with a longing so exquisite, so overwhelming . . .

"I can't," he said dully.

"*¡Carajo!* Do you know how long I've been running around at night like this? I can't *believe* you'd blow this off!" Rodolfo slammed his hand against the wall, then all at once his voice turned pleading. "Imagine it, Alonso. The two of us." He put a hand on Alonso's shoulder and shook him gently. "The insurrection is coming, 'mano. If you don't join now you'll be too late. You'll be stuck washing laundry when we take Lima."

Alonso choked. The vile air of the latrine was filling his

lungs like sewage. He wrenched free of Rodolfo, opened the latch, and stepped outside.

"I've got to go home," he said, gulping the chill night air.

Rodolfo said no more.

A man and a woman stood wrapped together beside the dance hall, their hands and mouths all over each other. They ignored the boys. There were no soldiers in sight.

Down at the highway, Alonso and Rodolfo waited in silence until a late-night *micro* stopped. Rodolfo handed over the fare for the two of them. They rode the long journey around Lima, switching buses twice, without ever saying a word. As the bus stopped near Canto Grande, Rodolfo stood up. "Ten A.M., *hermano*. At the bus station downtown." Without even a gesture of farewell, he walked down the aisle and got off the bus.

Alonso watched him go, and then he rode three more stops down the avenue. Hopping off the bus, striding up the hill into San Juan, he let his mind watch Rodolfo as he packed, caught a few hours of sleep, kissed his mother good-bye. . . . Reaching the shack, he banged furiously on the door. "It's me, Livia," he barked. "Open up."

The door swung open to a flash of lamplight. Alonso blinked. Before he could dodge, his father grabbed him by the scruff of the neck and dragged him inside. "What the hell are these, Alonso?"

Stunned, Alonso saw a sheaf of papers. Leftover fliers, announcing the armed strike. He blinked, confused, and then understood.

Carajo, he thought. *He went into my box.*

His old man's grip tightened, and the room started jerking back and forth.

"Answer me! What the hell are these?"

That son of a bitch went into my box.

No one was supposed to go in Alonso's box. It was a rule. It was the law. It was all Alonso had.

Something inside him, a string stretched so tight for so long that Alonso had almost ceased to feel it, finally snapped. "You drunken son of a bitch!"

He shook off his father's arm. Threw a wild punch, and felt a shock of joy and pain when his fist crashed into his father's jaw. His father stumbled backward and Alonso punched again. This time his father caught the blow easily in his hand. For a moment he held Alonso's fist, staring at it. Then he swung.

The blow went off like an explosion behind Alonso's eyes. Like being hit by a car on a dark highway. A blinding flash of pain.

A one-two punch slammed into his ribs and diaphragm, knocking the breath out of him. Alonso fell over, gasping, and tried to roll away. He pulled a chair over himself, and his father's foot slammed into it.

Alonso tossed aside the chair and rose, swearing with every insult he could dig from his bowels.

His father came roaring after him. "They killed your mother, you little prick! They killed your mother!"

All three kids woke up and started screaming, but it was Livia who saved him. She threw herself between them so impetuously that her father couldn't check the punch he was throwing. His fist caught her on the temple, and with a cry of pain she flew backward to the ground.

"No, Papi," she screamed. Sobbing, she scrambled to her feet and threw her arms around her father. "Don't hit him, please don't hit him!"

"*Oh, my God . . .*" Her father slumped to his knees.

"Please don't hit Alonso!" Livia clung to him, begging. "*Please*, Papi!"

"Livia, *hijita*, are you hurt?" With a wounded gasp, Alonso's father tried to lift her face, to see the damage he'd done. But Livia burrowed against his chest, black hair mingling with his as he rocked her, weeping.

Watching them, panting against the pain in his ribs, Alonso suddenly knew. Livia was okay. She'd always be okay. It was him his father hated, not the kids. It was him—he was the problem.

They'd all be better off without him.

Alonso lurched to the doorway and stepped out. His head felt as if it had split open. His side throbbed. But the mist was a damp caress on his face, and it was only a couple of kilometers to Rodolfo's house.

·TWELVE·

The bus hugged a curve in the highway, then plunged through a curtain of fog into blinding sunshine. Rodolfo slept. Alonso gazed out the window.

To their left, at the bottom of a long, steep dune, lay a beach, barren save for a tiny fishing boat dragged up on the shore. A net lay in a tangled heap beside it. Beyond the beach, the Pacific moved and glittered, arching into long, curved whitecaps and sprinting toward the shore. Alonso pressed his forehead against the glass. It felt cold, and his breath steamed it.

The bus turned inland, following the twist of the highway through dunes so high and smooth they looked like sifted mountains of golden flour. He'd heard about buses flying off these dunes when drivers took the curves too fast. But the dunes looked soft. As if the bus could tumble down and they'd crawl out unhurt at the bottom. Laugh, all of them, and race into the surf.

Alonso put his head back and shut his eyes. The engine hummed, as his mother might have hummed, rocking him on her lap long ago.

He's a kid, maybe eight years old. His parents are going to raise a batch of cuyes, guinea pigs. Alonso likes cuy. Sweet, greasy meat, roasted on a spit. His father brings home a wriggling sack and pours three dozen squealing baby cuyes into a little pen behind the house.

Alonso notices one. A little brown cuy, shaped like a cigar. With long hair and an oddly knowing look in its black beady eyes. It squirms softly in his fingers.

He names it Lucio, brings it fava beans from the kitchen. The cuy whistles when Alonso steps out the back door. Scampers to the edge of the pen to eat from his hand. Sometimes he carries it inside his shirt, soft fur tickling and tiny nails scratching his skin.

Rodolfo teases him. "That cuy's gonna end up roasted," he warns. "That cute little face, lookin' up from your plate. And you thinkin', Don't I know you from somewhere?"

The day comes. The cuyes have grown big and fat. Alonso's parents know how to slaughter cuyes, how to skin and dress them. They talk excitedly, making plans. The money from the cuyes will help pay for a roof, a real roof on the house.

Alonso hides Lucio in his room.

His father is baffled. "How'd it get out? Have you seen it, Alonso?"

"No, Papá. Maybe a hawk . . ."

But his mother hears Lucio that very night, rustling under the blanket. When his father comes home the next morning, she tells him.

Her betrayal hurts more than the spanking. It's just an open hand over his school trousers.

When Alonso gets home from school, Lucio is gone and his father is shoveling straw in the backyard. Alonso feels the tears about to explode and runs to his bedroom.

"Alonso! Get out here and help me clean this pen."

His mother's voice, soft, "Just let him be, cholito. . . ."

Alonso presses his face into the pillow. His father won't hear him. Won't know he's a crybaby.

The shovel scrapes against the hard ground. When Alonso finally emerges, dirty straw is piled in the corner of the yard. His father sits on the back step, turning a box of matches over in his hand. He glances sideways at Alonso and hands him the box.

Alonso strikes a match, carefully. He's never done this before. He tosses a tiny, flaming stick onto the straw. Then another. The matches catch, flare. Alonso sits down beside his father, and they watch the bonfire together.

□ □ □

"Wake up," Rodolfo said. "We're here."

Alonso groaned. His jaw creaked, frozen and stiff. Maybe his father had broken it. Cautiously touching the bruise, he looked out the window onto a thicket of tricycle carts. A rutted street ran between whitewashed adobe walls. Huaraz.

Alonso sat up. Damn! He'd missed it! He'd slept right through the Cordillera Negra, the black western range of the Andes where his mother grew up. All those times she'd told him about it, about herding sheep up rocky hillsides, and he'd snored right through it. Muttering, he snatched up the backpack Rodolfo's mother had packed for him and stepped off the bus into a shockingly cold dusk. Alonso gasped and fumbled with the backpack, tugging out Mariela's scarf and snaking it around his neck.

In the west, an orange blaze surged up from the horizon. It cast a fiery halo over the low cement and adobe buildings. Alonso sucked in a deep breath. The air tasted clean, cleaner than he had known air could taste. Across the street, a radio blared. Clarinets hummed and violins wheezed.

Rodolfo grinned at him. They both felt a little dizzy. A little drunk from the long bus ride. Still grinning, Rodolfo began to dance down the street, shuffling and hopping. When the *huayno* singer on the radio began to whoop exuberantly, Alonso felt like joining in.

A few blocks away, the Plaza de Armas was filled with people. Chatting, strolling arm-in-arm, lingering on corners. Heavyset little *campesinas* in felt hats and full skirts, their calloused toes sticking out of black rubber sandals. Townsmen in jeans and loafers. Tourists clomping around like astronauts in their hiking boots and fleece jackets.

Alongside the plaza, vendors had set themselves up with tables or just blankets on the ground. They were selling sweaters, jewelry, fluffy toys. The tourists clustered around them, pointing and speaking their garbled nonsense.

Alonso stopped to watch a tall, red-haired gringo argue in guttural Spanish with a tiny woman in a bowler hat. The gringo held a red alpaca scarf. "Seventeen *soles*," he said, putting the scarf down.

The *campesina* gave a little screech. She picked up the scarf, trying to shove it back at him. "Eighteen *soles*," she insisted. "Baby alpaca. Very good quality!"

"Seventeen," the man replied. He stuck his hands in his pockets, refusing to take the scarf.

Rodolfo spat in disgust. "For one *sol*," he said, cursing the gringo. He grabbed Alonso's arm and pulled him away. "That one *sol* means a hell of a lot more to her than it does to him."

Alonso looked back. The gringo was reaching inside his sweater, pulling out a pouch. He took some bills from it and handed them to the woman. Both of them were smiling as the woman folded the scarf and slid it into a little green bag.

At the corner of the plaza, they crossed the street and began climbing a hill so gigantic Alonso figured it must be a mountain, looming black against the indigo sky. After several blocks, the pavement faded to dirt, and the painted cement walls gave way to unfinished brick.

Alonso sighed at the familiar sight. Rough, unpainted facades. Flat roofs, waiting for a second story. Black rebar poking out. Shantytown houses. They were everywhere.

Puffing like a pair of locomotives, the boys climbed. A band seemed to have wrapped itself around Alonso's chest, and the more he walked, the tighter it gripped. "Slow down," he panted. "I can't breathe."

"It's the altitude," Rodolfo wheezed. "You'll feel better in the morning." He slowed his pace and Alonso found to his relief that he could breathe again.

Rodolfo seemed to know exactly where he was going. Halfway up that gigantic, looming hill, he stopped and rapped his knuckles on a metal door. It rang dully and they waited, shivering.

"*Who is it?*"

"Simón," Rodolfo replied.

The door opened and a woman's head poked out, her eyes dwarfed by an enormous pair of black-rimmed eyeglasses. She peeked up and down the street, then motioned them inside. Within a cement box of a room, a single blazing bulb hung from the ceiling on a wire. Beneath it sat a man, eating a bowl of soup. He didn't look up as the door clanged shut.

Rodolfo shook the woman's hand. *"Buenas tardes."* There were no introductions. They shrugged off their backpacks and the woman gestured for them to sit. The man went on slurping his soup.

Rodolfo had turned somber-faced and quiet. In the silence, the woman slipped into the kitchen, her jeans rustling. She brought them soup and a basket of flatbread, avoiding Rodolfo's eyes when he thanked her. Finally she sat down with her own bowl of soup, training her gaze downward.

Alonso tried not to look at her. He gnawed on the piece of gristle in his soup and thought about Rodolfo's new name.

Simón. Trust Rodolfo to have his *chapa*, his alias, all picked out. And what a choice. Not Simón Pedro, that obedient rock of an apostle upon whom Christ had built his church. No, it had to be Simón Bolívar, who had liberated South America from the Spaniards. That was more Rodolfo's style.

Alonso grabbed a piece of bread and dunked it in his soup. Simón Bolívar wasn't the only *Libertador*. There was also José de San Martín, whose army had swept up from Argentina to liberate Peru.

Comrade José. Alonso savored the sound in his mind. Simón and José. *Libertadores.*

As the spoons clinked against their empty bowls, the man turned to Rodolfo. "You should sleep now," he grunted. "There's a truck leaving the market before dawn. Look for the one with

'Guide me, Señor de los Milagros' painted above the cab." He showed them the bathroom, then gestured at the sofa. A thin mattress lay on the floor beside it. With a terse good-night, he disappeared beyond the kitchen.

"Not real friendly, are they?" Alonso kicked at the mattress, then pulled a blanket from his backpack.

"The less we know about each other, the better." Rodolfo sounded matter-of-fact. "And he's right. We should sleep."

But as soon as Alonso lay down, his head started pounding. *Thrum, thrum.*

"Ro—" He stopped himself just in time. "Simón," he whispered.

"What?"

Thrum, thrum. His brain was beating in time with his heart. "I'm José."

"Huh?"

"My *chapa*. It's José."

Rodolfo looked down over the edge on the sofa, frowning. "What kind of *chapa* is that? That's like calling yourself Juan. Can't you be more creative?"

"For José de San Martín," Alonso retorted. "The *Libertador*."

Rodolfo let out a soft chuckle. "Copycat."

Reaching up from his mattress, Alonso slugged him on the arm.

"*Ow!*" Rodolfo laughed. "Go to sleep. It's the only way to beat *soroche*."

"Beat what?"

"*Soroche*. Altitude sickness. If you don't rest, it can kill you. Water on the brain, or something. So go to sleep," he ordered.

"Yes, sir." Alonso saluted smartly. Both of them, *Libertadores*.

It seemed just minutes before their hosts were nudging them awake in the freezing darkness. He and Rodolfo gulped down steaming mugs of coca tea, burning their tongues. Then the man handed them a bag of bread and shoved them out the door.

They found the Señor de los Milagros truck, a battered old ten-ton Volvo. The driver, a taciturn man in a grease-stained sweater, seemed no happier to see them than the couple who had put them up for the night. He jerked a thumb at the truck's roofless cargo bed, leaving them to clamber up the tailgate and over lumpy sacks of potatoes.

Tossing a few sacks to one side, they dug themselves a hollow against the back wall, just above the cab. The last stars glittered above them as the driver started the engine. It turned over listlessly, giving several weary gasps. Finally it shuddered and, with a smoky black burp, started.

Rodolfo reached into his backpack and pulled out a blanket. "We should get some more sleep," he said, tucking the gray wool around himself. "It'll be a long day." He shut his eyes. And then, to Alonso's astonishment, he actually went to sleep while the sky paled to gray and yellow and the truck bounced out of Huaraz.

That's what a soldier ought to do, Alonso thought. *Sleep whenever he gets the chance.* But there was no way he was closing his eyes right now. Slipping on the sacks of potatoes, he stood and looked over the side of the truck.

They left the city and climbed to a high, flat plain. Vast and colorless, empty save for a few thatch-roofed huts and mud-brick corrals. A poncho-draped *campesino* emerged from a hut, and Alonso waved. One thin stick of an arm poked upward, waving back. When the sun finally rose, it did so suddenly, with a blaze of gold. The light poured westward, turning a distant range of snow-capped mountains into pyramids of fire. Alonso let the wind tug his hair. He drank in the cold air and felt his heart balloon with joy.

At the edge of the plain, the truck descended through dry hills. Then the driver turned onto a dirt road and they began to climb once more. During the two hours they climbed, they saw no cars. Just two enormous dump trucks, carrying loads of gravelly ore. Finally, the potato truck slowed to a halt beside a little stone hut. The driver got out of the cab, leaving the engine running.

Beyond the hut lay a broad valley, lush and green, walled in by shale-covered mountain slopes. A stream twinkled in the sunlight. In the distance, at the head of the valley, snowcaps glittered.

"There." The driver pointed a grease-blackened finger at a dirt trail. "Follow that to the pass. Don't lose it, because if you do you'll have a hell of a time finding it again. Take the left fork up the mountain, around to the other side. About two-thirds of the way down, there's a village. Tambo Matacancha. Tell them Hilario sent you."

"*Gracias.*" Rodolfo held out his hand.

The driver snorted explosively, like Rodolfo's hand was a bad joke. But he shook the hand and gave Rodolfo a plastic bag full of toasted corn. To Alonso he gave a two-liter bottle of Inka Kola. "Don't stop if you want to get there by dark," he warned. He turned and climbed into the cab. Alonso waved, but the driver didn't look down. He ground the engine through the gears and drove away.

▫THIRTEEN▫

Rosa tucked her blouse into her skirt. She looped a long curl behind her ear, puckered her lips, and gave herself a last look in the mirror. Her school sweater, bright red and unbuttoned, lay draped over her book bag.

Normal, she thought. She opened her bedroom door.

Mamá sat in the dining room, drinking coffee. Rosa had heard her during the night, heard the steady moan from the bathroom. Now gray half-moons shadowed Mamá's eyes. The half-moons came out whenever Mamá had a bad night.

Pain. Bleeding. Endometriosis. *We all have a cross to bear,* Rosa thought. That's what Tía Virginia said. She sat down and reached for the orange juice.

Papá strode into the dining room, smelling of aftershave and bending to kiss them both. "Feeling any better?" he murmured.

"Mmmm." Mamá ran a finger along his cheek. "Get the milk, will you, Rosa?"

Verónica was in the kitchen, pouring steaming milk into a little porcelain jug. Rosa slipped her arms around that wide, soft waist, and Verónica laughed.

Normal, Rosa thought.

Papá was folding his newspaper when Rosa returned. She set the creamer before him and sat down. Now was the time.

"I've decided not to see Andrea anymore." She spoke casually, as if it were a manicure she was canceling, and not the weekly sessions with her shrink.

Her father tipped a drop of milk into his cup. "I'm not sure that's a good idea."

Rosa fidgeted with her place mat. "I really don't need to anymore." She meant it. She was tired of sitting with Andrea every week. As if talking could change anything. "I'm fine. Really."

"That's not what Andrea thinks." Papá was stirring his coffee now, picking it up and taking a careful sip.

Rosa flushed. How could he know what her psychiatrist thought of her? Andrea had said their sessions were private. That Rosa could say anything she wanted and the words would stay secret forever, bottled up like a genie in Andrea's little *consultorio*.

Or maybe not, Rosa thought. *Maybe they talk about me. Diagnose me.*

She stood, her voice even. "Andrea's *my* doctor. You had no right to talk to her."

"Of course I do." Papá's gaze held hers, steady brown.

"Why? Because you pay her?"

"No, because I'm your father."

"Really?" Rosa shoved her chair against the table. "Then why don't you ask *me* how I'm doing, instead of Andrea?"

Papá put his cup down, so carefully that it barely clicked against the saucer.

"You don't really want to know!" Rosa exclaimed. "You just want Andrea to fix me so you don't have to think about me. Just like you don't think about Salvador anymore."

"Rosa, please." Mamá's voice slipped between them, pleading. "Enough."

Papá ran his fingers along the tabletop. Stroking it.

You make me sick, Rosa thought. First it was the new sofa, then a new carpet. Now they had a new dining room set. The apartment had been just fine the way it was, but with Salvador out of the picture, Papá was spending more and more time at his private practice in Miraflores. He was finally bringing in the money, the way Mamá's family had always wanted him to. *Such a talented doctor, wasting his time in a shantytown.* At last he was living up to their expectations. He was famous now, thanks to all that glowing research about the healthy kids in Salvador. People had read his name in the newspaper. His practice had a waiting list. He could afford to go shopping.

Alonso's brutal words came back to her, and without thinking she repeated them. "But why should you care about Salvador? Lima's full of *cholos* for you to experiment on."

Papá gasped, an in-breath so sharp it hurt to hear. Mamá stood and slapped Rosa across the face.

"*Mamá!*" Stumbling backward, Rosa pressed a shocked palm to her cheek. She had never been struck in her life.

But she saw no regret in the pale, angry face before hers. Mamá spoke in a voice so filled with ice that Rosa shivered. "Go to your room. Now."

Rosa turned. She ran. She slammed the bedroom door so

hard the frame shook. She saw again that wounded look in her father's eyes and hated him for it.

Magda should never have turned around to save her. She was her father's only child, but so what? That's what she wished she could tell Magda. *You shouldn't have come back for me!*

Oh, God, it was starting again. That wordless screaming, inside her head. Weeping, Rosa pulled a pillow over her face. No one else needed to hear. Not the sobs. Not the screams. Not the whispers that often came, unbidden.

Maybe Papá was right. Maybe she was crazy.

Five months had passed. Padre Manuel had written to say he was coming back, any day now. That was weeks ago. Nobody talked about Magda anymore. Not her parents, not the newspapers. Not even the politicians. It was time for Rosa to get over it. Move on. Go to school, do her homework, hang out in pubs. Date Jano. Life goes on.

Rosa tried to stop crying, but couldn't.

Yesterday Papá had brought Mamá some new painkillers. Strong ones.

How many pills would it take to kill pain like this? Twenty? Fifty? If Rosa swallowed them with a glass of milk, maybe she could keep down a bottleful.

Do something.

The voice. Not a whisper this time, but a voice, ringing in Rosa's head like a phone going off. And the thing—*but this is crazy*—the thing that made Rosa lift her head and look around the room, as if someone might be there with her, was that for the first time she *recognized* the voice.

Just do something, Rosa. Do it now.

The voice was peremptory. A little wry. Exasperated, perhaps, but hopeful. The way Magda always sounded. *Do something.*

With a sob, Rosa jumped from her bed. Hands shaking, she dug through the jumble of makeup and jewelry on her dresser. She found a few coins, a few bills. She pulled on the red sweater, grabbed her book bag, and ran.

□ □ □

Six hours and several mistaken bus routes later, Rosa hopped off a *micro* into a roadside jumble of kiosks and carts. She looked around, taking in the half-built houses, the smell of diesel. Two dirt roads rose above her, curving like brown snakes up the hill toward San Juan.

She was here.

A few meters away, a woman was cooking fish over a hissing propane stove. A half-dozen men crowded a bench, waiting for their lunch. As Rosa approached the woman to ask for directions, the men stirred. One of them stared hungrily at Rosa's chest. She halted, pulling her cardigan closed, and the man smiled. He had a thin nose and a shark's smile, all sharp teeth and odd, light-colored eyes. Rosa turned away. She felt his pale eyes pricking the back of her neck as she walked to a bodega on the corner.

Early November. The sun was veiled in gray, glowing modestly. Not much light made its way into the bodega, to illuminate the dusty shelves of noodles and canned sardines, the bins overflowing with vegetables. A heavyset woman in a black dress crouched in the shadows, wiping up some liquid that had spilled from a barrel of olives.

"*Buenas tardes, señora.*" Rosa pointed at the glass-fronted counter. "How much is that pound cake?"

"*Buenas tardes,*" the woman replied. Her gaze rested on Rosa's school uniform, on the red sweater with its private school insignia. She pulled out the cake. "Eight *soles.*"

Rosa gaped. "How much?"

"Eight *soles,*" the woman repeated. "Do you want it or not?"

Sighing, Rosa handed over a bill, and the woman slid the cake into a plastic bag. "*Señora,* can you tell me how to get to the María Auxiliadora School?"

"In San Juan?" The woman frowned, eyeing Rosa's school insignia. The red sweater was a neon sign, blinking. *¡Pituca! ¡Pituca!* The woman shrugged. "Three kilometers up the road. Turn right at the towers."

Stepping out of the bodega, Rosa pulled off the sweater and stuffed it into her backpack. The rest of her school uniform—gray jumper and white shirt—wouldn't stand out. Every kid in Peru wore gray and white on school days. She strode up the hill. If people wanted to stare, let them.

"Where are you going, *mamita?*"

Rosa spun around, and the man from the fish stand stepped from a doorway. The man with the shark smile. His eyes, a green so pale they looked almost yellow, met hers.

Rosa felt a chill through the thin cotton of her blouse. She turned and kept walking. "Nowhere," she muttered.

He padded beside her, his voice oily. "Nowhere's a bad place to go in San Juan, *mamita*. Especially alone, *no?*" His palm slid onto the small of her back, just above the curve of her buttock.

"Get your hands off me," Rosa snapped, stepping beyond his reach.

His sneakers whispered in the dust. "I'll just make sure you get to where you're going, *no, mamita?*"

For a moment, Rosa strode beside him, her skin crawling. She could scream, but who would care? She wasn't Dr. Pablo's daughter here in San Juan. She was just some *pituca* lost in a shantytown. She crossed the dirt road, dodging a skinny dog that was snarling to itself over a pile of garbage. Shark Eyes kept pace on the opposite side of the road. Above them, the sun gave up and disappeared.

Brick and cement gave way to *esteras* as Rosa climbed, stepping carefully around heaps of garbage and excrement. She could feel Shark Eyes watching her. When she slowed to glance at an adobe wall pasted over with Senderista fliers, he did, too. The fliers announced tomorrow's *paro armado*, the armed strike. Rosa didn't bother to read them. Last year, Sendero had announced a citywide *paro* with great fanfare. No one in Lima had paid much attention.

At the top of the hill, where the road leveled out, a string of electrical towers loomed like spidery gods above the shacks. Rosa heard pattering footfalls and turned to find four young girls around her, black-haired and ruddy with excitement. "*Gringuita, gringuita!*"

"*Gringa?*" she retorted. "Me?"

"*Sí, sí, gringuita.* Don't you have any candy?" A smudge-faced little girl in a torn T-shirt stuck out her hand.

"I'm not a *gringa,*" Rosa said indignantly. "I'm as Peruvian as you are!"

The oldest girl, bucktoothed and braided and wearing a gray school jumper, frowned. "But you're not from *here.*"

Rosa glanced across the street. Shark Eyes had turned, was slipping into the shadows behind a row of shacks. Rosa smiled gratefully at the bucktoothed girl. "I'm looking for my god-brother. I brought him a toy car. His sister goes to Maria Auxili-adora School. Livia Carhuanca."

"A skinny girl who never talks?" The bucktoothed girl spoke dismissively. "She's in my class. I can show you where she lives."

"Wait!" Squatting, the littlest girl pulled down her shorts. A stream of urine blotched the dust.

Watching her, Rosa felt a tug inside her chest. As if someone had very gently yanked open one of the chambers of her heart.

Magda used to boast about the Cesip's latrine brigades. They had built a decent pit toilet for everyone in Salvador. Rosa remembered laughing: *Latrine brigades! But Magda, it's too funny.*

"Come *on,*" the older girl urged. The little girl pulled up her shorts and scooted after them.

"Here's our school." They paused beside a gate, all scrap wood and rusty, exposed nails. "They're in the afternoon session."

Hundreds of voices poured from the gray cinderblock school. Teachers rapped out orders while children called the times tables. One voice rose above the rest, and Rosa smiled. *Don't leave us, brother, we love you so!* It was the Vallejo poem, about the dying soldier. She had recited it, too, back in fourth grade.

"There." The girl pointed at a windowless shack of *esteras* and flattened cardboard, with a splintered plywood door sagging off its hinges. "That's Livia's house." Her voice dropped to a whisper. "Livia's *papá* probably broke the door. He's a drunk." She paused, and all four girls gazed expectantly at Rosa.

But Rosa wanted them to go away, right now. She couldn't face that splintered door with this happy little mob around her. "Thank you," she said firmly. The girls glanced at each other. Rosa waited, unmoving.

Finally the older girl shrugged. "Well. Bye."

"Bye, *gringuita*," the little girls sang. Hand in hand, laughing, they made their way back up the street.

Barely breathing, Rosa approached the shack. She knocked, and the plywood slumped. The door's hinges were torn from the frame, and all that held it up was an inside latch.

"Hello?" She stuck her head inside. "Alonso?" She groped for a light switch, but felt only the frayed, crisscross weave of *esteras*. Through the shadows, her eyes adjusting, she saw a dirt floor ankle-deep in shirts and blankets and towels. Pots and pans scattered everywhere. Underwear and toys tangled over a toppled dresser. The television like a dead cockroach on its back, screen shattered.

"Alonso?" Rosa slipped on a comic book. "Tomás?"

Magda's kitchen table lay overturned. A mattress leaned against one wall. The other mattress had fallen to the floor, cotton bulging from a ragged gash.

Outside, at the back of the shack, Rosa found a few water

barrels and the charred remains of a wooden box. Footsteps in the dust, and scuff marks. Trembling, she turned to face the room. At her feet lay an open notebook filled with Livia's childish scrawl.

The familiar, useless tears begin to fall.

Magda had been whispering in her mind for months. But Rosa had ignored her. Done nothing. Cowered in Miraflores. And now they were gone.

She slapped at the tears, but they wouldn't stop.

Something rustled at the edge of the shack, skittering behind that upended mattress.

A *rat!* Stumbling over books and pans, Rosa fled. She was outside, pulling the door shut, when a little voice squealed within. "Livia, let me go!"

For an instant Rosa stood paralyzed. Then, violently, she shoved the door. She stepped inside to see Diana launching herself like a tiny guided missile.

"Rosa!"

She was filthy. She'd grown taller. Her round face was red and smudged with tears, but it *was* Diana! Rosa knelt, arms outstretched, and Diana dived into them.

"Rosa, Livia wouldn't let me go!" Another rustle sounded behind the mattress, and Gustavo crept out, sucking his thumb.

"Gustavo," Rosa breathed. She wanted to swallow him whole with her eyes. "Shhh, Diana, it's okay. Where's Livia? Is she behind the mattress, too?"

Diana rubbed her wet cheeks against Rosa's neck. "She won't come out. She's too scared."

"Scared of what?"

"The police."

"But why?"

With a long, wet sniff, Diana stopped crying. "Because they taked Papi," she said in a small voice. "In the night."

Not wanting to let go of Diana, feeling that if she did Magda's family might melt into thin air, Rosa took the fat little hand in hers and led Diana to the mattress. Behind it huddled Livia, a wiry ball in grimy pajamas. Rosa pushed the mattress to the floor and crouched beside her. The child's face was pressed against her knees, but on one temple Rosa saw an ugly, swollen bruise.

"Livia?" She touched the hunched shoulder. "Livia, it's me. Rosa." Livia flinched and Gustavo whimpered. When Rosa smiled, he tucked his chin into his chest, dodging Rosa's smile as if it were a fist.

He was thinner and taller than she remembered, his black hair hanging in long tendrils over his ears. A little boy, not Magda's baby anymore. He must be nearly three now. Rosa pulled the toy car from her backpack, but Gustavo refused to look at it.

Sighing, Rosa sat down on the mattress. Diana snuggled beside her. After a moment Gustavo snatched the car and sat down as well.

"Tell me what happened."

Livia's tight little body didn't stir, but Diana replied. "The police breaked the door. We were asleep. They wanted Alonso."

"Where is Alonso?"

"He went away."

Rosa couldn't believe it. Alonso would never leave his family. "Why?"

Diana tugged fretfully on a lock of hair. "Papi hit him too much," she whispered. She slipped the hair into her mouth and began to suck.

"Is that why the police took your *papi?*"

Diana shook her head. "They came for Alonso."

"But you said—" Rosa stopped herself. She put an arm around Diana, holding her voice as steady as possible. "I thought they took your *papi.*"

The dark little head nodded. "But they wanted Alonso. They thought he was in the mattress." She pointed to the long rip in the other mattress. "Then they thought Papi burned him up in his box." Diana's forehead wrinkled anxiously. "But Rosa, Alonso wasn't in his box when Papi burned it."

"No, of course he wasn't," Rosa soothed. "But why'd they take your *papi?*"

"He called them bad words. They all started hitting him. . . ." Diana's voice trailed off and Rosa braced herself for more tears. "They taked him away in a truck." Miraculously, Diana sounded almost matter-of-fact. "Alonso is coming back on Wednesday. Papi said so."

"Really?" The news brought Rosa a blaze of joy. "Livia, did you hear that? Alonso will be back tomorrow!" Impulsively, she reached for Livia, but Livia cringed away, and Rosa's hand caressed air.

There had been a stray dog, once, in the park on the *Malecón*. Rosa had befriended it, tossing it bits of bread. But when she finally got close enough to touch it, the dog had shuddered violently and shot from the park as if fired from a cannon. Rosa never saw it again.

Santa María, Rosa thought. Livia could disappear like that. Not physically, but in some strange way Livia could leave and never come back. And Rosa didn't have days to reach her the way she'd reached the dog. She had hours. Once darkness fell, it would be too dangerous to take the kids to the avenue to catch a *micro*.

"I'm hungry," Diana said.

Rosa smiled. A simple demand, something she could actually handle. "I brought a surprise."

While Diana and Gustavo wolfed down thick slices of pound cake, Rosa hauled the mattresses back onto the beds and picked up the clothes and books and pans. As she worked, she talked. She told the children about riding the bus here, about school. About how the sun was finally starting to come out and how summer would be here soon. Diana took a piece of cake to her sister, and after a moment Livia began stuffing yellow scraps into her mouth.

"Gustavo," Rosa said, "my *mamá* is your *madrina*. Remember her? I bet she'd love to see you."

Gustavo's lower lip slid out in a pout.

"What a good idea," Rosa went on. "We'll go see my *mamá*!" She looked at Diana. "Okay?"

Diana shook her head, hard.

"It's all right, Diana. You remember my *mamá*. She's Gustavo's *madrina*!" Rosa tried to sound firm. In charge. "Now come on. Livia, it's time to go."

Livia's plate fell to the floor with a thump. Rosa saw a pinwheel flurry of limbs, and Livia was back against the wall, arms folded around herself. Diana wailed, an eerie, despairing shriek. Gustavo stamped his feet and began to scream, his face turning purple.

Shocked, Rosa found herself bellowing. "NO!" she screamed. "STOP!"

Diana slid from her chair and darted across the shack. She scuttled like a beetle under the double bed.

"Diana, come out of there! Nobody's going to hurt you!" Rosa tried to speak more gently. "We can't stay, don't you understand? Please come out, Diana." She knelt to look beneath the bed. Diana scrambled across the dirt, out of reach.

"Papi said not to go outside!" Diana sobbed. "We have to wait for Alonso."

"But your *papi* didn't mean you couldn't go out with me! We'll leave a note. Diana, we can't stay here tonight!"

Diana's sobs rose to a howl.

Kneeling, Rosa begged. "Diana, *please* . . ."

With an angry shout, Gustavo ran around the bed and crept beside his sister.

Rosa sank to the floor, defeated, the dirt floor cool and damp beneath her cheek. Livia crouched, mute with fear. Gustavo and Diana sobbed, clenched together under the bed. How could she get them out of here? Magda would have known what to do, but she wasn't Magda. She couldn't think with so much screaming in her ears.

Get your papá, Rosa.

Papá could come and get them. She could call him at the university. He hated being called away from class, but when he got here, when he saw how they were, he'd understand. He could sedate them. He could get them out of here.

Rosa stood up. "Diana, stop crying. I won't make you leave. But I need to call my father. Dr. Pablo needs to know I'm here with you, okay? I need a telephone, Diana."

A few teary gasps, and then a long sniff. Finally Diana replied. "There's no phones in San Juan."

"That's impossible," Rosa said. "There's always a phone somewhere. In a bodega, maybe?"

Silence beneath the bed, then the same little voice. "Alonso said there was no phones. That's why he had to go away one day to call you." The voice got even smaller. "Papi came home while he was out. He got so angry . . ." The voice broke off. Diana began crying again, as if her four-year-old heart had already been broken more times than it could bear.

Suddenly Rosa couldn't stand it anymore.

She knelt again, peering under the bed at the little form huddled in the shadows. "Oh, Diana, Diana, listen to me." Diana turned away, and Rosa slid under the bed beside her. "No more bad things will happen, Diana. I promise!" She put her arms around Diana and was startled by how violently that little body shook. *Like the dog,* she thought. *Not you too, Diana.* "No more bad things," Rosa repeated. "I promise you."

Oh, she was angry now. She had never felt such anger in her life. Such rage. She wanted a sword. She'd stand in that miserable doorway and cut to pieces the next Evil that tried to darken this shack.

Hugging Diana, she raised her voice. "Do you hear me, Livia? I will not let any more bad things happen!"

Livia didn't reply, but Diana stopped crying. Gustavo slithered atop his sister, then slid over Rosa. He tucked himself under Rosa's arm and plastered himself to her side. The three of them lay on the dirt, staring at the wooden slats that held the mattress.

No more bad things. A crazy promise.

Rosa closed her eyes and wondered how she could possibly keep it.

·FOURTEEN·

The sun had slipped behind a mountain when the boys finally saw the village. A cluster of thatch-roofed mud hovels surrounded by scrub grass and veins of exposed rock.

Alonso slid to a stop. "Welcome to Tambo Matacancha," he croaked. A handful of sheep cropped at the patchy grass. Tendrils of smoke curled from a few huts. Otherwise, the village seemed deserted.

Then, from below them, a shout rang up the mountainside. A half-dozen dark shapes darted from the huts. They coalesced into a mass and charged up the hill toward the boys.

"What do you think?" Rodolfo asked nervously.

"They may not be expecting us. We need to tell them Hilario sent us." Alonso rubbed his hands together. The setting sun was sucking the warmth from the air.

Ponchos flapping, the shapes flew up the trail. Within moments six men surrounded the boys. Short men with wiry arms and wrinkled faces. Ancient as dwarves, with calloused, horny toes and gnarled fingers grasping wooden staffs.

"Ow!" Alonso yelped as one of the men jabbed him. "Hilario

sent us!" He grabbed at the staff. The man shouted at him in Quechua. A breathy stream of sounds.

"Hilario sent us!" Rodolfo repeated. But it did no good. Neither of them spoke Quechua. The men poked at them, shoving them down the trail and sending them stumbling over the stones.

Alonso could hear his own heart pounding, could hear Rodolfo panting by his side. Nobody spoke as they drew near the huts, squarish mud boxes with hairy straw roofs. A few old women watched from the doorways, and a scrawny dog the color of dust appeared from nowhere to begin snapping at Alonso's heels. One of the old men kicked it away, and its startled yelp echoed off the mountainside. Finally they stopped outside a hut. One of the men called softly in Quechua, and from the darkness, a hunched little man emerged.

He looked a hundred years old. *The King of the Dwarves*, Alonso thought.

A young woman followed, her face indistinct as she stared over the old man's shoulder. Inside the hut, a fire spat puffs of smoke toward the ceiling.

"Who are you?" The young woman spoke Spanish. Alonso wanted to cheer.

"Simón," Rodolfo replied. "And Juan."

"José," Alonso corrected, jabbing Rodolfo with his elbow.

"José," Rodolfo repeated. "Hilario sent us."

The girl nodded, and both boys exhaled in relief. The old man murmured something and she listened, watching the boys. "Comrade Ezequiel and his wife will feed you," she said. Her voice blended clipped Spanish consonants with rounded Quechua vowels. "And show you where to sleep. We'll talk in the morning." With that, she and the old man turned and went back into the hut.

A hobbling old man showed the boys to an empty hut on the western edge of the village. Above the mountain they had just descended, the sky glowed pale lavender, but the village was already dark. They waited outside the hut, fidgeting in the cold until an old woman approached them with two bowls of soup. When they thanked her, she muttered something incomprehensible and trudged away.

The soup tasted like hot water. "You did that on purpose," Alonso accused, gulping it down.

"Did what on purpose?"

"Called me Juan."

Rodolfo started to laugh and went inside.

"You did, didn't you?" Alonso followed, trying to see through the darkness.

"No, I didn't."

Alonso could hear him chuckling. "Very funny, comrade." He looked for a door to close but there was none. In the corner, a few chickens clucked drowsily.

Rodolfo was still laughing as he pulled a blanket from his pack and rolled himself in it. "Goodnight, Comrade Copycat." He gave a final squeaking guffaw. Within minutes, he was asleep.

Rodolfo could sleep anywhere, just like Diana. Get him horizontal and he was out.

Alonso wrapped himself in his blanket and lay down, listening enviously to Rodolfo's steady breathing. The longer he lay there, the colder he felt. Who said Lima was cold in winter? Cold was a doorless adobe hut four thousand meters above sea level. Cold was lying on a dirt floor with a wool blanket around you. Alonso pulled his knees to his chest, trying to conserve heat in a tight little ball. Oh, great. Now he had to pee.

Muttering a string of curses, he ran through the doorway. The air seemed to freeze in his nostrils. He found an enormous boulder near the trailhead and stepped behind it, shivering and laughing at himself. Who would see him, anyway, in this half-deserted gathering of huts?

Tambo Matacancha, Ghost Village of the Cordillera Huay-huash.

He unzipped his jeans, eyes tearing with relief, and tipped his head back.

And blinked in awe.

A thousand stars. A million stars. More than that. A white splash of light across the sky. The Milky Way. So that's what it meant. It really did look like milk, spilled over a velvety black tablecloth.

Back in Lima, a grubby pall hid the stars, all but a handful of them. If he stood in front of his house and looked up, he saw a few blurry specks. These stars were stabs of brilliance, billions of them.

The exhilaration he had felt in the truck returned. He wanted to dance. To feel this happy, twice in one day, seemed miraculous. He thought of Rosa, and a ravenous hunger swept through him. Ay, to feel her skin right now . . .

When the People's War ended, he'd bring her here. He'd make love to her beneath a sky awash with starlight. He'd make it up to her, somehow. He'd explain it all.

He was thinking about Rosa, about her curves and her hair and the way her jeans clung to her skin, when a rustle on top of the boulder startled him. He zipped up his jeans and stepped back.

A villager wrapped in a poncho lay sleeping on the giant stone. Alonso grinned. This guy was supposed to be guarding the trail into Tambo Matacancha. Some sentinel.

Still, if a *campesino* could sleep on that slab of granite, he himself—an EGP recruit!—ought to be tough enough to sleep in a hut. Creeping back inside, he lay down as close to Rodolfo as he could. He curled his body next to his friend's and they nestled together like spoons. Finally, not warm but warm enough, he slept.

□ □ □

"Hey, little girl, wake up!"

Alonso woke. Rodolfo's face lay before his, eyebrows raised. Light poured through the doorway.

"*Hola, mamita.*" Alonso yawned, rolling away. "It was freezing last night."

They stood up, stretching and scratching, and wandered out into the early morning. The sun was up, shining above a glacier-topped mountain. Alonso turned his face eastward and let tepid sunshine pour over his cheeks. The air still felt like an ice bath.

An old man carrying a wooden hoe shuffled past. Without

looking at the boys, he trotted down the trail to a terraced brown field below the village.

In the doorway of the hut next to theirs, a woman sat beside a pile of carded wool, spinning it onto a drop spindle. She was bare-legged and barefoot, and wore what looked like a dozen graying petticoats under her skirt. She ignored the boys, staring at her gently rotating spindle. They watched, mesmerized by the growing spool of yarn.

"*Buenos días, señora*," Rodolfo said tentatively.

"She probably doesn't speak Spanish," Alonso muttered.

"*Señores!*" A red-cheeked little girl ran toward them. She wore a bowler hat and layer upon layer of old clothes. Scarves and sweaters and blouses. At least three pairs of torn and grimy sweatpants. "*Buenos días*, comrades! The Political Commissar is waiting for you." The little girl bobbed respectfully and led them over the grass.

The village was as quiet now as it had been at sunset. A ghost village. Were all the villages up here like this? Just a few old women, spinning wool in the doorways. Chickens kicking up the dust in a listless search for insects. A couple of filthy, matted sheep. The little girl shoved one out of their way and showed them into a hut.

In the corner, an open fire hissed, sending a haze of smoke toward a roof vent. The young woman who had greeted them in Spanish sat at a table, spooning soup to her mouth and staring at a notebook. As they entered, she stood with a shy smile. The little girl scurried over to a pot above the fire and began ladling soup into a bowl.

"Welcome, comrades." The young woman shook hands with them, her dirt-etched fingers limp. The little girl brought them each a bowl of soup, then ducked her head with something like a curtsy and darted away. "Please sit, comrades," the young woman said. "Simón and . . . Juan?"

"José," Alonso corrected.

She looked down at her notebook, her finger sliding across the page. "You will be serving in the glorious People's Guerrilla Army, carrying your lives in your fingertips, ready to hand them over in the service of the People, the Party, and the Revolution?"

Rodolfo replied firmly. "Our lives belong to the Party. Death is natural and comes to all."

The young woman nodded. "I am Comrade Elena. I am Political Commissar of Tambo Matacancha."

Alonso tried to think of something to say, something Senderista, but nothing came to him. A few *cuyes* squeaked behind a platform bed piled with sheepskins. Finally Comrade Elena looked up from her notes and flashed Rodolfo a brilliant smile. "Comrade Francisco and his men may return today," she said. "You'll be able to join them."

Picking up the dented spoons the little girl had laid out, Alonso and Rodolfo began to eat. Alonso wrinkled his nose. This soup was as thin and tasteless as last night's. Water, really, with a few scraps of potato, some strands of wilted herb and not even a hint of salt. Suddenly he remembered yesterday's bread. He still had a few pieces of that flat, chewy bread from Huaraz in his pack, left over from the hike. "We have bread," he told Comrade Elena. "I'll go get it."

Her eyes and mouth spread wide with delight.

She's pretty when she smiles, Alonso thought. Big black eyes shaped like teardrops. Chapped cheeks glowing warm and ruddy over those flat cheekbones.

"Bread!" she exclaimed. "I haven't had bread since . . ." She broke off and looked down, leafing through her notebook. "We never go into Chiquián to the market anymore," she murmured. Finding what she was looking for, she ran a finger under a line of handwritten text. "'The insa—The insur—'" She frowned at the notebook. "'The insurrectional peasantry must starve the cities into submission,'" she read. "'We are becoming self-sufficient, so we must not sell or buy anything.'" She looked up, her expression sober.

"We didn't buy the bread," Alonso said uncertainly. "I mean, a comrade gave it to us in—"

"Just get the bread, José," Rodolfo snapped.

Flushing, Alonso turned on his heel and went out.

The sun was higher now, so bright that the sky around it seemed pale and silvery. In the east, jagged peaks speared the horizon. To the west, the trail snaked down the mountain they had crossed the day before, then cut through Tambo Matacancha to the rock-strewn field where the old man was working with his hoe. As Alonso watched him poke at the soil, a dozen men emerged from a gully.

Young men, in felt hats and brown ponchos, striding over the rocks. Wiry and tough, like the gnarled, reddish queñal trees Alonso had seen in the valley yesterday. A few wore rifles slung from canvas belts, and most carried machetes. Two of them were dragging a third, who stumbled and cried out. The old man dropped his hoe and trotted toward them, pulling off his hat as he drew near.

Comrade Francisco, Alonso thought. *It has to be.*

Looking up, a bearded young man in a broad-brimmed hat caught sight of him. He barked a command and two of the men shot up the trail. Alonso didn't resist when they grabbed him by the arms. They held him immobile as the rest of the platoon climbed to join them.

"Who are you?" the bearded man demanded. He had a pistol strapped to his side.

"José." Alonso looked steadily into the hostile brown eyes. "I came with Simón. Hilario sent us."

The expression of suspicion didn't vary as the man fired more questions. "Where did you come from? When did you get here? Where is this Simón?"

"We came from Lima. We got here last night, just after sunset. And Simón is with Comrade Elena, having breakfast. Are you Comrade Francisco?"

"I'll ask the questions," the man snapped.

The two Senderistas dragging the third joined them. The wounded man was moaning, his pant leg stiff with mud and dried blood. Something sharp stuck through the fabric below his knee.

Alonso whistled, then looked up at the leader. "I know first-aid," he said. "If we can get him inside—"

"There's no need," the leader retorted. "Get your comrade, and tell Comrade Elena to gather the people by the school." He nodded at the men gripping Alonso's arms, and they released him.

Alonso looked back at the wounded man. He slumped, arms

draped across the shoulders of his two comrades. His face was caked with dust and sweat, and his eyes were half closed.

Alonso stared at the leg. That jagged thing sticking out was bone.

"Compound fracture," he murmured. It was a miracle the man wasn't in shock. Alonso turned to the leader. "He needs help now," he insisted.

The leader's expression hardened. "Do as I tell you."

Alonso rocked slightly on his heels, staring at the horrific leg as the wounded man moaned again.

"Go!" the leader nearly shouted.

Shaking his head angrily, Alonso turned back to the village. He trotted to Comrade Elena's hut.

"Come on," he said, sticking his head through the doorway. "Comrade Francisco is here. He wants us all to meet by the school."

Rodolfo and Elena stood up so quickly that they bumped the table and spilled their soup. Elena began calling to the villagers in Quechua. *Campesinos* emerged from huts and came trotting from the fields. They gathered before a small adobe building, a dozen or more old men and women with wrinkled faces and sunken cheeks. Elena's eager little assistant raced toward them with a few old men shuffling in her wake.

The platoon was waiting for them, ranked in a semicircle in front of the school. Comrade Francisco stood beside the wounded man and the two guerillas who propped him up. A Senderista was hoisting a red flag onto a wooden pole. As the wind caught the flag and unfurled it, a hammer and sickle stood out against the brilliant blue sky.

Bobbing in a little half curtsy, Elena held out her hand. Comrade Francisco shook it and then turned to the villagers. His voice carried above the wind. "Comrades! The agents of the reaction are everywhere. They come with smiles and gifts, but they have only one goal: to serve the counterrevolution and keep the People forever oppressed in a situation of hunger, misery, and exploitation. They are doomed to fail! The victory of the People's War is inevitable!"

Comrade Francisco paused. In the silence that followed Elena began to speak in Quechua. The old men and women looked at her, their rheumy eyes flickering with comprehension as she translated. When she finished, Comrade Francisco spoke again.

"I have called you here for a People's Trial. Tambo Matacancha is the first in a shining chain of villages in the Liberated Zone of the Cordillera Huayhuash. Your loyalty to the Party is vital." He paused, and once again Elena translated.

With a jerk of his head, Comrade Francisco gestured for the two Senderista soldiers to bring forward the wounded man. Alonso winced as they forced him to put weight on his injured leg.

"We captured this dog of imperialism on the trail from Tambo Matacancha. When he and his two companions saw us, they fled. Why would they flee if they were not spies of the reaction? The friends of the People have nothing to fear from us." Comrade Francisco pointed at Alonso and Rodolfo. "Recruits into the People's Guerilla Army. You see? They didn't run from us."

Alonso gazed back as Comrade Francisco nodded. Rocking

slightly on his heels, he felt edgy. Distant, somehow. Like he was watching this scene from high up on the mountainside.

Francisco spoke again as Elena finished translating and the *campesinos* glanced at the two boys. "Only counterrevolutionaries abandon their comrades. When this dog fell into a ravine, the other two ran away."

The wounded man's eyes were open now. He listened closely as Comrade Francisco adopted a mocking tone. "He *claims* to be an aid worker. He *says* Tambo Matacancha was the first stop on his journey to bring a new livestock project into the Cordillera Huayhuash. He *says* he met here with leaders of this community." Comrade Francisco's voice rose to an angry shout. "He is lying! Tambo Matacancha is a liberated village. It supports the People's War!"

As Elena spoke, the villagers stirred. Francisco's eyes swept across their stolid faces like a searchlight sweeping a prison yard.

"We have brought him here for a People's Trial. If he is an agent of the reaction, he must be squashed like an insect. It is for you to decide."

Elena finished translating. A cool wind blew through Alonso's hair and tugged at the *campesinos'* ponchos. On the mountainside above them, a lamb bleated, answered by a ewe's low, reassuring rumble. Nobody moved. The *campesinos'* faces were dark beneath the brims of their hats. Uneasily, Alonso glanced at Rodolfo. He was staring at Francisco. Even the prisoner was motionless, collapsed over his captors' shoulders.

A stir in the crowd broke the spell. Slowly the *campesinos* parted to let a very old man wearing a red poncho step forward.

It was the ancient man who had emerged from the hut the night before. The King of the Dwarves. As he approached Comrade Francisco, a woman's high wail broke the silence, a protesting screech that fell off as abruptly as it had arisen.

"Don Fermín . . . ," Elena began. She bit her lip.

Don Fermín took off his hat and faced Comrade Francisco. "In the old order of oppression," he quavered, in Quechua-accented Spanish, "it was my turn to serve my community as President." With a gentle, backhanded wave, he gestured at Elena. "That was before we had the Party and a Political Commissar." Elena looked down at the ground. "Now we have the Party to guide us. But when the three aid workers," a gnarled finger pointed at the prisoner, "came over the mountain, I climbed to meet them. To speak for my community."

Comrade Francisco glared at the hunched figure before him. "Alone?"

"Sí, señor." Don Fermín nodded. "I was alone."

A shadow of skepticism passed over the commander's face. "When you met with these agents of the reaction, did you denounce them to the Commissar?"

"No, señor, I did not." With his hat in one hand, Don Fermín spread his arms apologetically. "We talked about alpacas. They said that they would bring us purebred alpacas. Their wool is finer than our sheep's wool. But I told them Tambo Matacancha is a liberated village. We don't need alpacas because we no longer sell sweaters to the tourists in Huaraz."

Francisco smiled slightly. Don Fermín's unsteady voice grew stronger. "I don't think you should kill this man. He is not a spy.

He is an *evangélico* from one of those sects that don't lie or steal. Send him away. Let him tell his people not to come back to Tambo Matacancha."

Comrade Francisco nodded.

A few feet shuffled. A few sighs mingled with the wind. Alonso let out a quivering breath of relief. Maybe he could dress the man's wound. Dr. Pablo had taught him first-aid.

I can do it, Alonso thought. *I can splint his leg. He'll make it up the mountain.*

Comrade Francisco pulled his pistol from its holster and stepped toward Don Fermín. The barrel was black, a metal tube that glinted in the sunlight.

Startled, Alonso looked around. The prisoner was quivering, holding his shattered leg above the ground as if the slightest weight were unbearable. No one else moved. The villagers. Elena and Rodolfo. Everyone was staring at Comrade Francisco. No one looked at Don Fermín.

The old man closed his eyes. Comrade Francisco placed the barrel against his forehead and pressed it there.

Then, before anyone could speak, he pulled the trigger.

·FIFTEEN·

The blanket was coarse gray wool, and it tickled each time Rosa breathed. She yawned, staring up at a ceiling made of flattened cardboard boxes. GLORIA EVAPORATED MILK, she read. TROPICAL RICE. The kids lay around her, still asleep. Gustavo's feet pressed into her back, and Livia's head rested on the crook of her arm. Wedged between them, Rosa tried to stretch without moving. CRISTAL BEER.

The night before, she had piled the other bed with books and pans and shoved it in front of the broken door. She'd tossed her school uniform atop the pile and slept in one of Magda's old T-shirts. Now she pulled her arm free and crept from the bed, crossing barefoot to the battered wooden dresser.

Tomás had kept all of Magda's clothes, the sweaters and blouses, the skirts and jeans. Why, in this tiny shack, had he bothered? Was he was trying to keep a piece of Magda? Did he ever slip a hand into the drawer, just to touch clothes that had once touched his wife?

Rosa opened a drawer and pulled out Magda's blue sweater. She could still see Magda wearing it. Could remember her smiling in the doorway of the Cesip.

That's why he keeps it, Rosa thought. Something of Magda remained in the sweater. As Rosa put it on, she felt the sweater wrap around her like a hug.

The children's heads lay close together, their bodies fanned like the spokes of a wheel. Rosa watched them breathing for a moment, then tugged the other bed from the door. Before they woke, she needed to find a market or a bodega. Somewhere she could buy a breakfast even Livia wouldn't refuse. Another pound cake. Chocolate. Candy. Anything. But even more than that, she needed a phone.

She stepped outside and pulled the door shut.

The sun was already gleaming behind the clouds, but the street was deserted. No men heading off to work. No baker pedaling a three-wheeled cart. No water truck rumbling through. A bodega stood on the corner, but it was closed, battened down behind bars and a sliding metal door. From within the windowless shacks, Rosa could hear voices and a few radios. A brassy salsa tune. The sharp accents of the *Radioprogramas* announcers. The life had been sucked from the street and bottled up in the shacks.

A few blocks away, she found a dusty little open-air market, as empty as the street. Perplexed, she wandered among the stalls, lifting plastic sheets and peering into wooden trays. She found nothing except a dried old potato. Above her, a breeze toyed a red banner tied to a stall. The banner opened tentatively, uncurling and subsiding. Rosa saw two crisscrossed golden shapes sewn onto the red.

A hammer and sickle. Startled, Rosa took a step backward.

Pasted to one of the stalls, she saw another of those fliers she'd ignored the day before. Her eyes ran down the words. *Paro armado*. Armed strike. Anyone who went to work or shop would be executed. *Ajusticiar*. Executed with justice.

¡Viva el paro armado!

A soft footfall padded behind her, and as Rosa turned a hand clapped over her mouth. A blade, thin and sharp, pressed against her neck.

Oh God, she was going to pee in her pants.

An oily voice whispered. "Not a good place to be alone during a *paro armado, no, mamita?*"

Shark Eyes.

He began to pull her backward, to a stall where blue plastic flapped against the wood. He cursed gently as he dragged her, then more roughly when he stumbled. For an instant his hand fell from her mouth. Rosa tried to scream, but shut her mouth with a whimper when the knife cut against her throat.

"Shhh," he whispered, turning her around so he could drill his yellow-green eyes into hers. "Shhh."

Her blood throbbed through the artery beneath his knife. She stared at him, unable to speak.

His nostrils flared. He liked what he saw. Liked her terror and the way it turned her mind to gel.

"I know," he said lightly. "Why don't we go home?" His voice friendly. His arm around her shoulders and the knife against her neck. "To your little house up the road?" Everything he said was a question.

Feeling as if her knees might give way at any moment, Rosa let him guide her toward the street. No one would see them. The stalls were empty. The shacks were shut tight, curled in on themselves. Shark Eyes would walk her, unseen, to the shack, and then he would open the door—

Rosa stopped walking.

"No, no, no." His lips brushed her ear. "Keep moving, *mamita*." The knife pricked as he shoved her forward.

"No," she whispered, locking her knees. *No more bad things.*

Shark Eyes cursed at her and tried to drag her forward. She managed the first high note of a scream before he slapped his hand across her mouth. Then he pulled the knife away and kicked her. She punched at him as he twisted her head in his hand. His fingers gouged her cheek. His palm smothered her cries. Rosa fought her way back toward the market.

Abruptly, he gave up trying to pull her into the street. The knife was at her neck again and Rosa felt a thin slice, almost like a paper cut. His nails scratched her scalp as he seized a fistful of hair.

She stopped fighting and stumbled backward, letting him drag her toward the stalls. Her eyes filled with tears of gratitude, as if he had showed her some unexpected kindness. *No more bad things.* Magda's children were safe.

Shoving her between two stalls, Shark Eyes forced her down, flat on her back. His knife still at her throat, he kicked her legs apart and knelt between them.

In the silence of the market, Rosa heard her own heart. She heard him breathing through his mouth. Maybe he couldn't breathe through that thin nose. His yellow eyes didn't leave hers.

Ants seemed to be crawling through her hair, out of the dust and across her scalp. She wondered who was behind the yellow eyes, if it was a person at all, if it had a name. And if it was a person and had a name, if it could feel pity.

"Please," she whispered.

He began to undo the metal button at the waist of Magda's jeans.

"Please don't." Cold sweat beaded her chest.

Shark Eyes smiled as the button slid free. He grasped the tab at the top of the zipper.

Oh God oh God oh God. Rosa began to tremble. *Not this. No, God, please, not this.*

But there was no answer, only a soft *zzzz* as he pulled down her zipper. With one hand, he jerked the jeans and her underpants down around her knees. Rosa put her hands between her legs, trying to cover herself, but Shark Eyes slapped them away.

Then, still kneeling above her, he began to unzip his pants. Rosa shut her eyes.

Oh, Magda, why didn't you just run? Why did you come back for me?

Her eyelids were clenched as tightly as her fists. She would keep his eyes out of her, if not the rest of him. It was all she could do, now.

There's nothing else I can do, she thought.

Magda's voice came, soft and unexpectedly peaceful. *Ay, hija,* she murmured. *You can always do something.*

"You shouldn't have come back for me," Rosa told her in a choked voice, feeling bitter. "You should have just left me there."

"What did you say?"

"You shouldn't have come back," Rosa repeated.

Do something.

I'm too frightened!

Do something!

With a sharp gasp, as if she were emerging from a long time underwater, Rosa opened her eyes. His face was close to hers. He was watching her, squinting and wary.

She cleared her throat and swallowed without moving. Her eyes on his, she struggled to grasp the feeling inside her, the breath of clarity Magda had brought. Above them, a red banner waved.

"Why not, *mamita?* Why shouldn't I have come back?" The knife stroked her neck. Up, down.

Rosa looked over his shoulder at the stall behind him. Another of the fliers was pasted there, with big words scrawled at the bottom. *¡Viva el paro armado!*

"*Viva el paro armado,*" she whispered.

She turned her eyes to his again, but she didn't see him at all. Instead she saw a boy. Soft brown eyes icing over with anger and a fledgling hatred. Rodolfo's words, spoken that long-ago April morning, glittered like a knife in her memory. "You know what the Party does to rapists?"

Shark Eyes dropped his knife and slapped her.

"Why do you think I'm here?" she asked him.

"Shut up, whore!" But his eyes broke from hers and the trap sprang open in Rosa's mind.

She knew all about fear. She had learned everything there

was to know that day in the Cesip. Her fear had made them strong and helped them kill Magda. But now Shark Eyes was frightened, and his fear was making her strong, filling her mouth with a metallic taste. A taste of knives.

She heard her voice turn cold, the way Mamá's sometimes did. "Do you think girls like me just walk into San Juan the day before a *paro armado*? Do you really think I *live* here? Look at me!"

"Shut up." His voice was weakening.

"You have about three minutes before my comrades arrive," she said. "So you can stay here and finish up"—she glared into his eyes, which were filling with confusion, a flounder flopping on a line, not a shark at all—"or you can get out of here now and not lose that filthy thing hanging between your legs."

His lips stretched back from his teeth. Rosa froze as he picked up the knife again, but she forced herself to look into his eyes, to stare him down without moving, without touching him.

He stood and began to zip up his trousers, yellow eyes darting and furtive. Rosa looked at her watch. "Two minutes," she said.

Shark Eyes turned and ran.

Two minutes, she thought, and began to shake. The taste in her mouth turned to acid. Two minutes.

He's gone. He's gone.

She rolled over onto her knees and vomited. Her pants were still down around her knees. She could feel cool air on her skin as she stood up, swaying and nauseous. *He's gone.* And still she shivered, reaching down and trying to pull up her underpants and jeans. Her vomit lay before her, a yellowish splatter in the dust.

Maybe it's true, she thought. *Maybe they were coming.* Suddenly she felt exultant. They were coming! Coming to castrate Shark Eyes and then kill him, because that's what they did, she'd read it in the newspaper. *You know what they do to rapists?* That's what they do to rapists.

Oh, yes, come! Give me the knife and I'll do it myself!

A wave of hatred crashed into her then, so powerful, so dizzying, that she almost threw up again. She leaned her head down, pressing her forehead against the edge of the stall.

She wanted that knife.

Tears pouring down her face, she tried to straighten Magda's jeans, which were all twisted, all tangled, but her hands were shaking too hard. She struggled then with the zipper, but her hands still shook too hard. She gave up and stumbled away from the stalls, away from the puddle of vomit. Finally she could breathe.

I'm okay, she thought. *I'm okay.* Trying to convince herself.

She ran clumsily. It was just a few blocks, but she was panting and drenched in sweat by the time she shoved open the door and stepped inside. She dragged the bed to block the door. Then her strength gave out and she sat down, her hands gripping each other in her lap. Blood, wet and warm, was drying on her neck.

Rosa heard the blanket rustle on the other bed. She looked up into Livia's wide, black eyes.

"I'm okay," Rosa whispered. "Really." With a superhuman effort, she put her hand over the sticky cuts on her neck and stood up. Trying to breathe normally, she crossed to a washbasin on the table. She rinsed blood from her neck and face, wincing. One of his nails had left a scratch on her cheek.

She walked to Livia's side. "I'm okay," she whispered. "I . . . I saw a rat, and I fell trying to run away." She forced a smile. "I hate rats, don't you?"

Livia looked away, and Rosa sat tiredly on the bed. "Everything's going to be okay," she said. "Alonso will come back. And my father will get your *papá* out of jail. You'll see. We'll be okay."

Livia pinched Rosa's sleeve and began rubbing it between her fingertips. Rosa watched, wondering. "This was your *mamá's* sweater."

Almost imperceptibly, Livia nodded.

"I don't think she'd mind that I borrowed it, do you?" Livia didn't reply. "When I saw it in the drawer, I remembered how your *mamá* looked in it. It made me sad. But it felt right when I put it on. Like she was still here, taking care of us."

And she is, Rosa thought. *She is*.

"Remember the time I spent the night at your house? Your *mamá* gave me a big T-shirt to wear and I slept in your bed with you." Rosa pulled up the sweater from her waist. "Look. I found the same T-shirt last night. It's small on me now."

Livia cocked her head as Rosa spoke. Diana woke with a kittenish yawn.

"The next morning, Alonso got up to go to the *comedor*, you remember? You and I went with him. When we got back, we had breakfast together. Diana, you were just a tiny baby. Gustavo wasn't even born yet."

Glancing at Diana, Rosa smiled. Memories flowed like a quiet river. "While we ate, your *mamá* told us about when she was a little girl in the Sierra. She used to take the sheep up the mountainside. Her mother would give her a poncho and a little pouch of toasted corn. She'd stay out all day and all night. She had to watch the lambs to make sure the foxes wouldn't get them. One night, there was a hailstorm and she nearly froze. But she stayed anyway, taking care of the sheep. When she got home, her mother gave her hot soup. She said it took three days before she felt warm again."

Diana smiled. Livia's fingertips went on rubbing Rosa's sleeve.

Shark Eyes was gone. No more bad things. Please, oh please, Santa María, keep us safe.

"Padre Manuel came over, do you remember? He hadn't been in Salvador very long, but he and your *mamá* were already friends. And then my father came to get me. Your *mamá* made coffee, and they all talked about Sonia, the little girl my father had taken to the hospital the day before. A little girl who got burned. She was going to be okay, my *papá* said. I'll never forget—your *mamá* started to cry when he said that. Padre Manuel gave her his handkerchief, and she blew her nose and said she was being silly."

The three girls sat in silence.

"I'm hungry," Diana said.

Rosa laughed, and a glint of humor seemed to flicker across Livia's passive face. "Okay, Diana. Let's see about breakfast."

There was a crate of oranges, and Rosa found a few eggs. She served them, fried, over some leftover rice. Diana ate her own breakfast and then pulled Livia's plate across the table and ate hers. Livia swallowed a glass of orange juice.

They listened to the radio during breakfast. From some of the shantytowns, breathless reporters announced empty streets. Vacant markets and shuttered stores. The Army was patrolling the city. But Sendero had tossed a Molotov cocktail into a *micro* with the driver inside, and all the bus lines had shut down.

Rosa clicked off the radio.

After breakfast, she heated water and gave the children sponge baths. Shining like wet seals, Diana and Gustavo laughed and splashed, tossing drops of water onto the dirt floor. Livia lifted her arms so Rosa could peel off her T-shirt. She winced when the collar squeezed her bruised temple. Trembling, she held Rosa's hand as she stepped into the washbasin.

Rosa ran a washcloth down those chopstick legs and began to speak of summers at the beach. Of burning sand and icy waves and fishing boats dragging their nets through the sea. She spoke softly as she rubbed water and suds over jutting bones and loose brown skin. After a while, Livia stopped trembling.

With the kids finally fed and clean and dressed, Rosa took a deep breath and inventoried the supplies. She felt like a military commander under siege.

They had a head of cauliflower and a half-dozen potatoes. The crate of oranges and enough rice and beans to last a week. They'd stay inside. They'd survive. Rosa soaked a pile of beans in water, and as the afternoon drifted toward evening, she lit the stove and began to boil them. Gustavo was playing with the toy car she had brought. Diana was watching Rosa peel a clove of garlic, slipping the smooth white kernel from the skin. Livia sat on the bed. For the past hour she'd been staring down at her feet, dangling from her spindly little legs.

Tomorrow would be better. Tonight they'd eat dinner, and then Rosa would tell them a story. They'd all sleep together in the big double bed. But they'd be safe tomorrow. The Army would take back the streets. She'd find a telephone. Papá would do something to make Livia start eating again. Mamá would know that Rosa was alive, that she'd only done what she had to do. Tomorrow, her promise to Livia would come true.

Everything would be okay tomorrow.

·SIXTEEN·

Her voice raised in a high-pitched, singsong wail, the old woman fell to her knees beside Don Fermín's body. But before she could lay hands on him two other women, thick squat women in bulky skirts and ragged sweaters, grabbed her. They dragged her to a hut, where their voices joined hers in a screeching lament.

Something hot and wet had splashed Alonso's cheek when Don Fermín's head burst open. He wiped it off, staring at the glistening red smear on his hand.

The villagers had uttered a soft, collective moan when the gun fired. Now they bunched together silently, their eyes veiled and unseeing. Rubbing his bloody hand on his jeans, Alonso looked at Rodolfo. His eyes narrowed to slits, Rodolfo was staring down at Don Fermín.

Comrade Francisco shoved his pistol in its holster and turned to the prisoner. Grasping him by the hair, Francisco forced him to look at the corpse.

"You see the price of weakness," Comrade Francisco said. "The Revolution will sweep away the forces of reaction in a river of blood."

The wounded man's eyes were bleak, dead pools.

"Are you a spy of the reaction? Answer yes or no!"

"No," the man croaked. Comrade Francisco released him and his head flopped forward.

"Does no one have *anything* to say?" The Senderista commander sounded fed up. But no one spoke, not even Elena. She stared straight ahead, her face pinched and resolute.

Comrade Francisco shook his head in disappointment. "Then we execute him with justice," he said.

The word he used, *ajusticiar*, rang a tinny little bell in Alonso's mind. He was back in Comrade Felipe's cell. "Do you know why the Party executed your mother?" *Ajusticiar*. Executed her with justice.

Alonso felt his skin prickle. Then, with a violent shudder, he left it. Floated right out of his body and rose above the clearing in front of the school.

Looking down, he saw everything. The square adobe building with the red flag waving before it. The prisoner, slumped between the two guerrillas. The semicircle of Senderistas, watching the proceedings with cold boredom. Comrade Francisco, as fierce and arrogant as a hawk. Facing them, the villagers, who stared at nothing while Rodolfo kept his eyes on his commander.

"Lay him down," Comrade Francisco told his men.

Roughly, the two Senderistas lifted the injured man's arms from their shoulders and threw him to the ground. As they stretched out his arms, two more guerrillas grasped his feet. One tugged on his shattered leg, ignoring his screams. He went on screaming as the four of them crouched and pinned him, spread-eagled in the dust.

Comrade Francisco barked an order. Two of his men strode

from the clearing to an open field, where they each pried a small boulder from the ground. They returned slowly, their arms dragged down by the weight of the stones.

The wounded man looked up at them, his eyes darting in terror from one impassive face to the other. "Not with stones! Please, just use your gun! Not with stones," he begged. Tears traced dark tracks through the dirt on his temples.

No one but Alonso seemed to hear him.

Comrade Francisco looked at the *campesinos* and pointed at Elena.

As she stepped forward, one of the Senderistas handed her his stone. She staggered slightly under its weight, her face expressionless as the man on the ground went on begging. "Not with stones, not with stones!" Then suddenly Elena was screaming. She lifted the boulder high and hurled it down onto him. It landed with a soft thud in the middle of his body and Elena turned away, stumbling back toward the villagers.

The man's eyes were open. The boulder lay on his stomach and he was retching, retching and gasping. He was, Alonso saw, fully awake, fully aware of what was happening to him, what would continue happening to him until he was dead. Comrade Francisco shook his head, disappointed again.

He wants his breakfast, Alonso thought. It had been a long hike, dragging the prisoner along with them. Alonso floated off to the trails through the Huayhuash, to the mountains and the blue sky.

Francisco pointed again. He beckoned, bidding Alonso to approach.

The prisoner lay moaning softly, stretched on the ground between the four Senderistas.

Rodolfo shoved Alonso forward and Alonso watched as a boy he knew to be himself walked to the man's side. Then he watched the boy accept a flat boulder from the second of the Senderistas.

"It will go faster at the head," Comrade Francisco said.

Alonso stepped beside the man's head.

The eyes were open, looking straight up into Alonso's. They were brown, a sort of tea-colored brown. Like Dr. Pablo's eyes.

This could be Dr. Pablo lying here, the boy thought speculatively, watching himself raise the stone. It was heavier than he'd thought. For a moment it seemed he wouldn't be able to raise it high enough to get any leverage. Then he shifted and heaved, and the stone was up. His arms locked. He held it above his head as the boy who was Alonso looked down at the prisoner's tear-streaked face.

The cracked lips were moving. A little blood trickled from the mouth and the man began to pray. Alonso paused, waiting. The man's eyes reflected the sky as he whispered, "And deliver us from evil."

Slowly, Alonso lowered the stone. Without letting go, he stepped backward. One step, two steps.

A soft footfall beside him, and the whisper of a pistol being drawn from a holster. Comrade Francisco gently, almost tenderly, placed the barrel of the gun against Alonso's temple. The metal felt cool and smooth, the way Alonso had always known a gun would feel.

He rocked backward on his heels and let the stone fall to the ground, barely missing his own feet. It spat up a puff of dust as it landed.

A cry rang out at the edge of the crowd. "Don't kill him! Comrade Felipe sent him!" Shouting, Rodolfo lunged forward, and like a camera lens zooming to close-up, Alonso found himself back in his own body. He watched Rodolfo run to him, pleading. "Comrade Felipe sent him! Don't kill him!"

Rodolfo bent and picked up the stone Alonso had just dropped. His back strained as he turned and lifted it high in the air, where it poised against the blue sky. Then, with a scream, Rodolfo hurled the boulder down on the man's head. Falling to his knees, he lifted it and smashed it again and again into the now-silent, bloody face until the face disappeared and Alonso could watch no more.

▫ ▫ ▫

Night was coming at last. In the aftermath of the stoning, that cloudless blue sky had been the hardest thing to bear. From his place in the hut Alonso watched with relief as the light outside softened to yellow and then gold. Footsteps paused beside the doorway, and a pair of wrinkled brown hands placed a bowl of soup there. Alonso couldn't see who owned the hands. Perhaps the toothless old woman who had fed them yesterday. If only his parents had taught him to say "thank you" in Quechua.

"*Gracias,*" he called. There was no reply. He crept over and sat in the doorway.

Watching, unmoved, as the setting sun lit the mountains on fire once more, Alonso sipped the watery soup. This morning, he had thought he would never eat again, though it had been Rodolfo who lost his breakfast. Spattered with blood, Rodolfo had crawled away from the body and vomited at the edge of the clearing. One of the Senderistas had joined him there. When Rodolfo had finished throwing up and was wiping his pale, sweating face on his sleeve, the guerrilla had laughed and slapped him on the back. Apparently, vomiting after first blood was not an offense.

The offense was refusing to take that blood, and as Alonso sat alone with his soup, he knew he wouldn't be forgiven a second time. He had no doubt that Rodolfo had saved his life. Not just by killing in his place, but by mentioning Comrade Felipe, whom every Senderista in the country had heard of.

He shuddered. He had come that close to dying. Even now, he wasn't sure if it had really been him out there, dropping that boulder to the ground.

For all the good it had done the prisoner. One of the Senderistas had made Alonso help carry the bodies to a rocky ravine north of the village. With a swing of their arms, they had hurled the corpses over the edge. The bodies had sailed through the air and landed with a thud, among at least a dozen other bodies down there.

After seeing the bodies, tossed and twisted among the boulders, Alonso finally knew where the people of Tambo Matacancha had gone.

Anyone who could flee had fled. They weren't sticking

around to plant orchards of red flags. They had picked up their children, bid a tearful farewell to those too old to make the trip, and headed over the mountain. It must be a long hike to the road with a child in your arms, and it was an even longer hike to Chiquián. But everything except power was an illusion. Power and the strength of a rifle. If you had neither, you ran.

Alonso forced himself to swallow more soup. Rodolfo had refused to look at him since the stoning. He was eating with the Senderistas now, over in the school. Alonso could hear them laughing and shouting, having a good time as they got to know each other.

Tilting the bowl, he swallowed the last of his soup, then withdrew into the hut. Rodolfo would have to come for his blanket, even if he was going to sleep with the Senderistas. As darkness settled around him, Alonso wrapped himself in his blanket and sat leaning against the wall. A new moon crept over the horizon.

The doorway was a pale rectangle of moonlight when a shadow finally stepped through it, a slender shadow Alonso would have known anywhere. The shadow didn't speak as it walked to the edge of the hut and lay down, pulling Rodolfo's blanket over itself.

With a knot as big as a grapefruit in his throat, Alonso tried to find the words he needed. None came. Rodolfo was soon asleep, his breathing low and steady. Once he cried out in his sleep, a sharp cry of protest that quickly subsided.

The rectangle of moonlight shifted, creeping across the dirt floor. Alonso sat, not really thinking. His eyes open in the darkness, he watched the doorway. Finally he slept, perhaps a few minutes, perhaps few hours. When he opened his eyes again he was still sitting against the wall, still wrapped in the blanket. The moonlight had dimmed and the sky was filling with clouds.

Rodolfo was sighing by the far wall. Alonso crept to his side. He could barely see his friend's face, but he knew it by heart. Dark and slender, framed by those wild black curls Alonso had always envied.

"Rodolfo," he whispered, shaking him gently. "Rodolfo, wake up."

Sounding a little like Gustavo, Rodolfo whimpered and tried to roll away. Alonso shook him again and Rodolfo's eyes flew open. He sat up, mumbling. "What is it, *hermano?*"

At the endearment, *brother,* which he had thought he might never hear again, Alonso had to blink back tears. But when Rodolfo spoke again, his voice was cold. "What do you want, José?"

Dry-mouthed, Alonso tried to respond. "I want . . . I want . . ."

"Go to sleep. We leave first thing in the morning."

Alonso shook his head, desperate for the right words. "We can't," he choked.

"What are you talking about? Just because you chickened out . . ."

"I didn't chicken out," Alonso said, anger giving him back his voice. "That man didn't do anything wrong. You heard Don Fermín."

"What did he know? These *campesinos* are ignorant, Alonso. Especially the old ones. Ignorant and stubborn."

"I thought they were the People."

"I'm going to sleep." Rodolfo tried to lie down, but Alonso grabbed his arm.

"We shouldn't have come here."

Angrily, Rodolfo threw off Alonso's hand. "What did you expect us to do? Have tea parties?"

"I didn't expect us to murder *campesinos* and aid workers."

"Only war will end war. You know that."

"This isn't war! Go look in the ravine! Francisco might as well be a *pishtaco*! Don Fermín did nothing! And that man just wanted to give these people some alpacas so they'd have better wool!"

"Reactionary promises. Cushioning the misery. The only way they'd use alpaca wool is for those stupid scarves they sell the tourists."

"What's wrong with that?" Alonso whispered fiercely. "Maybe they could buy a little salt!"

"They've got to be self-sufficient." Rodolfo's voice softened, became reasonable. "*Hermano*, the *campesinos* can't keep trading. They're supposed to strangle the cities, starve them into submission. It's not about buying salt—it's about overthrowing the bourgeoisie! Don't you see? They can't be selling alpaca scarves. They need to grow food for the EGP!"

"But killing Don Fermín! Bashing that guy's head in—"

"Oh, would you forget him! He was revisionist scum—another useful fool. They say they're trying to help, but they make things worse! He was just like your mother, Alonso. Don't you see that? If it was okay for the Party to kill your mother, why do you care so much about him?"

Startled, Alonso stumbled to his feet. "I never said it was okay!"

"Then what are you doing here?" Rodolfo stood up to face him. "If it wasn't okay, what are you doing here?"

"It wasn't okay," Alonso repeated, backing up. "It was necessary. Comrade Felipe said—"

"Comrade Felipe would say it was necessary to kill that aid worker, too."

Alonso felt himself beginning to shake.

Useful fools. Executed with justice. *They killed your mother, you little prick!*

Alonso retreated until the wall slammed into his back. How many people like his mother would he have to kill? How many aid workers and Don Fermíns? A river of blood.

"Face it, that guy was just like your mother, *hermano*."

"Like my mother." Alonso shook his head, feeling his hair brush the adobe. "But that's what you said. . . ." A flash of clarity made him blink, and he stepped forward. "Rodolfo, do you remember what you said, when you told me about the night the cops raided your house? Do you remember?"

"What?" Rodolfo snapped.

"You said no one came to help. You said it was because . . . you said, *there's no one here like your mother*."

Rodolfo shrugged impatiently. "So what?"

"What kind of a country are we going to have after we kill all the people like my mother?"

When Rodolfo replied, his voice was bitter. "It'll be a hell of a lot better than the one we have now."

"With people like Comrade Francisco in charge?" Alonso

spat. "I don't think so, *hermano*. If my mother and that aid worker were useful fools, we'd be better off in a world of fools!"

They faced each other, both breathing heavily, as if they'd been wrestling and were exhausted but didn't know how to stop.

And yet, at last, Alonso knew what he wanted.

"Let's leave, *hermano*. Right now. We can get away—the sentry probably fell asleep out there. He did last night—" He broke off as Rodolfo shoved him against the wall.

"Are you crazy? Nobody walks into the EGP and then just walks out again. We're in this now, together!"

Alonso pushed him away. "No. I'm not in this."

"Yes, you are."

"No, I'm not!"

"Yes, you are!"

Listen to us. Alonso nearly smiled. They'd had a million arguments like this, when they were kids. They'd known each other forever. "Please, Rodolfo," he begged. "Come with me."

"Who says I'm letting you go?"

"You're my best friend. Don't stay here."

Outside, lightning flashed, followed by a loud crack that seemed to explode from the mountaintops. "It's going to rain," Alonso said, stepping to the doorway. "It'll cover us."

Rodolfo stood beside him. "You're not going."

"I have to."

"Boy, you sure change your mind fast, don't you? Why? Why, Alonso?"

But Alonso had no answers anymore. "Please come with me, *hermano*."

Lightning blazed. In the burst of white light Alonso saw a glimmer of yearning on Rodolfo's face. A few big raindrops tumbled from the sky, thudding like marbles to the ground. Then, with a loud rush, a torrential rain began to fall.

"We'll kill you if we catch you," Rodolfo said. "So you better run fast."

Before Alonso could reply, Rodolfo shoved him out the doorway. For a moment they watched each other through a curtain of rain. Then Rodolfo turned and disappeared into the darkness of the hut.

There was nothing Alonso could do then but turn his face toward the mountain and run.

◻ ◻ ◻

He ran.

He ran and he ran and he ran.

Alone in the pouring rain, he ran through the night. With every step he grew more afraid. He thought of guns and stones and machetes and he wanted to scream with panic.

By the time the rain stopped and the sky began to lighten, he was racing down the far side of the mountain. His feet slipped on the steep path, arms flailing as he fought to keep moving without falling. The storm had turned the path to mud, slick and treacherous and studded with rocks.

But he couldn't fall. Not now. Not with the valley finally in sight, a flat green runner spread between the towering shale and granite walls of the mountains. *Not now, not now.* Not with his heart thudding, panicked and insane. If he fell, he'd freeze. He wouldn't get up again. The Senderistas would find him paralyzed, like a chicken tied by its feet in the market. After a while they stopped struggling and just waited for the knife.

A thousand meters above the pass, the trail leveled out. As it crossed through a moraine, Alonso's stomach wrenched. He bent over, retching miserably onto a lichen-spattered boulder. Finally he straightened up and tried to spit the taste of acid from his mouth. Water. He needed water. The *soroche* was making him vomit, sucking him dry. He hadn't lost two baby brothers to dysentery without learning that dehydration could be as deadly as a bullet.

Eyes cast down, he stumbled through the gray boulders of the moraine. Finding a tiny, transparent pool, he dropped to his hands and knees. His arms trembled as he lowered his mouth to the puddle. His stomach cramped, but he fought down the nausea and sucked up all the water he could.

Carajo, it was cold up here. Too cold. And too damned high, thousands of meters up in the Andes. He was shivering uncontrollably, soaking wet, so cold that his bones ached and his teeth chattered. He wanted to curl up into a ball, huddle like a boulder and sink down into the thin soil of the mountainside.

Oh, my God, he thought. *I am going to die. I'm going to die and I don't want to.*

I don't want to!

Across the valley, above the western rim, a hulking snow-capped mountain burst into color, shifting from white to pink to fiery gold in the light of the rising sun. The clouds were clearing out, tumbling down the valley and scattering blue flags of open sky in their wake. Below them, the valley was green, like Rosa's eyes. The green stretched northward between the flanks of the mountains.

The *soroche* was making his heart pound. Crouched on his knees, Alonso listened.

Then he stood up and began to run.

He ran and he ran and he ran.

▫ SEVENTEEN ▫

As the dump truck rolled past his outstretched thumb, Alonso's legs began to tremble. His whole body seemed to quiver, swaying like a reed beside the little stone hut where Hilario had dropped them off. He had run to keep warm, run to stay alive, run all the way out of the valley. Now he could barely stand.

Fifty meters down the road, the truck stopped. A few chunks of ore tumbled out over the tailgate, bouncing as they hit the road. Then, like an ugly forty-ton angel of mercy, the truck backed up. Alonso was hardly inside the cab when the driver gunned the engine and they began zooming down the road.

Wide-eyed, Alonso looked around the cab. The driver was a solid lump of a man, with big hands and shoulders hunched from too many years at the wheel. He had a little plastic-covered picture of Sarita Colonia stuck to the dashboard. Padre Manuel said Sarita wasn't really a saint, but a lot of people carried her image around as if she were. Sarita kept her mournful black eyes on Alonso, and he felt strangely comforted each time he looked at her.

The trucker barreled down the mountain. He didn't say a

word or slow down until they got to the highway. Then, as the tires hit the asphalt, he handed Alonso a thermos of black coffee and a little plastic bag of that flat bread from Huaraz. Alonso wolfed it all down, hunks of bread and swigs of searing coffee.

They didn't talk much, except to share that the driver was taking his load of ore to the port in Callao, and Alonso was headed to San Juan. It was past midnight when they got to Lima and the man pulled over. He flipped on an overhead light, reached into his pocket and handed Alonso a wrinkled ten-*sol* bill.

"I gotta get to the port," he said. "I can't take you to San Juan."

Alonso stared at the bill. Ten *soles*. A fortune.

"Take a cab. You look like you're about to keel over." He ignored Alonso's stuttered thanks and drove away, his headlights two shining tunnels through the darkness.

The taxi dropped Alonso off on the avenue, because the cabbie took his ten *soles* but refused to drive him up the dirt road into San Juan. So Alonso walked the last few kilometers home, leaving behind the streetlights on the avenue and climbing past endless rows of darkened shacks.

One foot in front of the other. The hill seemed as high as the mountain beside Tambo Matacancha.

Comrade Francisco's Senderistas would have reached the road by now. They'd get word to Lima by tomorrow. Alonso was going to have to tell his father that. That he'd run out on the EGP and they'd probably come looking for him. He wasn't going to hang around waiting for them, but he needed to warn his family. And before his old man threw him out, he hoped he'd get a chance to say sorry.

But no belt. Never again. That boy was dead.

Finally he passed the school and saw his own door. Light streamed through a hole in the plywood, and Alonso cursed. His old man had kicked the door in.

"Papá." He knocked. "It's me. Alonso."

With a soft mumble of wood scraping dirt, something was dragged from the door. The sheet of plywood jerked open and Alonso saw a teenaged girl, silhouetted against the light.

They're gone, he thought. *They've disappeared!*

He stared. "Rosa?"

She stepped back and he entered. He watched her scrape the door shut and push a bed against it. Then she turned to him, trying to smile. But all at once she gave a little moan and her arms flew around his neck, hugging him so tightly that he nearly choked. He tried to hug back, but just as abruptly she broke free, wiping her eyes.

"I came back," he said. He didn't know what else to say. He looked around. The kids were asleep in the double bed, three rounded heaps under a blanket.

Rosa nodded. "Are you okay? Have you eaten?"

He tried to remember how long ago he had eaten the bread, drunk the coffee. He shook his head.

He looks half dead, Rosa thought. Sunken-eyed, exhausted. A bruise spread like a squashed plum over his cheek. Where had he been? What should she tell him? She turned to the stove and flicked on the propane. Her hand shook as she struck a match. Then she put on a kettle of water and poured some oil into a pot.

Alonso stepped closer, watching her chop a clove of garlic into tiny pieces. The knife thudded into his mother's old wooden chopping block.

Rosa swept the garlic into the oil and was reaching for the rice when he grabbed her hand, surprising them both. He lifted it and pressed his lips against her birthmark, that little brown oval on her wrist. Then he turned her hand over and kissed her palm.

"I've got garlic on me," she protested, trying to pull away. She wanted perfumes for him, sweet and wild. Something so beautiful he'd never want to leave again. Not garlic.

But he drew her to him and kissed her mouth. It was so soft there, so warm. . . . Her fingertips brushed his cheek, and his hands buried themselves in her hair.

A fire was kindling inside him. He wanted to stay here forever. Holding her like this. Touching her like this. Deeper and deeper. If only she'd let him stay. . . .

Come inside, Alonso. Come home.

During the long hours of waiting, Rosa had feared that if this moment ever came, Shark Eyes would come back with it, thrusting himself between them. Instead, she felt only Alonso. Like the sun, his body seemed to draw hers into its orbit. A feeling hot and liquid and almost painful.

Finally she stepped back, her eyes bright. Alonso felt suddenly lightheaded.

"Sit down," she whispered. "You need to eat."

He sat, unable to take his eyes off her. She cooked him rice in his mother's dented aluminum pan and pulled a pot of beans from the refrigerator. Finally she squeezed some oranges and poured him a glass of juice. He swallowed it in four gulps, barely tasting it, and she made more and he drank that, too.

"What are you doing here?" He smiled at her. She was beautiful. She was a miracle. "Where's my father?"

Rosa sat down beside him. "He's been arrested."

Alonso choked. "What?"

She repeated herself, and then, as gently as she could, told him of her arrival here, of everything Diana had told her. "I don't know why they arrested him. Diana said the police were looking for you and your father started cursing at them and they . . ." Her voice faltered. "They took him away."

Cops? Looking for him? But how? And why? He'd used a fake I.D. to get into the prison.

He thought of the night he and Rodolfo had pasted all those fliers here in San Juan. Those two drunks they'd seen and laughed at. He felt his hands shaking in his lap.

He had led the police to his family. He clenched his fists but couldn't stop their shaking.

"Where have you been, Alonso?"

"I went to the mountains," he said. Suddenly he registered how much time had passed. "But you said you came on Tuesday. What is it now, Wednesday? Thursday?" He sat back, horrified. "Couldn't you have done something?"

Done something! Rosa stood and ladled beans onto a plate, then scooped a mound of rice from the pot. As if she'd done nothing! She thought of telling him about Shark Eyes and touched the cut on her neck.

"Do you realize," she finally said, "that Livia is an absolute basket case, and Diana's not much better? I couldn't get them out of here. They went into hysterics. And while you were in the *mountains*"—she drawled the word, as if he'd been on holiday—"we had a *paro armado*! There were red flags up in the market! What was I supposed to do, leave the kids here and walk home?"

The *paro*. He had completely forgotten about the *paro*. A *paro armado*, and Rosa and the kids alone in San Juan. "No," he whispered. The food on his plate seemed to move, and the room with it.

"It's all right." Her voice softened. "Eat. You'll feel better." She pushed his plate closer.

Alonso stared at the sticky, steaming hump of rice. Then, suddenly ravenous, he started shoveling in mouthfuls. He didn't say a word until he was nearly finished and had drained the glass of juice. "*Gracias*," he said, abashed.

On the bed, Diana cried out. Rosa stood, ready to go to her, but Diana fell silent once more. All three children lay unmoving, flat on their backs beside each other like paper dolls.

It's time, Rosa thought. A chill crept over her. But he was so tired. She couldn't tell him now. She should wait . . . maybe tomorrow . . .

But by tomorrow the kids would be awake, and then what? Then she'd be back in Miraflores, suffocating on the *Malecón*. If she didn't tell him now she never would.

She put her hands on the table, one on top of the other. "Alonso . . ."

He should know. He deserved to know.

"I never told anyone what really happened in the Cesip that day." Her thumb slid over her birthmark, but she held it still. "When the Senderistas came through the back door . . . When they walked in, your mother was already leaving. She was going out to look for you."

Don't, Alonso thought. He felt so tired he could barely see. *I already know what a bullet does to a person's head.*

"I was by the lab," Rosa went on. "And I just sort of stood there. Like I was frozen. Your mother came running back and she pushed me. She made me get away first. One of them was already aiming at her—" Rosa broke off and looked at the ceiling. "She could have gotten away, Alonso. I mean, if she hadn't come back for me."

Rosa blinked, about to cry.

Please don't, Alonso thought. He didn't think he could take it if she cried. *It wasn't you,* he wanted to say. Sooner or later, they were going to kill her anyway. Because she wouldn't let them have the Cesip. Because of who she was.

Rosa put her face in her hands. "I don't know why she came back," she moaned. "I wish she'd left me there!"

Alonso tried to find his voice. To explain. He knew what he wanted to say. What Rosa had to understand. They killed everyone who got in their way. His mother. Don Fermín. Everyone.

He pried Rosa's hands from her face. "Rosa, she loved you! My mother loved you!"

Rosa hunched over his hand, her shoulders heaving.

Oh, God, he had to make her see. She had to understand. But as her tears splashed his arm and her fingers wove through his, Alonso's throat seemed to close. And as he thought of his mother, and how much she'd loved them all, he couldn't help himself. He put his head down on the table and wept.

Raggedly. *He cries like a man*, Rosa thought. *Not a child*. He sobbed as her father had, the day of the funeral. Her own tears dried as she watched him.

Tentatively, so softly that at first she barely touched him, she began to stroke his hair. It was thick and black and straight. She had always loved his hair, so different from her own.

Alonso didn't hate her. He didn't even seem to blame her. But she found with a kind of numb surprise that it didn't make much difference. Because Alonso could love her, but he couldn't absolve her. He couldn't heal the part of her that had been maimed inside the Cesip.

Of course Magda had come back for her. *She loved you!* Magda wouldn't have been Magda if she hadn't come back. Rosa might spend the rest of her life wishing she hadn't frozen, but she had. Whether anybody else blamed her, whether they offered some kind of cheap grace—*it's not your fault*—it didn't matter.

What mattered, maybe, was to live a life worth the price Magda had paid.

Alonso cried and cried, as if he might never stop. His sleeves grew damp from his tears. Finally, his sobs subsided to a weak moan and he looked up, his lashes spiky and wet.

Her eyes looked dark, almost black, in the weak light cast by the kerosene lamp.

"You're exhausted," she whispered.

Drawing a shaky breath, he nodded. She blew out the lamp and stood. Like a child he followed her, let her remove his sneakers and sweater and lay him down on the bed beside his brother and sisters. She kissed him and his longing for her returned, so hot and sharp that if he could have spoken it would have been to beg. She brought over a chair and sat down, taking his hand once more.

Her hand followed him into his dreams, and remained with him all night.

▫EIGHTEEN▫

Thump, thump. Darkness swathed the shack. *Thump, thump, thump.* Someone was banging on the door.

Alonso let go of Rosa's hand. Peering outside, he saw a night writhing with fog. A shadow of a face, hidden behind a black ski mask. Yellow eyes glowed through the slit.

The ski mask spoke. "People's Trial in the market. Bring your family out."

Alonso tried to speak, but fog swirled into his mouth. Maybe he no longer had a voice. Maybe he had wept it away, the night before.

The yellow eyes narrowed. "You see the price of weakness."

Not with stones, Alonso thought. He shut his eyes and started to tremble. *Please God, not with—*

"Mamá!" A high-pitched voice cut through the fog. "Did you see?"

Alonso opened his eyes. He was lying in bed, sweating. Livia lay beside him, the blanket framing her face like a monk's cowl. Her eyes twitched, a ghostly flicker behind closed lids. She was dreaming, talking in her sleep. They'd both been dreaming.

Alonso sat up and looked around.

Sunrise lit a gray glow behind the *esteras*. His mother's jeans lay folded on a chair beside the bed. Diana and Gustavo slept with their arms outflung. Rosa was snoring lightly, her mouth open.

Alonso steadied himself, watching her.

One of her curls lay above her head, a brown spiral cast upward on the pillow. She'd be so embarrassed if she could see herself.

Leaning across Livia, he felt Rosa's breath, the intermittent warmth against his cheek. He bent closer, closer. He was kissing her. The soft snore stopped. Rosa's lips curved. When he finally opened his eyes, she breathed his name.

He wound that lone, upflung curl around his index finger. "We should go," he whispered.

She nodded. "Go find a taxi. I'll get the kids ready."

He went out into the early morning light and followed the road out of San Juan. The *paro* was over and everything was the same. Down on the avenue, trucks and *micros* sped past, diesel fumes hanging in their wake. Men clustered around the newspaper kiosk, reading tabloids clothespinned to strings. Some of the tabloids had pictures from the *paro*. A burned-out bus, a market hung with red flags. Others had pictures of half-naked showgirls. As if nothing had happened at all.

A *combi* passenger van skidded to a stop in front of him. "Get on, get on!" The ticket boy hung like a monkey from the van's open door, trying to wave Alonso aboard. Alonso shook his head and the *combi* roared off. Finally a little Volkswagen sputtered by, a dull gray one like Padre Manuel's, but with a red taxi sign stuck to the windshield.

He was afraid the driver would ask for the fare upfront, but the guy didn't even blink. He just nodded and drove up the long hill into San Juan. As Alonso stepped from the car, Diana tumbled from the shack. She threw herself into Alonso's arms and Gustavo came running behind her, screaming with delight.

"WONZO! WONZO!" Alonso carried them inside, laughing and choking. Gustavo clung to his neck while Diana covered his cheek with kisses.

Rosa had stuffed some clothes into a couple of bags and put on his mother's blue sweater and jeans. "Come on," she said to the kids. "Help me carry these to the car." She tipped her head at the bed. "You'll have to carry Livia, Alonso."

Livia sat at the edge of the bed, rigid and silent.

Rosa stepped through the doorway and the little ones dashed outside with her. Alonso could hear them, their sharp little yaps of excitement, as he approached the bed.

"Livia," he murmured. She seemed very pale. Shrunken, as though something had been drained from her. "It's me, *hermanita*. Alonso." Livia twitched, as if in pain, and collapsed downward over her knees. Both arms went over her head.

His mother's little flower.

She shut her eyes as he slid his arms beneath her. She seemed to weigh less than Diana.

Rosa was already in the taxi's front seat, with the kids bouncing in the back. He put Livia on Rosa's lap, and she pressed her face against Rosa's neck as Alonso climbed in behind the driver. Then, with a little gurgle, the Volkswagen turned around and rolled down the hill.

It was a long ride to Miraflores, even in a taxi. Diana and

Gustavo exclaimed at the cars and trucks, the purple and red and white *micros*. Rosa gazed out the window, stroking Livia's hair. She didn't say anything until they reached Miraflores. "This way," she murmured to the driver.

The Volkswagen rumbled onto a side street, a little canyon cut between high stucco walls. Open sky lay ahead, with a tang of brine and seaweed in the air. At the end of the street, the taxi turned onto the *Malecón*. Beyond a narrow, grassy park, Alonso saw the green and rippling immensity of the Pacific.

"There." Rosa pointed at an apartment building with peeling paint. "That's it."

Clambering from the backseat, Alonso heard a loud and very Spanish-sounding curse above their heads. "*¡Coño!*" He squinted against the bright sky. Above him, looking down from the third-floor balcony, he saw a man in black. A squat man, with a white clerical collar.

Diana scrambled from the Volkswagen as Alonso lifted Gustavo out. "Hold his hand," he told Diana. He stepped around the car to take Livia from Rosa's lap.

He was straightening up with Livia in his arms, and Rosa was stepping from the car, when he saw them. Three adults, running out the front door of the apartment building and slamming to a disbelieving halt.

"*Mamá!*" With a sob, Rosa ran into her mother's arms, mumbling that she was sorry, she was so sorry. . . .

"*Coño*," Padre Manuel murmured.

Dr. Pablo devoured Rosa with one look. Then he glanced at the little ones and stared hard at Alonso. He was morphing from father to doctor before Alonso's eyes. He looked down at Livia, huddled in Alonso's arms, and his expression changed. "Give her to me," he said quietly.

Alonso's arms tightened, clenching Livia to his chest.

"Alonso." Dr. Pablo touched his shoulder.

Alonso looked down. Diana stood at his side, gripping Gustavo's hand. She was sucking her hair again, eyes wide. She had not asked him, yet, where their father was.

Alonso loosened his hold and Dr. Pablo took Livia. Padre Manuel began to shepherd them all inside, through the glass doors and into the elevator and upstairs, to a carpeted living room that looked out over the sea. Alonso wanted to hold Rosa's hand, but she was in her mother's arms now—out of his reach.

He turned to the priest, who was gray with exhaustion but beaming. "Padre." The priest reached out an arm to pull Alonso into a hug, but he sobered as Alonso shook his head.

"We need to get my father out of jail," Alonso told him.

□ □ □

The Clínica San Martín was painted the pale green of sour apples, with six stories of windows that caught the sun like dozens of glassy eyes. As Padre Manuel pulled into the parking lot, Alonso stared in wonder. It had taken the priest one call to the Archbishop to get his father out of jail and into the best private hospital in Lima.

The room where Alonso's father lay smelled of plaster and Lysol. Sunshine, pouring through a window, mottled the floor. Near the window stood a bed with its head cranked up. A sheet covered the body in the bed, but when Alonso saw what the cops had done to his father's face, he nearly turned and ran.

Shredded lips. Broken teeth. One ear a swollen red balloon. One hand groping unsteadily toward Alonso while the other, swathed in bandages, lay unmoving on the sheet. Swallowing, Alonso stepped forward.

"*Hijo*." His father's voice was hoarse. "Are you . . . the kids . . . ?"

Alonso slipped his hand into his father's. "We're okay, Papá. All of us."

His father's eyes were black slits behind bloated lids. "Where did you go? Were you with Rodolfo?"

A cold fear splashed over Alonso. "Is that what you told the cops?"

"I didn't tell the cops anything," his father retorted. "Where were you?"

Alonso glanced at Padre Manuel, and the priest stepped out to the hall, speaking in a low voice to a nurse in white polyester. Alonso replied in a whisper. "We went to the mountains. We were with them."

"Them?" His father gasped. A hurting sound, like he'd taken another blow to the gut. "You went and—"

Alonso began to stammer. "I didn't do what they wanted me to. They . . ."

But his father was looking away now, like he couldn't stand to look at him anymore. Out the window, straight at the white light.

Alonso clenched his jaw. "I'm sorry about the cops, Papá." He turned for the door. "That was my fault."

"Where are you going?"

"I can't stay. They know where we live."

"Do they know you're in the hospital?"

Alonso shoved his hands in his pockets. "The Party has a thousand eyes and a thousand ears, Papá."

"Don't believe everything they told you. They'd have said whatever it took to convince you." His father shook his head, incredulous. "The son of Magda Rios. They reeled you in like a fish, Alonso." His father sat up, wincing. "You see that, don't you? Or do you think it was *you* they wanted? Alonso Carhuanca?"

Balling his fists in his pockets, Alonso stared at his father. He imagined tabloids, hanging from newspaper kiosks. He imagined headlines. SON OF MAGDA RIOS JOINS SENDERO LUMINOSO.

No wonder Comrade Felipe had been so glad to see him. Orchards of red flags. No one hungry. Victory was inevitable. Even the sons of the victims knew it. Even the son of Magda Rios.

"I don't believe anything they told me," he muttered. "Not anymore."

"Then come back here." His father gestured tiredly at a vinyl chair. "Sit."

"I have to go, Papá."

"*Carajo*, Alonso!" His father sounded more frightened than angry. "Is that what your mother would have wanted?"

Alonso wheeled on his father. "What do you care what my mother would have wanted? She was a fool, remember?"

"I never said that!"

"You did! You said she was a fool for me!"

His father half rose from the bed, then gave a gasp and sank back, shaking his head. "Not just for you," he muttered. "For all of us."

"She was the bravest person I ever knew," Alonso snarled.

"I know, *hijo*." His father turned his broken face toward him. "But she's gone." He blinked, wincing. "It's just us now."

"Us and that belt?"

"No." Above the stringy collar of the hospital gown, Alonso saw his old man's throat twitch. "No, Alonso. No belt." He cleared his throat. "Not anymore."

Alonso glared as Padre Manuel entered the room, brisk and smiling. "Tomás, you'll be able to travel in a week." The priest rubbed his hands together. "Which is wonderful. Because . . ." He looked from one to the other and smiled uncertainly. "I have good news. Spain has offered you asylum."

Alonso bounced on his heels. He felt like a goalie waiting for a penalty kick, not knowing which way the ball would come. "What's a *sylum*?"

Padre Manuel's smile broadened. "It means you go live in Spain. Be safe."

And leave Peru? Alonso thought of Rosa and shook his head. "I'm not going."

"Then none of us will."

Alonso stared at his father. "But you have to."

His father shrugged, ever so slightly.

"Don't be nuts!" His father was a lunatic. A stubborn, idiotic—"I am not going, Papá."

"Then we all stay."

"You can't stay! Look at yourself! You trust *cops* to keep

you safe? And what about the kids? What about—?"

His father's mummy-wrapped hand rose, silencing him. "What about *you*, Alonso?"

"I can make it on my own," Alonso snapped. "You did."

"*Ya.*" His father nodded. "I did." He breathed quietly for a moment, eyes nearly shut. "But if they come after you? What'll you do?"

"I don't know." Alonso folded his arms, pinning his fists. "I'll do something."

"*Do something?*" The bruised and swollen eyelids opened wide, and then, to Alonso's astonishment, his father smiled. An easy smile, rising like mist from some deeply buried memory.

Suddenly Alonso heard her, too. *You can always do something,* she said.

The wave crashed through him then, grief, tearing the air from his lungs. He pressed his arms against his chest, feeling like he might split in two. What would she want him to do, now that she was gone?

"I won't leave without you," his father said.

□ □ □

The clouds had returned and the sky was darkening to dusk by the time Padre Manuel's little Volkswagen came sputtering back down the *Malecón*. Rosa watched the Bug park across the street, saw Padre Manuel's door open, saw Alonso step out on the passenger side. She was crossing the living room when her father intercepted her.

"*Rosa.*" His voice was a warning.

She stopped, not wanting to look at her father's haggard face, his bloodshot eyes. He had told her everything, earlier in the day. Padre Manuel had kept his promise. He'd gotten Magda's family asylum in Spain.

Papá put his hands on Rosa's shoulders. "Don't make this harder on Alonso," he begged. His voice so hoarse he sounded broken inside.

Rosa nodded. Her father wanted a look from her, a promise, but she broke from him and ran down the steps. The doorman swept open the big glass door with a flourish. "¡Señorita!"

Alonso and Padre Manuel were leaning against the car. Alonso turned at the sound of Rosa's footsteps, and the look in his eyes nearly melted her on the sidewalk.

Go *away*, she thought fervently. Padre Manuel should go, now. But he was too busy telling Alonso about his trip to Spain, and about his brother, who'd been diagnosed with cancer right after Padre Manuel reached Madrid. The doctors had taken out his left lung, leaving an empty space around his heart. Padre Manuel shook his head sadly. "Now his heart is enlarged. Misshapen. Because of that empty space."

"I thought he was a soccer referee," Alonso said.

"He was. Now he can barely blow a whistle."

Alonso scuffed at the sidewalk. "So what did he do?"

"He despaired," Padre Manuel said. "Told me to go to hell."

Startled, Rosa and Alonso glanced at each other.

Padre Manuel cleared his throat. "I went to see him before I left. He told me he was learning to live again." Nodding slightly, Padre Manuel fixed his gaze on Alonso. "Learning to live with a misshapen heart. And with all that empty space around it."

Alonso sighed, and Rosa wondered if all priests were like that. Walking homilies. She slipped her hand into Alonso's. "Want to go for a walk?" she whispered.

A rueful expression crossed the priest's face. "Don't go far, you two."

As soon as his back was turned, Alonso pulled Rosa close and kissed her.

"I missed you," she said.

His hands slid down her back. "Your doorman is staring at us."

Rosa glanced across the street. "That's because you look like a pirate." She touched the dark bruise on his cheek. "Did your father do that? Before you ran away?"

Alonso winced, pulling away, and they started down the sidewalk with their arms looped around each other's waists. "He went crazy for a while."

Rosa thought of Magda's clothes, so carefully stored in the shack in San Juan. "Is he all right now?"

"They broke his hand." Alonso walked a few steps in silence. "And a couple of ribs." He tilted his head so it rested against Rosa's as they walked.

At the edge of the park, the grass petered out and the sidewalk dropped off in a steep slope to a dusty lot. Alonso gazed across the dust at the ocean.

"You want to go down there?" Rosa asked.

Alonso grinned. "Someone'll think I'm mugging you."

She laughed and they slithered down the slope, slipping and sliding with stones tumbling before them. At the edge of the field, where jagged cliffs sliced into the land, Alonso kissed her again, with that flat gray sea behind her.

"Like a movie," Rosa teased.

"Nah." Alonso nuzzled her. "No sunset."

"Next time," she said.

He leaned his head against hers, rubbing like a cat till their hair tangled. "Rosa . . ." She watched his Adam's apple slide up and down. "Padre Manuel says—"

"I know." Rosa spoke quickly. "My father told me."

His arms tightened around her. "I have to go," he muttered. "They need me."

Rosa buried her face in the warmth of his chest. The salt breeze chilled her back. Their bodies breathed together, and something inside Alonso grew still.

He drew back with a lopsided smile. "So I guess I'll have two empty spaces, *no?*" He held up two fingers. "Around my misshapen heart."

The grin spread crookedly across his face, and Rosa tried to smile back, she really did. But then she started to cry, though she didn't want to, though she had promised herself not to, because she had to let him go, she had to help Alonso take this chance, because it might be his only real chance in life.

Boys like Alonso don't get many chances, Papá had said.

Alonso held her face in his hands. With his thumbs, he wiped away her tears.

□ □ ◻

Jet engines were screaming overhead. Rosa tilted her head to look through the rear window. She could see blue sky, but not the plane. It was already climbing, rising westward over the Pacific. It would follow the coastline north. It would fly over Central America and turn east to cross the Atlantic. Sometime tomorrow, it would scream again, and approach the earth once more.

At the first red light outside the airport, a little girl no older than Livia stood up from the curb and stuck a slender, dirty hand through Papá's window. She had a baby strapped to her back in a blanket. The baby looked into the car with eyes that seemed to have perfected the art of pleading. Eyes of hunger.

"No, *hijita*," Papá said softly. But Mamá opened her purse and pulled out a coin.

"You just encourage them," Papá said, after the child had darted to the next car. "You encourage them to risk their lives begging in traffic."

"Do you really think she'll stop begging if I don't give her anything? There are more of them every day, Pablo." Mamá snapped her purse shut. "And I don't think it's because we're all giving them too much."

Papá rolled up his window without replying. He turned onto the winding road down the cliffs so they could drive to Miraflores on the beach road. There were no stoplights or beggars down there, just garbage dumps and rocky beaches and the wide, green sea. The Pacific came into view, so big and unfettered that even the garbage couldn't make it ugly, and they all rolled down their windows.

A breeze blew through the car, full of salt and dust and the smoke of burning garbage. The sunlight broke into pieces as it hit the waves, and the ocean looked as though it went on forever, the way Rosa had thought everything would go on forever, back when she was a kid.

Papá drove slowly, putting off the inevitable moment when they would walk into a silent apartment, bereft after a week of Diana's chatter. Bereft of Gustavo's funny, half-human names for the cars and trucks on the *Malecón*. Of Livia's ghostly, nearly invisible smile.

Even Magda had fallen silent.

Standing by the immigration counter at the airport, where a bored-looking young woman had stamped his passport and was waving him on, Alonso had looked back one last time. His face anxious, he had searched desperately, on tiptoes, until he found Rosa. She was standing outside the security area, watching him. When their eyes met he smiled, and held up two fingers.

Two fingers, upraised in a V, the way hippies used to make the peace sign.

Watching him, Rosa had felt the breath leave her body, and thought that if she wasn't to cry she might never breathe again. For a moment all she could do was gaze at him, over the heads of the passengers and immigration officers, over all the gates and barriers between them.

And then she smiled, and held up two fingers.

Magda and Alonso. Two empty spaces, around her misshapen heart.

Then Tomás put his hand on Alonso's shoulder, and they were gone.

▫ **AUTHOR'S NOTE** ▫

On September 12, 1992, Peruvian police arrested the leader of the Shining Path, Abimael Guzmán, alias Chairman Gonzalo. They captured Guzmán and several other Senderista leaders after months of careful intelligence gathering and without firing a shot. It was a far cry from the brutality of the twelve previous years of war.

After Guzmán's arrest, and in the face of growing resistance by the *campesinos* they claimed to represent, Sendero Luminoso rapidly collapsed. Though remnants of Senderista columns remain active even today, Sendero's capacity to slaughter at will has ended.

Throughout the war, Peruvian human rights activists struggled courageously to document the horror engulfing their country. But the full extent of the suffering of ordinary Peruvians did not become clear until August 2003, when the country's Truth and Reconciliation Commission released a nine-volume report about the war.

According to the Commission, nearly 70,000 Peruvians died in political violence between 1980 and 2000. Three-quarters of those who died were native speakers of Quechua or other indigenous languages, among the poorest and most vulnerable Peruvians. About 15 percent of the murdered were children under the age of eighteen. More than half the deaths occurred at the hands of Sendero Luminoso. Nearly a third of the dead were victims of the military and police. Hundreds of thousands of Peruvians fled their homes to escape the violence. The torture and rape of civilians by the military, the police, and Sendero Luminoso were common throughout the conflict. The Commission's report makes clear that both Sendero Luminoso and the government frequently acted with deliberate and almost unimaginable cruelty.

This novel is a work of fiction. Unfortunately, the horrors described here are not.

Blessed are the peacemakers, for they shall be called the children of God.